WICKED WISH

DRAGON'S GIFT: THE STORM

VERONICA DOUGLAS
LINSEY HALL

For our cats. All of them.

© 2021 MAGIC SIDE PRESS
MAGIC SIDE PRESS
MAGIC SIDE, CHICAGO
Gilbart Rock
Breakers
Bentham Prison
Shoreline
The Circuit
Flyby
Hyde Park
Hall of Inquiry
Exposition Park
Midway Den
Dockside Dens
Jackson Park
Old Mud City
The Flats
South Shore
The Indies
South Chicago

1

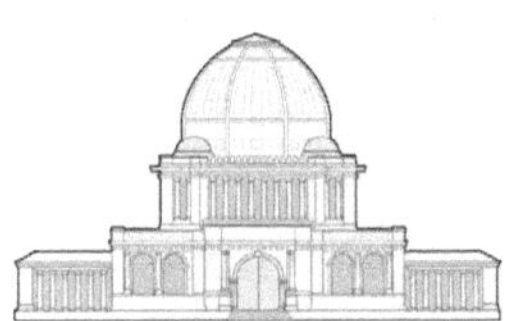

The air hummed with the magic of books wanting to be read.

They whispered irresistible secrets and promised power to those who would turn their pages. After years of working in the Order of Magica's Archives, I was used to the murmuring books and immune to their siren call.

The Order's Archives, one of the largest magical libraries in the United States, contained the secret history of the world—one written by sorcerers and vampires, werewolves, and demons. Their stories filled the endless stacks that descended deep below Lake Michigan. Tall marble columns supported the library's domed roof.

I wound my way through the bookshelves to my desk, hidden in a lonely alcove at the back of the archives. A precarious wall of stacked books, scrolls, and old reports formed a fortress around my laptop.

A stack of three new forms covered my keyboard. I groaned and snatched them up. Research requests. Partially completed.

Still on my feet, I waved the forms in the air. "Who left these? I was gone like fifteen minutes. *Who* even uses these anymore? Email me, people."

No response from the empty room.

I'd spent years compiling research for other people's cases while trying to work my way up to detective. So far, I hadn't gotten a lot of credit for my work, and my requests for advancement were always ignored.

I'd fight a raccoon for dumpster dominance if it meant a shot at detective.

I pushed aside my to-do pile and slipped a hidden folder out of my desk. It was full of notes I'd compiled on a recent string of supernatural kidnappings. I wasn't assigned to the case, but if I could crack it on my own, or even—

My gaze fell on a book that hadn't been sitting on my desk when I'd left for break. *Arabian Nights*, flipped open to the middle. My heartbeat quickened as I leaned over to read the words scrawled across the page. In ink, of all things.

Neveah Cross. Meet me at Exposition Park at eleven p.m. and your secret is safe. Tell no one.

Oh shit.

I swallowed hard, fear rushing through me. Could they know what I—

My phone rang, and my heart missed three beats. I fumbled for my cell, barely catching it before it tumbled onto the floor.

"Neve?" It was my best friend, Rhiannon, a detective with the Order. "Where are you?"

Tell no one. The note's words echoed in my mind, and I put on a casual voice. "Same place as always. Night or day."

"Neve. Sumerian demons are loose at the Oriental Institute Museum. We need a banishment spell." She was out of breath.

My heart raced.

This was bad.

While I lived in Magic Side, an all-magic suburb of Chicago, the Oriental Institute was located in Hyde Park, which was mostly inhabited by humans. The primary purpose of the Order of Magica was to keep the existence of magic hidden from the rest of the world, and a demon rampage in a public place like the OI Museum would take weeks to cover up.

What if they killed someone?

I shoved the note to the back of my mind as my fingers raced over the keyboard. "It'll take time to find the right spell. What kind of demon?"

"No time. Grab whatever books you need. The lieutenant wants you with us. Meet downstairs in five."

Holy shit. I was on a case.

A *real* case.

Not just books, but danger and demons. A chance to prove I could do this.

Finally.

My personal problems would have to wait. I tore the note out of the book, guilt streaking through me, and shoved it in my pocket. Heart pounding, I raced through the upper floors of the Archives, leaping over an oaken banister.

One of the long-nosed library imps buzzed by me on leathery wings. "No running in the Archives!"

I grabbed the little creature by the arm and spun it around. "I need books on Sumerian demons! Lives are at stake. I'll hit special collections. Can you check the stacks?"

Since the stacks spiraled sixty-seven floors below Lake Michigan, it was only practical to search them if you could fly, like an imp.

If only I could fly.

The imp glared, then nodded and darted away. I dashed into special collections. Technically, I wasn't allowed in here either, but right now, that didn't matter.

My fingers danced across the spines until I found the book I was looking for—an old musty leatherbound volume that vibrated with dangerous magic—the *Manual of Ancient Demonology*. The other books on the shelf had inched away from it, just to keep a safe distance.

Smart books.

I snatched the sinister tome and spun around, colliding with a dwarf.

He glared. "You're not allowed in here."

"Take it up with my boss." I faked right and ducked left out of his reach, then ran back through the library.

The imp caught up with me and dumped a load of books in my arms. "You need to check these out before leaving."

"Thanks!" There was no time. Books in hand, I backed through the massive doors to the Archives, setting off the library alarms. The furious imp shouted at me as I raced across the skybridge and down through the Hall of Inquiry.

Man. I was going to get reprimanded by at least three department heads for this little stunt. But then again, I never got to go into the field, and there were lives at stake. If this worked, they'd let me off the hook. And if it didn't... Well, it was my only shot.

Totally worth it.

I burst out the front doors, dashed down the steps, and slammed straight into a brick wall of a man who seemed to appear out of thin air.

My books flew across the pavement.

"Hey, watch it!" As the words left my mouth, a wave of magic surged over me. Scents of ancient forests. The taste of sea salt. The sound of waves. His magic was so powerful that it would have knocked me on my ass if I weren't already on it.

I looked up and locked eyes with him.

My breath caught.

Streetlights cast shadows across his face, but they couldn't conceal his lethal beauty. Or deadly physique.

His piercing green gaze skated over my form, sending shivers down my spine.

Who *was* he?

Perfection.

Terrifying perfection. An entrancing darkness radiated around him, like shadows cast by candlelight.

The world pivoted while he stood immobile.

It lasted just a moment, but time refused to move forward. My heartbeat drowned out everything around me until Rhiannon's voice cut the moment.

"Come on, Neve!"

His spell released.

I scrambled after the fallen books, scooping them into my arms.

"You forgot this one." His whiskey voice stroked over my nerve endings, and I tried to suppress another shiver. He held out the dusty book on demonology, its dark magic twining with his.

My instincts said run, but my feet were glued to the pavement.

His eyes drew me in with a gravitational pull, and

unable to speak, I took the book. My fingertips nearly brushed his, and an arc of electricity passed between us. I swallowed hard and looked away.

"Now, Neve!" Rhiannon shouted.

Sucking in a sharp breath, I took the book and high-tailed it to Rhiannon and the waiting car. I opened the door and turned back toward the mysterious man.

But he was gone.

2

We sped over the long bridge that linked Magic Side to Chicago.

Our city was located on an invisible island in Lake Michigan, just offshore of South Side. If you didn't have magic in your veins, you couldn't see it. That kept most of the normal people out, though every few months, someone found their way over.

My boss Gretchen—aka Lieutenant Bitchface— drove. Unfortunately, she despised me. Books and research weren't her thing. If she couldn't use it to crack somebody's skull, she wasn't interested.

She yanked the wheel hard left, and we squealed onto the invisible onramp near Harold Washington Park and raced down Lake Shore Drive.

There was no time for thoughts of the mystery note or my meeting at eleven. I tried flipping through the books in the backseat of the car, but my stomach lurched with every sharp turn.

Before I could find all the spells I likely needed, we screeched to a halt in front of the Oriental Institute Museum, located on the University of Chicago's campus. I grabbed the *Manual of Ancient Demonology* and followed Rhiannon and Bitchface through the Museum's ornate bronze doors and into the lobby.

Although the Museum was in the human part of Chicago, the Order had cleared the building so we could use our powers.

We were going to need them.

The Mesopotamian gallery crackled with magic and reeked of sulfur. These were some pretty heinous demons by the feel of it, but I couldn't see them in the massive room.

I ducked down behind a case of Mesopotamian cylinder seals and pressed my back against the glass.

Rhiannon crouched beside me. Clutching her samurai sword, she peered around the corner and whispered, "What the hell are those?"

"Good question." I peeked from behind the case and barely caught a glimpse of the two strange creatures. They were short, gangly humanoids, and they seemed to be oozing black tar from their stony flesh. Their large, bulbous eyes scanned the Mesopotamian Gallery, and I ducked before they saw me.

Leafing through the *Manual of Ancient Demonology*, I found the page immediately—I had a knack for books.

"They're gallu, ancient Sumerian demons that stalk the mortal realm. They can inhabit statues and make them come to life. Whatever you do, don't let them grab you with both hands."

"Why?"

"They'll drag you into the underworld."

"Greeeat."

On the other side of the room, Lieutenant Bitchface hissed at me, "I don't care what they are. How do I kill them?"

I flipped the page, reading quickly. "We can't kill them. We need to turn them back into stone statues with a binding spell. Gimme a minute, I know where it is."

Her lips pulled back in a snarl, and she twisted her heavy cudgel in her hand. The thrill of the impending fight flashed in her eerie yellow eyes. She was a shifter, and though she *probably* wouldn't transform in the museum, she'd still fight like an animal. And win.

Though I didn't love the fact that she was on my case all the time, I did respect her track record for kicking ass.

A crash sounded from the gallery behind us.

"Nope. Time's up." Bitchface pointed at Rhiannon. "Let's go!"

"The book says whatever you do, don't damage them!" I shouted. "They'll—"

A howling gallu leapt from behind a case, ran along the wall, and hurled itself at Rhiannon. She dove for cover, but its demonic claws raked her face.

Bitchface kicked it in the chest and slammed her cudgel into its skull before it could get both claws on Rhiannon.

The creature's head separated from its body with a resounding crack and rolled across floor. A thick plume of oily smoke billowed up from its neck.

Then its head reformed.

"Oh, *hell* no," Rhiannon hissed.

I pivoted right, looking for the severed head. It had rolled to a stop by a wooden cabinet. It grew a new body of black smoke that hardened into living stone.

"Damaging them makes them multiply!" I shouted. "*That's* what I was trying to tell you."

"Well, shit!" Rhiannon sheathed her sword. "This isn't going to be any use."

The demons cackled with delight and dashed down the hall toward the Khorsabad court.

"Not so fast, assholes!" Rhiannon jumped to her feet, pulled a bolas from her hip pouch, and spun the weapon overhead. The two heavy weights whirled uncomfortably close to the glass cabinets full of fragile, priceless artifacts, and then Rhiannon let it fly.

The bolas zipped through the air and wrapped

around the legs of the fleeing demon, which skidded through the gallery. The weapon moved as if it had a mind of its own—which it did, as well as a name —Hercules.

Gretchen raced after the demon's twin as Rhiannon shouted, "One down!"

I flipped open the book in my hands. "I can turn them to stone, I just have to memorize this spell!"

The fleeing gallu slashed at the Lieutenant's torso as she rounded the corner of a display case. Rage flooded Gretchen's eerie yellow eyes, and fur bristled along her skin. She leapt at the demon with a roar, shifting into a snarling black wolf mid-air.

Well, there she goes.

Bitchface slammed the demon to the ground, trying to pin it with her mighty paws.

"Don't let it get two claws on you!" I shouted.

At that moment, the third demon howled above me.

I dodged out of the way as it dropped from the ceiling. The monster grabbed for my arm. I deflected its strike with the book, but it caught my wrist with its other claw, searing my skin with its foul magic.

One more handhold on me and that would be it— the demon could drag me into the underworld.

Thankfully, I was trained for moments like this. In a world filled with demons, you had to know how to fight back.

I pivoted as the demon lashed out, then stepped

closer using the dance-like movements of Silat, a South-east Asian martial art and knife-fighting technique. With a single fluid motion, I deflected its arm and slammed my open hand against its wrist, breaking the creature's hold.

I kicked out the demon's left foot, spun it around, and pinned its arm behind its back.

I controlled the dance now.

Closing my eyes, I chanted the words of the ancient Mesopotamian binding spell and prepared for magic to pulse through me.

Nothing happened.

Well, shit.

Ancient Sumerian was damn near impossible to pronounce, even with training from ghosts.

The gallu kicked its clawed feet into my stomach, sending me reeling into the adjacent display cabinet. The monster raced toward the museum entrance.

I scrambled to my feet. "Don't let him escape!"

Rhiannon stepped out and clotheslined it with her sheathed sword. The demon slammed onto its back with a crack, but didn't split in two.

This is my shot.

I dove to her side and slammed my palm down on the demon's chest. It flailed and wrapped a clawed hand around my ankle.

Agony flared as desperation coursed through my veins. I chanted the Sumerian spell, wishing with all my strength that it would work. A raging torrent of magic poured through me and into the monster. It howled and hardened into solid rock.

"Stone cold!" Rhiannon shouted.

I yanked my leg out of the demon's solidified claws, shredding my favorite jeans and leaving a trickle of blood on my skin. "Damn it!"

Glass shattered in the rear of the museum. Bitchface clamped her jaws down on the demon she was fighting, pulled it from the wreckage of a display case, and threw it against the wall.

I silently cringed. "Gentle, L.T.—with the cases and the demons!"

The Lieutenant pinned the demon to the floor with her massive paws, though it fought like a thing possessed. I darted to her side, dodged its grasping claws, and cast the spell. The monstrosity hardened to stone with a dying wail.

Exhausted by the powerful magic, I staggered back to the demon entangled in Rhiannon's intelligent bolas, Hercules. With the last of my strength, I uttered the incantation again, petrifying the last gallu and sending its soul—if it had one—back to the underworld.

A black, bituminous slime coated my hand as I peeled it away. "Ew."

To my relief, the residue began to dissipate in a stream of foul smoke.

Rhiannon slapped me on the back. "Nice spell work!"

Picking up the *Manual of Ancient Demonology*, I flopped onto the cold, hard floor and stared at the patterns that adorned the Oriental Institute's ceiling. As much as I adored museums, this was one of the unintended consequences of amassing ancient artifacts—you were never quite sure what people dug up in the early twentieth century.

3

"I'm so screwed." I glared at my drink. My Southside cocktail was strong, but it hadn't quite mellowed my mood.

Rhiannon and I had decided to nurse our wounds at The Hideout, our go-to bar on the corner of Stone Giant and 60th Street. Despite its name, the place was well lit by the Edison bulbs hanging from the ceiling. We sat at a long granite-topped bar, staring at the collection of strange and familiar liquor bottles on the shelves.

Conveniently, The Hideout was also located near Exposition Park, where I'd be meeting the mysterious note writer later tonight.

A chill ran through me, but I bit my lip. *Tell no one.*

I desperately wanted to tell Rhiannon, but there was no way I'd put her at risk. I'd handle this problem just like I handled most others. On my own.

Anyway, I had a lot of secrets. The note writer might not even know the *big* one.

"You're not screwed." Rhiannon sipped her crisp pint of Old Style. "It's not a total disaster. Gretchen was really impressed with your spell casting."

I jabbed at the mint leaves in my glass, relieved for once to focus on work problems. "For all of five minutes. Until she got fifty-thousand angry phone calls. Now she's in total *bitch mode* again."

After we had busted the demons, Gretchen had been screamed at by the head of special collections, the head of circulation, and her direct supervisor, the department chief.

Apparently, saving the day did not make up for robbing the library.

"Yeah. The chief apparently tore her a new one."

"And it all trickles downhill. I got *such* an earful. She hated me before. I'm never gonna make detective while she's running the show."

"Well, maybe stop putting salt in her coffee whenever she's not looking. It's the wrong way to get noticed, and she's got to know it's you by now."

I brushed aside a whisp of my red hair. "You're right. I've gotta think of a new trick."

Rhiannon laughed and threw a handful of beer nuts into her mouth. "The shifters on the force only see you as a researcher. You've got to start using your powers, Neve. Show off a bit."

"*What* powers? So I can planes-walk. The most hazardous and *indirect* form of travel."

She leaned in closer. "We both know you're capable of more."

I swallowed hard. Of all my secrets, this was the big one.

No, don't think of it now.

The note writer might not know that I was half-djinn, one of the four elemental species of genies. I wasn't sure what I was capable of, or how to control my powers. Worse, if the wrong Magica found out what I was, they might try to capture me and force me to grant wishes—which I certainly couldn't do. As much as I wanted to explore my power, I needed to do so discreetly.

I shook my head. "I can't risk people finding out what I am. You know what happened the last time I used my magic. I won't do it again. I can't."

Rhiannon frowned. We had done this dance many times before. Rhia hadn't mastered her own powers yet, either. She was a time traveler, a talent that was extremely dangerous to use without years of practice.

Lucky for her, Rhiannon could also use her powers to look into the past—a super valuable skill for a detective. Even though we joined the Order of Magica at the same time, she'd climbed the ranks while I was stuck in neutral.

Eager to change the subject while killing time before

my meeting, I leaned in close. "Do you think the gallu have anything to do with the string of supes gone missing?"

It was the topic on everyone's mind. For the past month, supernaturals had been disappearing at an alarming rate throughout Magic Side. Nobody at the Order of the Magica had any leads—which was why I'd started surreptitiously researching the case on the side.

"Maybe. Perhaps the gallu pulled the missing supernaturals into the underworld." Rhiannon idly glanced at her watch. "Aw, crap, it's late. I have to go."

"You're leaving already?" It would be for the best, though. I didn't want to have to ditch her suspiciously at eleven.

"I'm beat, and I've got a date with my bed." She gave me a wink and put her fingers to her forehead, like a seer. "Anyway, I've been to the future. And tonight is the night that a tall and handsome gentleman buys you a drink and makes you a proposition you can't refuse."

I rolled my eyes. "One, you can't travel to the future. You can't even travel to the past unsupervised. Two, it would be more convincing if you didn't predict the same thing every other week."

She laughed and winked at me. "Well, I'm gonna be right one of these days. Have a good night."

Rhiannon dropped some cash on the bar, and waved to the bartender. "See ya tomorrow, Di. Unless the tap runs dry."

Diana waved back. "It never does. You're the only one who drinks Old Style here!"

Rhiannon maneuvered out of the bar, switching her black stilettos for a pair of flats she pulled out of her oversized handbag as she went.

I caught Diana's eye. "I have no idea how many pairs of shoes she can fit in there, but I love that girl like she's my sister. It has *nothing* to do with the fact that we have the same size feet."

The tall bartender laughed. "Enjoy your book, hon."

"You know me too well."

I pulled out my evening's reading and stared blindly at it. Normally, *The Sorcerer and I* would suck me right in. Now, all I could think about was the upcoming meeting in the park. Just an hour to go.

Two pages in, Diana slipped a cocktail in front of me. The vivid yellow liquid glittered in the short Delmonico glass.

Intriguing. This wasn't my usual order.

"What is it?" I asked, breathing in the herbaceous scent of anise, lemon, and elderflower.

Diana smiled. "Elder Monk. With gin, your favorite."

Rhia and I had known Di for at least five years. If she brought you a drink, it was usually worth checking out. Plus, she was good about vetting the weirdos.

I took a sip. It was tart, light, and surprisingly refreshing. "This is so good!"

"It's from the handsome guy standing at the end of

the bar." Diana nodded in his direction, then turned to serve another customer.

What the heck? Guys never sent me drinks in bars.

I glanced over my shoulder and unintentionally locked eyes with him.

Whoa.

He stood, and I had a moment of vertigo. He must have been six-three. Jeans, T-shirt, black leather jacket—he wore them like armor over his chiseled form. He strolled toward me, but I couldn't pull my eyes away from his. They were dark green, penetrating, and spoke of danger. The opposite of mine, which were an icy blue. My skin prickled, and I shifted warily.

"You." My heart thundered. "You're the one who knocked me down outside the Hall of Inquiry."

"I prefer to think of it as being the one who helped you back up." His deep voice brought to mind visions of broken shores and windswept peaks.

As he moved closer, his magical signature hit me like a rogue wave, its strength overwhelming me. A faint heat caressed my skin. His magic smelled of juniper, sea salt, ancient forests...and something that was just at the periphery of my senses. I'd missed it earlier. A scent that had gone missing somewhere along the way.

Powerful supernaturals had signatures that hit all five senses. Though I knew he had to be strong, he was concealing part of his signature well. What was he hiding?

We weren't at Exposition Park, but had he written the note?

He shot me a dark smile and pulled back the stool. "May I join you, Ms. Cross?"

"How do you know my name?" I demanded, heart racing. I shifted on the stool, ready to flee.

His dark green eyes locked on mine, pulling me toward him with an irresistible force. "I'm a seeker, and I've been looking for you."

Ice rushed over me. "*You* wrote the note."

He nodded. "I'd planned to meet you at the park, but then I saw you here. Convenient that we were waiting in the same spot, isn't it?"

"Convenient isn't exactly the word I would use."

Did he know I was half djinn? Was I being hunted? I wanted to bolt, but I had to figure out what he knew. "What do you want?"

"I have a job proposition. I need your expertise to help me find something."

"What do you mean, my expertise?"

As he took a sip of his whiskey, my eyes traced the sharp line of his jaw. "Let's get acquainted first." He smiled. "I'm Damian. Damian Malek."

I nearly choked on my drink. *Damian Malek*? Shit. I knew who he was for sure. Elite bounty hunter. Gangster. He was a central figure in the Chicago Underworld, and worse, one of the Fallen.

A dark angel.

No wonder my alarm bells were ringing. This guy was bad news.

I studied his face. I'd missed it before, but at that moment, I saw a trace of those too-perfect angelic features and a dark glow at the corner of his eyes. I had misread his aura, thinking it was simply sinister and dangerous. Nope. It was the dark radiance of a fallen angel.

Much worse.

I took a breath and tried to calm my nerves. "You realize I work for the Order, right?"

His lips twitched in contempt. "Yes. Which is unfortunate. You're wasting your talents."

Malek was notoriously lethal and elusive. Word on the street had it he ran a ring of bounty hunters who did jobs for all the crime families in Chicago, dispensing some form of Underworld vigilante justice. His activities often ran crosswise with the Order, though his wealth and connections had kept him beyond our reach so far.

"I could lose my job if somebody sees me speaking to you, so spit it out. What's your end game here?" *What do you know about me?*

I wanted to shout it, but bit my tongue instead.

"Come now, Ms. Cross. This is not the first time that you've had Underworld liaisons in this bar."

"What? I have no idea what you're talking about."

"We both know that you're not afraid of anything.

Not even the Devil himself." Knowledge glinted in his eyes.

The Devil himself? It dawned on me—he didn't mean the devil in a general sense. He meant the Devil of Darkvale, *the* crime boss from Guild City, London's supernatural district. I'd met him here a few months ago. How did Damian know that?

Damian smiled and rattled the ice in his glass. "I see you understand me. I know about your meeting. Your employers don't...for now. Maybe you should hear me out."

Oh, thank fates. *That* was the secret he had on me.

The threat was a bad one, but not nearly as bad as if he'd known my species. I could handle a little fall out with the Order. I could *not* handle getting mixed up with Damian Malek. "No. I'm not getting involved with the Chicago Underworld."

"Come on. You've dealt with the Devil. Why not an angel?"

"You mean fallen angel. There's a bit of a difference."

Damian shrugged. "This has nothing to do with the Underworld. More to do with you."

What did he mean by *that*?

He read the question on my face. "I need to get to the Realm of Air, and I need a planes-walker to get me there."

I froze.

He knew.

But *how?*

Rhiannon was the only other person who knew I could planes-walk to the Realm of Air. I'd only done it once before, and it ruined my life.

I set my drink down slowly and stalled for time. "I'm afraid I can't help you with that."

He examined me, trying to peel away the barriers I had wrapped around myself. "I think you can, Ms. Cross. You're half djinn."

I stopped breathing. *Shit.* This was exactly why I had concealed my nature. Fumbling for an out, I managed, "I'm sorry, but you're mistaken."

He put his drink down on the granite bar and leaned in closer. "Ms. Cross, I have a gift for reading magic. I know what you are and what you can do."

I shook my head weakly but couldn't force a denial past the lump in my throat.

Seeming to sense my rising panic, his voice lowered soothingly. "No need to worry. I understand you don't want anyone to find out what you are. So much so that you've kept it a secret from everyone, including the Order."

I searched his dark green eyes for his intentions but came up short.

He sat back. "You should know that I'm in the business of secrets. And if you help me out, your secret will be safe with me."

My mouth was dry, and I was holding my breath

again. Releasing it, I said through clenched teeth, "Blackmail?"

He smiled, the barest movement of his lips.

A predator. That's what this man was. A predator wrapped in a beautiful shell.

I glared. I was trapped, no way around it. "I won't even contemplate helping you until I know what you're after."

He nodded, seeming to understand. "I don't normally discuss details until a contract is signed, but I can tell you this—there is an evil djinn on the loose, and I need to get to the Realm of Air to find it and trap it. You're the only one of your kind that I could locate."

I did some quick mental calculations.

The bad: he knew I was half djinn, and his plan indicated that he had enough power to trap a genie. I could feel the magic emanating off him, and I didn't doubt it.

The good: I didn't seem to be his primary target. At the moment, at least.

I looked for a way out.

"I haven't planes-walked for fifteen years," I whispered, which was the truth. "I can't control it. I'm sorry, but I'm not the one to help you." I grabbed my purse and rose to leave.

He reached out and his fingers brushed my arm, sending a wave of electricity across my skin. For a second, I didn't want to move away. His touch lulled me and drew me in, almost by hypnosis. With a sharp breath, I cleared my head and came to my senses, snatching my hand back.

He looked surprised.

This man was not used to being refused.

He met my gaze, recovering quickly. "I can help you harness your power and planes-walk." With a smile, he added, "Plus, I'll make it more than worth your time."

My cheeks flushed.

"And...if you help me," he continued, "I will keep your secrets. Your origins. Your dealings with the Devil of Darkvale."

It was a barely veiled threat. Naked as a hairless cat.

Again, I turned to leave, but he stopped me. "Nevaeh, this is an opportunity to see the world you came from."

How did he know so much about me? I desperately wanted to see the Realm of Air, a world lost to me as a child...but I couldn't think. Not at the moment.

I needed to get the hell out of there.

4

I caught a cab outside The Hideout and made my way to Rhiannon's place. Hopefully, she didn't have a guy over. Not that it really mattered. I was going to storm in anyway. Rhia would forgive me anything. We'd been through countless tough times together, and she'd want to know that I'd just met the actual Damian Malek.

I pulled my cell phone out and called her. No answer. *That's strange.* She'd pick up in the middle of anything.

My fingers raced over the screen as I tapped out a text: *You're not going to believe who I just met. Need to talk. Heading over now.*

What was I going to do? Essentially, a fallen angel and underworld boss was blackmailing me into using powers that I couldn't control and didn't understand. No way this would end well.

To clear my head, I rolled down the window and sucked in the cool night air.

What were my options? I could search my books for a spell to bind his tongue so that he could never speak of my half-djinn secret to anyone. Would a spell like that even work on one of the Fallen?

I could go straight to the Order. Now. Tell them I was half djinn and that he had threatened me. Unfortunately, as far as I knew, he was untouchable. He'd still get what he wanted out of me, one way or the other.

And who knew what the Order would do? Genies were supremely powerful and dangerous. Sure, I wasn't a full djinn, but I couldn't control my powers, and that made me a loose cannon. I would get fired, or worse, slapped in magicuffs and thrown in Bentham Prison. And what if outsiders found out? The Order leaked secrets like a sieve...

I choked out a gasp. I had been holding my breath, a terrible stress habit.

Damian said that he could help me master my powers and the ability to planes-walk. Was it possible?

He had offered me a chance to explore the Realm of Air. Could I find clues to my past there? I'd been to the Realm of Air only once, fifteen years ago, the day I'd accidentally used my powers and planes-walked away from a family I'd never found again. Pain seared me at the memory of my lost mother and father, an ache that never really went away.

I'd attempted to find my way back to them, but I became further and further lost between this world and the other. So I'd buried my magic in the back of my mind and hadn't unlocked it since.

I looked at the time. 11:04 p.m. Rhia would know what to do. After all, she had a similar predicament: she could travel back in time but could barely control it and had to hide some of her magic from the Order as well.

The cab bounced over potholes in the poorly maintained road as we pulled up to Rhiannon's. She lived in a third-floor walk-up on 69th and Ravensclaw.

I had keys, so I let myself in through the front door and took the stairs two at a time. As I neared the landing, I stopped cold. Her door was ajar.

The hairs on my neck prickled. I instinctively reached for my curved dagger, a khanjar, which was sheathed at my hip.

I pushed the door open, and my heart stopped. A whirlwind had been through here. Books and papers laid strewn about the room, with overturned chairs and a broken table in the center.

Holding my breath, I crept into the room, ready to strike.

I cleared the rooms, one by one, but found no sign of her. Rhiannon was gone, as well as whoever had taken her. Because someone *had* to have taken her. No way she'd have left her apartment like this. And if she were chasing down the culprit, she'd have called me for backup.

Heart pounding, I pulled out my phone and dialed Lieutenant Bitchface—*Gretchen*. I had to start thinking of her as Gretchen. As annoying as she was, she was the best one to have on a job like this. It only took a minute to describe the scene and convince her to head over.

As I hung up, a shimmer near the ceiling caught my eye—a band of golden writing burned along the top of the walls.

Holy shit. What had I walked into?

The script ran continuously along the perimeter of the room, and I grabbed one of the toppled chairs and climbed up to inspect it. Superficially, it flowed like Arabic calligraphy, but the individual letters were different. I had never seen anything like it. The writing had to be some sort of spell, but what *kind*?

I closed my eyes and took a mental image of the writing, then snapped some pictures with my phone just to be sure. My photographic memory was good but not perfect. Still, I had a sinking feeling that I knew what the writing was. There had been too many coincidences tonight.

The lieutenant barged into the apartment with Detective Miller in tow. She scanned the room, then fixed me a flabbergasted stare. "What in the hell are you doing up there, Neve?"

"I'm reading the writing on the wall."

"*What* are you talking about?" Gretchen snapped.

She couldn't see it? Confused, I looked at my phone.

My photos showed bare walls. I glanced back up. The emblazoned writing was still there.

My stomach turned.

Something tugged at the back of my memory. Had I seen this before?

It felt like a sound at the tip of my tongue. A word I couldn't pronounce. If my suspicions were right, there was no way I could explain why I was seeing the writing without letting them know what I was.

"Neve?" Gretchen prodded.

"Nothing. Thought I saw something, but I didn't." I got down from the chair and gave my statement to Gretchen and Miller. Despite Gretchen's cantankerous exterior, she was kind. She was obviously concerned about Rhiannon, doing her best to muscle down the worry and focus on her job.

I would definitely stop putting salt in her coffee.

I left out the details about Damian in the bar. That could potentially tank my career—plus, I couldn't risk letting them on to what I was. I didn't mention the writing on the wall again, either. Gretchen seemed to have forgotten it, or perhaps she'd assumed I was out of my mind.

My duties done, I slipped out as more officers arrived.

I hailed a cab and headed home, replaying my

conversation with Damian Malek. He was tracking down a loose djinn. Could it have kidnapped Rhiannon?

Things began to fall into place. I was the only one who could see the writing...was it because I was half djinn? Could it be a language of the djinn? Had the kidnapper left a message?

I tapped the driver on the shoulder. "Change of plans. I need to go to the Hall of Inquiry."

He dropped me off about twenty minutes later, and I bounded up the stairs at the front of the building. Security was used to me visiting at odd hours, and the guards didn't ask too many questions as they walked me through the East Wing and over the annex skybridge to the Archives.

The magical doors to the Archives were decorated with constantly shifting scenes of bizarre animals and monsters, scientists tinkering with equipment, astronomers studying the heavens, and a myriad of depictions representing the breadth of knowledge contained within.

I swiped my keycard and entered the vast domed space that was shrouded in shadow. Even at this hour, the librarians—fiendish imps—were flying in and out of the stacks, retrieving and shelving books. Every muscle in my body relaxed. This was my true home. Even in the dead of night, I was more comfortable here than anywhere else on Earth.

After an hour of hunting, I found a dusty tome

written in the 1920s, *The Language of the Djinn*. While I flipped through the cracked and yellowed pages, something tickled the back of my mind. A long-lost memory. Something intertwined with my childhood.

I closed my eyes and recalled the words I had seen on the walls. As I located them in the book and scanned the translation, my skin went cold. The inscription was a binding spell of the djinn—a trap laid for Rhiannon that would have prevented her from slipping away through time.

A lump rose in my throat. My best friend had been kidnapped by a djinn.

The djinn had hunted down a time traveler.

Shivering, I swallowed hard.

I had to find Damian Malek.

5

———

I woke with my face smooshed against the pages of *The Language of the Djinn,* still haunted by a series of strange dreams. Somehow, I had fallen asleep reading, searching for more answers.

My phone display flashed 8:30 a.m.

Crap!

I had to get a move on.

I could smell the stink of the gallu on my shirt, an unfortunate reminder of last night. I paused in horror. Had I actually gone to the bar smelling like this?

Before anything else, I needed a shower, coffee, and a fresh set of clothes.

I took one last mental image of the djinn binding spell before returning the tome to its slot, then I booked it home.

I spent the cab ride fretting about Rhiannon. Like

djinn, time travelers were also hunted by nefarious types who would exploit their powers to change the past. Normally, I never worried about Rhia—she was tough and resourceful, and she could use her magic to jump away if things got dicey. She might not be able to control where she went in time, but she could always get home. I couldn't even do that if I planes-walked.

I leaned back against the seat, staring up at the ceiling as my eyes pricked with tears.

I couldn't lose her. She was all I had.

Finally, the cab pulled up outside my place, an old red brick building with a wild, inlaid art deco entrance. It must have been built a century ago, and I loved it. Bleary eyed, I got out. I had to clear my mind and wake up.

Hurrying, I swung by the Magic Bean, a coffee shop located across the street from my apartment. It was a chain, but the brew was half decent. Their scones, though...those were a crime against pastry.

Equipped with coffee, I entered my building and found the elevator empty. It crawled upward to the ninth floor at an agonizingly slow pace. I sipped my coffee and savored its nutty aroma, trying not to freak out about Rhia.

I had a lot of decisions ahead of me. Most of them were strewn around my apartment.

The interior of my abode resembled an unkempt clothing bazaar, with outfits scattered over every available surface. I needed something professional to get me inside Malek Tower, but something that also said, *I'm prepared to kick ass and take names.* If it also made me look irresistibly gorgeous, that would be good, too.

Hmm.

I raced through my shower, and with no time to spare, I threw on a reliable look: a pair of gray moto jeans, my favorite white silk blouse, and a tan leather jacket. I went over last night's events in my head as I adjusted the necklace Rhiannon had given me a couple years ago, an opal pendant dangling at the end of a long gold chain.

Last night, Damian Malek tried to blackmail me to help him hunt down an evil djinn, and I'd turned him down. Now I desperately needed whatever information he had to track my friend.

I had to look confident. Convincing. Like I wouldn't take no for an answer. I glanced at my beauty table, then topped my look off with some red lipstick. Because when in doubt, wear red.

I ditched my purse for a small backpack and stuffed it with a few essentials, including my khanjar.

Boots—check. Outfit—check. Face—check. Dagger —check. Coffee—check.

Let's do this.

I burst out of my apartment, only to then be forced to wait ten minutes for an Uber that got lost twice on the way. I mentally castigated the driver as I tapped my toe.

Magic Side, like the rest of Chicago, was on a grid system, and my apartment shouldn't be difficult to find. Twitchy in my impatience, I fiddled with the opal around my neck. My best friend was missing, and I had to get her back.

I checked the time. 10:30 a.m.

Damn.

I should probably call work, I thought, but as I reached for my phone, I paused. What would I say? *Hi, Gretchen, I can't come in today. I'm meeting Damian Malek, nefarious Underworld boss and bounty hunter.*

I wouldn't call. She had an instinct for lies, and I couldn't tell the truth. Instead, I tapped out a text: *Feeling sick. Worried about Rhiannon. Can't come in today.*

The Uber dropped me off out front of Malek Tower, a jarring juxtaposition of modern glass architecture and gothic elements. The top of the tower came to a sharp point, like a black glass harpoon thrust toward the heart of heaven. I stormed through the lobby doors but was stopped by a burly security guard.

"I have an urgent meeting with Mr. Malek," I lied, crossing my fingers that Damian was actually there.

Twelve minutes later, and after a series of phone calls, I was finally allowed on the elevator. It rocketed up to the 107th floor.

The elevator doors opened to reveal a dark reception area with walls of carved ebony. Shadows made it hard to discern the details of the decoration, but it reeked of power.

In the middle of the room, a receptionist sat behind a large desk, half of her face illuminated by a single green lamp. She fixed me with a vacant, reptilian stare. "You must be Ms. Cross. Mr. Malek will be with you shortly. Please have a seat."

I fumed. *Are you kidding me?* Between the cab, the doorman, and the elevator ride, I had wasted enough time already.

"No more waiting!" I snapped, and barged through the set of double doors.

Well, I tried to. They were locked.

Irritated, I pounded on the door, and Damian's voice sounded over the secretary's speaker phone: "You can let her in."

I shot her a triumphant look, then turned to push on the door...which was *still* locked. My glare turned wrathful, and the secretary gave me an unnaturally slow blink in return.

"Sorry." She smiled and reached under her desk to push a concealed button. The doors clicked, and I finally went through.

Damian stood at the far end of the room, gazing through a wall of windows overlooking the expanse of Lake Michigan and Magic Side below. He cut a striking silhouette against the sky, a black shape against white clouds. His tailored navy suit fit perfectly, accentuating his tall, athletic form.

"Ms. Cross." Damian turned. "I've been waiting."

His signature rolled over me like an ocean wave. He had repressed his power last night in public. Now, barely restrained, his magic crushed against me like the pressure of the deep.

I could barely breath, but I steeled my resolve. I would not let him intimidate me.

I strode halfway across the room. "Last night, you asked me to help you find a djinn. Thirty minutes later, I discovered my best friend was taken by one. What do you know, and what haven't you told me?"

Damian frowned. "Do you mean the woman you were with last night?"

I nodded. "Rhiannon Holloway. She's a detective at the Order."

"How do you know she was taken by a djinn?" He crossed the room, and I was taken aback by his broad shoulders and tall frame. His magic rippled off him, searing my skin with a radiant heat and igniting a flutter in my stomach.

My pulse quickened, and my senses heightened.

I stepped back, trying to focus. "I found her apartment in shambles, and there were remnants of a djinn binding spell emblazoned into the walls."

"If that's true, do you know why the djinn would have taken her?"

I didn't dare reveal Rhia's powers to him, so I gave a half-truth. "Rhiannon's been investigating a string of disappearances. They're probably related to your djinn."

"I am sorry. If the djinn is responsible for your missing friend and others around the city, then we have to act now. You need to help me."

"Not until we set some ground rules. Otherwise, I go straight to the Order." I walked over to the glass windows and gazed out across the vibrant city and the churning waters of the lake. "Priority one is we need to find Rhiannon."

Damian joined me at the window. "And the djinn?"

He was right. We had to stop it, or the disappearances wouldn't end.

"Fine. After we get Rhiannon, I'll help you with the djinn. Then you can do whatever it is you want with it." I turned to him, meeting his intense gaze. "And one more thing, you'll have to sign a binding magical document to never tell anyone what I am."

"Of course." Damian crossed to his desk and pressed the intercom. "Erica. Bring me a binding contract, please."

A minute later, a brown-haired girl with icy eyes, black horns, and a grey skirt swept in with the contract and a pen. The paper shimmered with deadly magic. As Damian scrawled his promises across the page, thin trails of smoke rose from the letters, filling the air with the pungent scent of brimstone.

Clearly, this was one hell of an enchantment.

He handed me the paper, and I read it three times. The language was tight. Maybe there was a way for him to weasel out, but I couldn't find it in the pressure of the moment.

In exchange, all I had to do was transport him to and from the Realm of Air. My stomach knotted. Not because I was agreeing to work with one of Chicago's biggest crime lords, or that I was making a pact with a fallen angel to track down a djinn, but because I was agreeing to return to the Realm of Air.

All in all, I wasn't on the hook for much. But the contract still scared me. These things were dangerous.

I looked up and met his intense green eyes. "I wasn't lying. I don't know how to control my power or navigate between the elemental planes."

He smiled. "I did promise to help you, didn't I? I never break a promise. I know you can do this."

I eyed him suspiciously, though something about the way he said it calmed my nerves. Perhaps it was the low tone in his voice, or the confidence.

Or maybe I was just going mad. Working *with* Damian Malek? I shook my head to clear it. There was a good chance I'd end up either fired or dead at the end of this mess.

But I didn't have a choice.

Holding my breath, I pushed the terror from my mind, and signed my name.

"How did you get involved in this?" I asked.

Damian looked down at me with a disarming smile. "The genie was released unintentionally, and it's my job to bring it back."

"Who released it?"

He paused. "I don't know. But it's a powerful djinn, and I suspect it's creating a stronghold in the Realm of Air."

Djinn were one of the four types of genies, and they ruled the Elemental Plane of Air. Efreeti ruled the Realm of Fire, dao the Realm of Earth, and marids the Realm of Water. Because I was part djinn, I could innately travel to the Realm of Air, but not the other three.

Damian rapped pointedly on the window with his knuckle. "As you know, djinn are unbelievably powerful beings, and there's no way to defeat one outright. I consulted with a mage, and our best option is to try to trap it in an object, like the lamp to which it had been bound. But to do so, we'll need to go to his palace and collect something precious to him to help with the binding spell."

"Wait a second...you said he was trapped in a lamp. How could you know that?"

Was Damian concealing something about this job?

He pulled a shiny brass object from his pocket. Part of a lamp. "Because I was charged with finding the djinn. To do that, I needed something that belonged to him. It helps focus my seeker magic."

He moved closer, sending shivers across my skin. "I understand you may find the idea of binding and trapping a djinn distasteful, but it's a destructive entity that needs to be stopped."

The proposition was terrible and brought a lump to my throat.

Could I trap and bind one of my own kind?

Hell, I hadn't even met my own kind. The thought excited me. I might learn more about myself. My powers. My family—

No. I'd give it all up for Rhia, if I had to.

"Rhiannon is my family. I'll do anything to get her back." I had lost my family once. It was not happening again.

"I understand." Damian nodded. "I respect that."

He turned and crossed to the far end of the room. I relaxed a little now that his magic wasn't making my skin tingle.

Damian traced his hand in an arc along the wall beside his desk. A flare of light revealed a ring of emblazoned runes. "I have something for you."

He stepped forward and vanished through the wall.

I approached cautiously—I knew very little about this man or his magic.

He returned a moment later, carrying a wide, leather-bound book with gold lettering embossed into the cover. "I'm led to believe that you're fond of books?"

Curiosity consumed me, and I moved closer. "What is it?"

The book hummed with magic. Rather than smelling like a dusty old volume, it exuded scents of incense and distant lands. It was deliciously ancient.

Damian placed the tome on his desk and stepped back, gesturing for me to approach. "It's the *Atlas of the Planes*. There are only three copies known to exist. It was *extremely* difficult to come by. I had hoped to use it to hunt down the djinn myself, but I don't have the gift."

"The gift?" I ran my hand across the leather cover. It was warm, as if it had been sitting in the sun.

"The ability to see what is within." Damian stepped closer, looking down over my shoulder. "To me, it's just empty pages."

My breath caught.

I opened the cover.

"What do you see?" he whispered, sending shivers dancing up my spine.

There were only a dozen or so pages within the large atlas. Dense calligraphy covered the initial leaves. I turned them over to reveal a map of the Realm of Air, sketched in detail with white ink.

I stared down at the shapes and figures on the page, and they began to move and dance before my eyes. I was drawn in by the vast realm of sky that appeared on the paper, pierced by floating cities wrapped in clouds. They were just specks in an open expanse, but as I looked at them, I felt myself tumbling closer. Spires rose from the mist, and birds wheeled through the air.

Damian grabbed my shoulders and pulled me back to the present.

I gasped and looked up at him, disoriented from being suddenly yanked back to this world.

"Careful, there. You almost left without me." His hands were still firmly planted on my shoulders, and my stomach did flips.

I hadn't been prepared for either of those things—tumbling headfirst into a book, or the strength of his touch—his power was haunting.

I took a deep breath. I yearned to return to the page and fall back into that realm. It called not just to my heart but to every fiber of my being. What was this sensation?

I flipped the page.

More text and a map of the Realm of Fire inscribed in red ink. Heat rose off the page, as if the paper would spontaneously burst into flame.

Flipping to the Realm of Earth, a strange sense of revulsion surged through me. I coughed, as if breathing in a cloud of dust, and felt my throat closing. I slammed the book shut.

"What?" Damian said, curiosity streaking his face.

"Nothing."

I opened it again and returned to the first pages. The text recounted the far travels of the tenth-century explorer, al-Muqaddasi. He described the denizens of each world and the method for focusing one's mind to pinpoint your destination.

I sat at the desk for hours, studying the manual. Damian might have passed in and out of the room while I read, but I hardly noticed. At one point, he brought me a roast beef sandwich and a latte, which I devoured ravenously, before returning immediately to the book.

I internalized everything I read, making memories of the pages.

Finally, realizing my back ached, I looked up. Damian stood before me dressed in blue jeans and a black T-shirt and jacket. When had he changed his clothes? I measured his form. He was a man shaped from steel or stone. Beautiful but austere.

He hefted a pack over his shoulder. "Are you ready?"

"I don't know if I'll ever be ready." I looked down at the book. "But I suppose we have to go."

I got up and staggered, my legs having fallen asleep. How long had I been reading? It was night, and the lights of the sprawling city shone like stars.

I gazed out the window, stretching my legs, and trying to get my bearings. I could see the Hall of Inquiry and the Gaslight District beyond. My apartment was somewhere to the south, in the part of Magic Side called Old Mud City.

Damian joined me. "It's a hell of a view at night."

I nodded and looked up at him. Dark shadows crossed his face, hinting at a dangerous past I couldn't even imagine.

Fallen angel.

What had he done to lose his wings? I shuddered, unnerved. His kind had impossible power, and I'd heard he was the strongest of them. I could feel his power even now, washing over me like a warm wind. His silhouette was magnetic. I felt myself take a step, longing to be closer, drawn in by the angelic lines of his face...

Fates. What was I thinking? This man was the devil.

"Why did you need to build such a tall tower?" I glared at him. "Who are you trying to impress?"

"No one except the clouds." Traces of a smile ghosted his lips. "In truth, I like to watch the storms roll in—and to keep an eye on Magic Side below. Someone has to."

I scoffed at that.

"What? I provide a simple service. I recover things that are taken. I bring back people who have strayed from the path."

"You work for gangsters. You're a thief and a hitman."

"Don't kid yourself. This city is run by criminals. They *are* the law. Everyone else is just going through motions and filing paperwork. The sooner you understand that the Order is a farce, the more clearly you will see the world."

I scowled. Was I *actually* going to work with this man? A criminal? We needed to get rolling before I lost what resolve I had. "I have to freshen up before we go. I've been reading for hours."

Damian pointed me to a bathroom, where I splashed cold water on my face. I leaned on the counter and looked at myself in the mirror. Was I really doing this? My reflection gazed back at me, slightly skeptical. I steeled my resolve and nodded. "Yes," I muttered. "I'm doing this."

It wasn't much of a pep talk, but it was all I could muster in the face of having to leap from Magic Side to a completely different plane of existence. Not to mention that I barely knew my traveling companion.

I strode back into Damian's office, slightly refreshed and pushing down my jitters.

"Were you talking to someone in there?" Damian asked.

"Absolutely not. Why?"

His gaze locked on me, like he was reading my thoughts. "Never mind. Before I forget, do you have an item that belongs to Rhiannon? It'll help in tracking her."

I hesitated for a moment. The thought of him being able to track Rhiannon scared me, but what choice did I have? He was a seeker and my best chance to find her. I reached for my opal necklace. "Will this work? It belonged to her a long time ago, but she gave it to me."

"Good. I can use it to find you both—not that you'll go missing."

My heart clenched at those last words. I was becoming less and less confident about the plan. Maybe I should've let Gretchen know what I was up to—but that would have raised way too many questions. I'd already gone too far.

I turned to the *Atlas* on Damian's desk. A faint force tugged at my chest, urging me toward it, compelling me to open it.

Weird.

I delicately opened it to the map of the Realm of Air. I'd never planes-walked like this before. Heck, I'd only ever planes-walked *once*. I reached my palm out to Damian. Did we have to be touching if he was going to come with me?

He took my hand in his, and I felt a calm wash over me. How odd. Sensing the strength of his magic, a part of me was glad to have him beside me.

I put my other hand on the page, visualizing the destination in my mind. I sucked in a deep breath, summoning the power buried within me. The *Atlas* drew me in, as it had before.

We whirled downward. The magic tore and ripped at us, pulling away every vestige of the material realm around us. Terror washed over me as my earthly form disintegrated, leaving only our ethereal bodies.

My grip on Damian's hand began to slip as the howling vortex of magic threatened to tear us apart. He pulled me closer, wrapping his arms around me, as every element of our beings was stripped away.

Suddenly, I was whole again. My stomach dropped as we plummeted into a realm of blinding blue sky.

Wind rushed around us, buffeting our clothes.

I gasped.

We were free falling and spinning out of control.

6

This is all wrong!

Panic shot through me as Damian and I plummeted through a vast reach of blue sky stretching in all directions.

Disoriented, I looked around for a landmark. Nothing.

Damian clutched me close as we spun. Oh, *fates*! In using the book, I must have focused on the Realm of Air and not a specific point in space.

I clenched my eyes shut and summoned the images from the *Atlas*. I saw a city in my thoughts, rising from the clouds. There was a great open square. I focused on that point and drew upon my power.

The air exploded around us in a *whoosh*, and we collided with stone pavement.

Sprawled on the ground, I took stock of my situation. I ached, but nothing was broken, thank fates. The world reeled around me as I tried to regain my bearings. My head pounded, and my arm tingled.

Damian helped me to my feet. "Nice save. Where are we?"

We stood in a square in the middle of a vast city. Massive spires rose around us. The buildings seemed hewn from fog, built as if they were of gray, semi-translucent stones. In the far distance, at the end of a long, uninterrupted street, a gray fortress towered above the clouds. A thin mist enveloped us.

I looked around, feeling queasy. "Specifically? I have no idea. I just picked a cloud city from the *Atlas*."

We were not alone. The street was filled with exotic beings going about their business. Some looked like us, while others were avians—birdlike people with wings, beaks, and taloned feet. Cloud-like creatures darted between the buildings.

I drew closer to Damian and breathed in the city's heady aroma of fruit and spices.

The people paid us no heed, as if our sudden arrival was neither surprising nor uncommon.

Two black ravens alighted on the ground near us and looked at us quizzically with beady eyes.

"Welcome!" someone squawked.

I turned, but nobody was there. "Hello?"

"Hello!" it squawked again. "Are you new?"

I looked down. It was one of the ravens.

"Huh?" I turned to Damian. He looked bewildered.

"Are you here to see the fine city?" the other raven said in a high voice. "Many fine sights."

A third raven flopped down on the stones. "I can show you the city!"

The first raven hopped closer to me, saying, "Do you have precious things?"

The ravens looked like any normal ravens would, but they were talking to me. Two more birds came down from the sky. "I'm the best guide to the city," said one of them.

The bird beside him pecked at his feet. "No, I'm the best guide to the city!"

"We're new here. Can you tell us where we are?" I asked, just going with the moment. I knew Damian was going to use his seeker sense to track Rhiannon and the djinn, but I figured we could use all the help we could get in navigating this foreign place.

One of the ravens flapped its wings. "The city of Tayir! In the wind-blown isles, of which Madinat al-Nasim is crown jewel."

I recognized Madinat al-Nasim from the *Atlas*. It was the capital of the Realm of Air and seat of the Grand Caliph, who was a djinn. I hadn't read about Tayir. It must be one of the many small strongholds in alliance with the capital.

"Do the djinn rule here?" I asked the birds.

Another raven hopped close to me. "This is the fortress of titans."

A third raven pecked at him. "No more without precious things!"

Damian put his hand on my shoulder. His eyebrows raised. "Are you talking to the birds?"

"Do you not hear them?" I asked.

"I hear them, but they sound like birds." He was looking at me like I was half mad.

I could still hear the birds muttering intelligibly below. Maybe I *was* mad.

"It must be because I'm part djinn, and at least partially native to this realm. *That*, or I hit my head too hard on landing." I related to Damian what little I knew of the place and looked back at the flock that had begun to surround us. "They're offering to show us the city."

"Perhaps that'd be a good idea."

A raven pecked my foot. "Precious things!"

"What do you want?"

"Shiny things!"

I unslung my backpack, which by some miracle I still had. I dug around and found my wallet, pulling out a few coins. I showed the raven a dime. "Will this work?"

It pecked at the coin. "These are good things!"

Grabbing the coin with its beak, it flew off.

"Hey!"

The other birds crowded in around us, squawking for shiny things.

"No!" I clenched the coins in my fist. "Not until you show us the city."

The birds looked slightly dejected.

One said, "Fine, follow!"

The flock took off into the air, leaving us in the middle of the square.

I looked quizzically at Damian. "Our guides seem to have just abandoned us."

Some of the ravens returned, landing at our feet. "Why not follow?"

"We can't fly," I said.

"Everybody can fly! You are of this realm, of course you can fly!" The raven cocked its head, squawking. It stood up straight and flapped its wings at me to demonstrate the process, as if I was slow on the uptake.

"It wants us to fly," I told Damian.

He shrugged.

A much larger raven landed amongst the flock. In a sudden whirl of feathers, it rose upward, and the bird transformed into a crooked old woman. She cocked her head at me. "Can't fly, eh?" she said in a crackling voice.

I took a step back. "Can you all transform?"

"These scallywags?" She pointed to the ravens around us. "No! They're just opportunists. They can't tell one city from the other. You're lucky they didn't rob you blind."

One of the ravens squawked, "Mother's unfair!" It stalked off, stomping its little clawed feet.

The old woman came close, inspecting me with myopic vision. She wore a gray shawl, and several shiny trinkets were slung on a string around her neck. Her magic tasted like fresh wheat and smelled of dried herbs. She grabbed my wrist unexpectedly, gently moving my arm up and down. I was too surprised to respond, but Damian stepped forward protectively. The old woman paid him no heed. "Yup, you can fly!" She looked me in the eye, staring up from her short stature. "Half djinn."

It was not a question. It was a diagnosis.

I gaped, unable to summon a response.

She took my other wrist and seemed to weigh each of my arms together, waving them up and down. "Hmmm....but which half?" She looked at my right hand, then my left hand, and let them go. "Humph! Doesn't matter. Can fly either way." Glancing around the square, she asked, "If you don't know how to fly, how did you get here?"

I looked at Damian for some sort of cue. "You can understand her, right?"

"Probably not, he seems kind of thick!" the old woman cackled.

I stifled a smile, looking back at Damian.

He shrugged off the barb. "Yes, I can understand her, all right. Are you *sure* we need her help?"

Before I could answer, the old woman quipped, "Big rooster, gets his tail feathers all in a bunch."

Damian sighed.

I leaned close to him. "I think this woman knows something about me and what I can do, so just go along with it."

He nodded.

I turned to the woman. "I planes-walked us here."

The old woman eyed me. "Hmm...but you don't know where you are. So you're not good at that, either. No one ever taught you anything?"

I hesitated, but the old woman waited for my response. "When I was young, I planes-walked away from my family. I never found them again." What the hell, I figured. My secret was out now.

I glanced at Damian, and something flashed across his face. Surprise?

The woman tapped me on my chest with a bony finger. "So the little chicky fell out of the nest. Very sad! Still...has to learn how to fly." The woman muttered to herself, "Can't fly and comes to the Realm of Air. Like a book taking a vacation to the Realm of Fire. Or a rock swimming in the Realm of Water. Half djinn, maybe only half smart."

"Can you help me or not?" Irritation fluttered in my chest, and I was beginning to lose my patience.

"Yes! Do you have precious things?"

I opened my palm and showed her my pocket change.

"Bah! I know when I'm being swindled."

Damian unslung his pack and drew out a small gold coin. He held it out for her to inspect. "Will this do?"

She looked closely. "Yes, very nice."

She reached to grab it, but he palmed it away from her. "After you help her."

"Mmmm. Fair." She pried my hand open and took a nickel out. "Also, I like this one! Now, listen, little chicky. Flight is all about *lift!*" she continued, pocketing the coin. "You must ask the wind to lift you up."

"How do I do that?"

"You must call the wind by its name. Do you know its name?"

I shook my head.

She whispered the name in my ear, then stood back. "It is not a secret. Everybody knows the name of the wind. But it is best never to say it too loudly, lest you attract the wind's attention. Also, you must say it breathing *in*, and not breathing out. In a whisper!"

The woman spread her arms out and walked in a slow circle. "You must ask the wind with your thoughts to lift up your body. You try it!"

I was deeply skeptical. Was I really learning how to fly from a bird-woman?

I closed my eyes and stretched out my arms. I sucked in a breath and called the name of the wind, imagining myself lifting slowly in the air.

A very different thing happened, though.

A gust of wind hit me, and my feet rose into the air.

Only my feet. The world was, for a moment, upside down, and then it was primarily comprised of pavement. The flock of ravens around me took flight as I hit the ground.

Pain flared through my skull as Damian helped me up. "That was rather good," he soothed, but gave me a look that said, *You asked for this.*

I glared at him. *Smug rooster.*

"No, no!" The woman shook her finger. "Too long thinking with two feet. Feet are unimportant. Think with your whole body. *Lift* your whole body. Balance on the wind."

Irritated, I tried again. I focused my energy on my whole body, imagining it lifting into the air. That time, the wind curled around me, buffeting my clothes, and I slowly began to rise. I caught my breath in elation as I drifted a few feet above the ground. Suddenly, I began to slowly tilt forward. I pushed myself back with the wind, but the sky spiraled violently out of sight, and I flipped completely over and smacked into the pavement.

"Uhhhhh..." My elbow screamed. My neck, too.

Damian pulled me to my feet, forcing back what looked like a smile. "Are you okay? You hit pretty hard that time."

"I'm fine. Just a minor case of whiplash. And some bruised elbows."

"Ten points for style."

I harrumphed. At least I hadn't landed on my head.

On the other hand, I was rapidly drawing the attention of those around. Why did I pick a crowded spot to learn?

I was angry and more determined than ever to succeed. *Third time's the charm*, I told myself.

It wasn't.

It took nearly an hour for me to even be able to balance slightly on the wind. But the sensation of tapping into powers and energies I had no idea I possessed left me feeling euphoric. Even better, Damian got good at catching me before I dropped out of the sky. By then, I had abandoned my embarrassment, and the crowd, having seen my early struggles, cheered my reasonable success.

"Yes, very good!" the old woman chirped, clapping her hands.

Joy surged through me, and I beamed at Damian. "Well, I guess I can fly now. What are we going to do about you?"

"Bah! He can already fly," the old woman grumbled.

I whipped my head around. "What?"

"All angels can fly! Even those who've fallen. He probably should've taught you. But he doesn't know the name of the wind. So best he didn't. He's like a rock that hurls itself through the air. Not elegant like a bird."

Of course. I had assumed that he'd been stripped of his wings when he'd fallen. Apparently not.

"It's true." He shrugged. "I assume that you, Ms.

Cross, understand the value of keeping one's abilities private."

"You did not know he could fly? But you knew he was fallen," the old woman interjected, and then thought for a moment. "Did you know that he is…"

This time, Damian shot her a look that was so forceful, the ravens around us took flight in a massive whirl of black wings.

The woman cringed. "…an upstanding gentleman."

I frowned. "What were you actually about to say?"

She pursed her lips, clearly unwilling to speak of it. Well, I'd get to the bottom of it eventually. He had secrets, and I'd discover them. I turned to Damian, changing tactics. "So, you can fly. What else can you do?"

His eyes darkened. "Much."

His magic crackled and flared around him, his aura shifting through a kaleidoscope of colors. It roared like uncontrolled flames but tasted of the ocean. I could feel the heat coming off him. It was immense. Overwhelming.

So *this* was the magical signature he'd been hiding when we'd first met.

Whew.

I took a step back, and he must have seen the look on my face because his demeanor suddenly changed. He smiled, and his raging aura subsided.

I should not have gotten so comfortable with this

man. He was charming, and I was drawn to him, but in truth, I knew very little about him or his magic. I'd never met an angel before. They were among the most powerful beings. And a fallen one...

I shuddered.

The woman broke the silence. "Now, why are you here? Where are you headed?"

Damian stepped forward. "We're looking for a djinn that is newly arrived to the area. Sometime in the last one or two months."

She scowled. "You should not tangle with the djinn. Their plans are unfathomable, and they could crush you with a wink. Even you!" She pointed to Damian. "Probably."

"We know our business," Damian replied.

"I do not tangle in the affairs of the djinn or angels. My services are rendered." She held out her hand, and Damian gave her the gold coin. Satisfied, the old woman reached down and plucked a feather from one of the ravens near her, who gave a mighty squawk. She pulled out a bit of garish red string from a twisted bundle in her pouch, then tied it to the feather to make a necklace. She whispered something unintelligible to the charm and handed it to me with a smile. "This will help you keep right side up. Fly well, little dove!"

In a rush of black feathers, she transformed once again into a raven and flew off into the shimmering sky.

As I hung the charm around my neck, Damian raised an eyebrow. "I don't think it's magic."

I clutched it to my chest. "It most certainly is!"

There was an awkward moment between us.

"So, you can fly. Where are they?" I craned my neck and peered at his back.

"I keep them hidden." He reached into his pack and pulled out a fragment of the lamp that had once held the djinn. "It's time we get moving."

He was *definitely* changing the subject.

"How, exactly, does that work?" I centered my gaze on the shiny brass object in his hand.

"I'll use it as a focus for my seeker magic. The farther away a target is, the harder it is to track. The signal gets weak, so to speak. This lamp was once very significant to the djinn, so I can use it like a divining rod to amplify the signal. That's why I need your necklace to find Rhiannon."

Damian clutched the brass piece in his hand and closed his eyes. I felt his magic thrum, like plucking the low string of a guitar. He was still for a moment, then opened his eyes and frowned.

"They're not here in this city. They're far away, but I'm not certain of the distance, but they're far." He rose decisively and pointed. "That way."

7

We left the square, turning down narrow streets crowded by a dizzying array of vendors. Spices. Silk. Scarves. Fruit. Trinkets. Tools. The scents overwhelmed my senses. Citrus. Fresh bread. Coffee. Incense.

Wings and elbows buffeted and bumped us as we maneuvered together through the crowd. Some of the people were avians—part bird, with human bodies and clawed feet, hawkish features, and wings. Others looked human, though they were dressed in flowing silks decorated with exotic patterns.

Yes, I thought, *my wardrobe definitely needs some of these outfits.*

Damian took the lead, and the crowd cleared naturally before him. As he moved forward, my eyes traveled down his body. He was *built*, an athletic man with chiseled muscles. And he looked mighty fine in fitted jeans. A smile tugged at the corners of my mouth.

Damian looked back and caught my gaze.

Oh, fates.

I craned my head, pretending to look anywhere other than his butt. "The architecture is just amazing here."

"There are some very fine sights."

I glanced at him, only to discover that he wasn't looking at the scenery. My cheeks burned, and I tore my eyes from his. "The buildings—it's like the stonework was formed from clouds."

"Is this place what you expected? What you remembered?" He started walking again.

I remembered nothing of my youth, nor if I had even spent any time here. What had I expected? Not this— the exotic people, the cloud buildings, the strange creatures in the air— none of it. Vertigo overwhelmed me.

"Honestly? I didn't expect us to make it this far. I didn't think I was going to be able to get us here."

He looked back, raising an eyebrow. "But you tried anyway, despite your doubts."

"I had to. I have to get Rhiannon back." My stomach rumbled.

Apparently, I also had to find something to eat. How much time had passed since we'd left Magic Side? Was time even the same here?

Damian glanced surreptitiously down at my stomach.

Oh, fates, I thought. *He heard that.*

"Maybe we should get some food for the journey," he said as nonchalantly as possible.

At least he was a polite criminal. "Yeah, seems like a good idea."

All around us, the peddlers offered a dizzying array of foods and fruits. I didn't recognize a thing.

"How will we pay?" I asked.

"Gold seems to spend, judging from the old crone's reaction." Damian pressed a few coins into my palm. His fingers lingered for a second, gently brushing the back of my hand, sending an arc of energy up my arm.

Gods, was this going to happen every time we touched?

I haggled with merchants at a few of the stalls and came away with a sack of fruit and bread, as well as two steaming bowls containing some type of stew set upon a yellow grain. We sat side by side on the curb, watching the strange procession of people. His shoulder brushed mine, and heat pooled inside me. Trying to ignore my body's inconvenient—and frankly, annoying—reactions, I chewed slowly, focusing on the flavors that were unlike anything I had tasted before.

"I'm exhausted." I had planes-walked twice, and I'd been flying all morning. Or was it even day? I couldn't tell. I hadn't seen the sun, and there were only ephemeral shadows here.

"I bet you are." He turned and examined me with that intense gaze, causing my chest to tighten.

Trying to act casual, I leaned back against the gray stone wall behind us, closed my eyes, and stretched out my legs, hoping the movement would force the image of his face out of my mind.

Briefly, I cracked an eye and stole a glance at him.

His carved features exuded a lethal beauty, and I was sure being an angel had *nothing* to do with it.

Damian's voice interrupted my stream of thoughts. "I think it will be too far for us to fly on our own, especially since you've just left the nest."

"Mm." I nodded, suddenly aware of the problems at hand. I could fly, but not well. I'd need more practice before I could be sure I wouldn't fall out of the sky.

"Let me see if I can find someone who can arrange transport," he said. "Will you be okay if I step away for a moment?"

"Yeah, I'm fine." Perfect. This would give me a chance to focus without him flooding my thoughts.

In the silence that followed, I opened one eye again, only to find Damian standing before me, looking concerned. "I'm not going anywhere," I insisted. "Go find us passage. Or whatever that amounts to in this place. I'll be fine."

He started to walk away but turned. "Stay put. I'll be back soon."

Unfortunately, that proved to be untrue. While I mulled over my options, I studied the oddly dressed people passing by. I could ditch him. Try to find Rhia on my own.

No, that was a terrible idea. He had the necklace I'd given him, and he'd be able to find me. He'd said so himself. Plus, I didn't have the slightest clue where Rhiannon was. Like it or not, I needed him.

My back ached, and I stood to stretch.

A merchant next to me sold an extraordinary array of scarfs, silky and adorned with strange patterns. I perused his wares, trying to pump some blood back into my legs. It would be a shame not to have a souvenir from this place.

A woman in a saffron dress caught my eye beside his stall. Her garment was ornate and subtle at the same time, and my gaze followed her as she headed down the street.

Wait—was that a book shop?

I knew I shouldn't dally because Damian might return at any moment, but I had to take a look.

The shop was empty save for the owner, who was sitting at the counter, bent over a book. He was short with wiry eyebrows. A dwarf? The walls were crowded with books, and his wares looked old.

The owner glanced up. "Can I help you with something?"

"Yes, I'm looking for a book on the Realm of Air," I raised my eyebrows hopefully.

"Over there."

"Thanks." I made my way to the shelf he'd indicated in the far corner and set my backpack down while I scanned the selection.

Legends of the Arrowhawks. Nope.

Food and Customs of the Planes. Nope.

A Practical Guide to the Realm of Air. I grinned. There we go.

The bell hanging over the door rang as a customer came in.

I pulled the blue leather-bound book from the shelf and scanned its contents. It had a section devoted to the djinn and one on the various cities in the realm. This would be perfect.

As I perused through the book, the hairs on my neck prickled, and I sensed someone approaching from behind. His magic smelled pungent and floral. I reached for my dagger as I turned, but he shoved me hard. I collapsed into the bookshelf as he darted out the door, and then down the street.

"What the hell?" I yelped, then looked down and noticed my backpack was missing. "Shit!"

I reached into my pocket, grabbed one of the gold coins Damian had given me, and slammed it onto the counter. I didn't know the price of the book in my hand, but I bet it was enough. Clutching the *Practical Guide*, I bolted out of the store.

The thief was a good twenty paces ahead of me, but I was fast. I sprinted after him, dodging passersby as I weaved through the crowded street. I gained on him, stride by stride. When he careened left into an alley, I cut the corner and jumped over a box of what looked like oranges. *Bastard!*

Could I call the wind to knock him down? I knew nothing about my powers, but I had to try *something*. I whispered the name of the wind under my breath. Instead of feeling a gust around me, though, a swirl of energy rose around my hand.

Huh.

The cutpurse was gaining ground, and I instinctively reached out my arm toward him. I wasn't at all sure what I was doing, but it felt right.

Energy exploded from my palm, and the thief flipped into the air, propelled by what appeared to be a gust of wind.

Holy fates! Did I just throw wind at him?

I caught up to him, and he sprang to his feet in a defensive crouch. He pulled a knife, and I felt a strange surge of energy pulse off him. His magic reeked of putrid roses.

I saw his face now. He was some sort of humanoid

half-breed. His lips pulled back in a snarl, revealing rows of razor-sharp teeth.

I didn't feel the energy in my palm anymore. I must have spent it when I cast that gust of wind, or whatever it was I did. I whispered the name of the wind again but felt a wave of exhaustion overcome me.

A knife fight it was, then. That was fine—I was used to relying on my khanjar.

I tucked the book in the back of my jeans and unsheathed my long, curved dagger. My body pulsed with the thrill of the fight.

He lunged at my left flank, hoping to catch me off guard, but I stepped to the side as he reeled forward. I brought my elbow down onto his back as he flew by, using his momentum to push him into a merchant's stand behind me. The stand exploded into a flurry of colors as fruit flew through the air. We had caused such a ruckus that the locals were beginning to gather, watching us with concerned glances and whispers.

I stepped forward and grabbed my backpack from the middle of the alley. The thief rolled over and glared.

"What's going on?" Damian barged through the crowd, his gaze on me and then the thief on the ground. He looked worried. "What the hell happened? I told you to stay put."

Okay, never mind. He looked pissed.

The thief took advantage of the moment and darted forward, slashing out with his knife. I leapt to the side, but his knife hit its target. A sharp pain shot across my shoulder blade, though the adrenaline in my veins quickly dulled it.

I spun around to face him. Had he targeted me? Or was he just a thief?

The creature lunged at my face, and I ducked as the blade cut through the air, inches above my head. I kicked, knocking him off balance. He crashed to the ground but scrambled upright and jumped for me. I raised my dagger, seeing just where I would strike with the pommel to knock him out cold. I'd have him this time.

Suddenly, before I could make contact, his body jerked away from mine. He contorted, teeth clenched.

"What the..." I whispered. Was I doing this with my magic?

But then Damian appeared at my side, and I saw that it was his doing.

I balled my fists. I didn't need help—I'd been just fine.

The air around Damian vibrated softly, and I felt his magic, a tingling sensation that set off all my alarm bells. Damian's eyes were dark, and his expression...*cruel*. He watched the man before him, his focus intense. Consumed by rage. Horror filled me as I realized that he was squeezing the life out of the thief. I'd never seen anything like it.

"Damian, stop!" I reached for his arm, hoping to

break the spell he was obviously casting. But he stood there unflinching, focused entirely on the thief. Suddenly, he came back to me, as if waking from a trance. The thief's body relaxed and slumped to the ground.

Onlookers crowded around us, speaking in hushed tones. They were clearly just as shocked as I was at the scene that had just unfolded.

I ran over and crouched beside the thief, feeling his neck for a heartbeat. His skin was warm to the touch, but there was no pulse. He was dead.

I glanced at Damian across the way. He stood there, emotionless. No guilt or remorse.

Fear chilled my bones.

I'd killed before, but always out of self-defense, when there was no other choice. The way Damian had looked terrified me. It was like some kind of evil specter had overcome him…

The cacophony around us startled me back to my senses. The crowd of spectators had grown, and I heard yelling down the street. I didn't know what sort of laws there were here, but I was sure we'd broken a few. We had to get out of there *now*, before whatever authorities ruled this place showed up.

"Let's go." I tugged at Damian's arm, and we pushed through the wary onlookers.

"You're hurt." Damian nodded to my back, his muscles tense.

Was he seriously worried about my back after he just killed that man in cold blood? Anger coursed through me, dulling the unease I'd felt earlier.

"I'm fine. It's just a scratch." My shoulder blade throbbed where the thief had sliced it. Luckily, I was wearing my jacket. I'd check out the wound shortly. *I'll live.*

We ran through the back alleys of the city with no real heading. I pulled up short as we rounded the corner onto a busy street. Shoppers haggled with merchants, and nobody seemed to notice us. I stepped back into the alley and pushed Damian against a brick wall.

"Why did you do that?" I demanded. "I almost had him! I didn't need your help back there. You killed him!" My voice came out harshly. This guy was hitting all my nerves. I didn't need his saving or his arrogance.

Anger flashed across his face. Protectiveness.

"He was lunging for your throat, and by the looks of it, he was going to kill you. I had to." He shot me a piercing look that only irritated me further.

"You didn't have to *kill* him."

"He was likely sent by the djinn. He probably targeted you. We can't leave any loose ends, or its your friend's life at stake." Damian put his hand on my arm. "Come on, we have a boat to catch."

So quickly he changed the subject, as if he hadn't just killed a man. I frowned as I followed him toward the docks.

Perhaps he was right. The thief was likely one of the djinn's minions. But killing him still sat wrong with me. My gaze roved over Damian's back as we walked, imagining that I was seeing his wings.

Fallen angel.

Dark. Dangerous. He'd done what he thought he had to do, but I hated it. How could I ever trust a man like him?

8

———

We wound our way through the streets of Tayir for half an hour, and my anger cooled off a little. Although we were unfamiliar with the city, Damian's seeker magic guided us directly to the sky docks, where he had booked us passage on the *Jewel of Tayir*, a flying merchant ship that sailed—or rather, flew—between the sky islands.

My breath caught as we founded the corner and entered the wharfs. We stood at the edge of the world. While a normal island would have been surrounded by water, Tayir was surrounded by sky. Step off the docks, and you would step into infinity.

The sky docks bustled with activity. Dozens of oddly sized wooden vessels hung in the air, bobbing gently in the wind. Many were ornately carved and brightly colored. My heart raced. I had never imagined anything like it.

As we approached our ship, Damian leaned close and said, "This is a merchant ship that runs between the sky islands. We'll get off at Azura. It's about twelve hours from here. The captain drove a hard bargain, but it was the only ship heading in that direction."

The captain who met us at the gangway was a hawk-faced man dressed in wildly colored robes. He wore a stern expression and had seen a lot of sun. He threw his arms out wide when he saw me and beamed.

"Welcome, welcome. I did not know we'd have the good fortune of carrying a half djinn. What an honor."

I smiled weakly. Did everybody in the Realm of Air know what I was?

"Your servant did not tell me we would be transporting such an illustrious person. We will have good luck on this voyage! Do you have bags?" He headed up the gangway. "Have your servant bring them up."

I shook my head and glanced at Damian with a smirk. He scowled.

We boarded the *Jewel* with several dozen other passengers. It was primarily a grain hauler, though it was taking a load of fruit to the outer isles. The sleek and streamlined vessel had a raking bow and stern but was broad amidships. Magic runes carved into the bow and stern kept it afloat. They glowed and flickered whenever the wind rose.

As we departed the docks, the ship unfurled three massive triangular sails. Two were like wings, while the third rose from the middle of the deck. The crew climbed aloft, shouting to one another from the rigging. At first, it seemed like chaos, but I quickly realized it was a gracefully orchestrated dance.

I found a seat on the upper deck. The sails billowed in the wind as we rose above the buildings below. Up there, the city didn't seem as large as it had from the ground. It was built on a massive chunk of rock—maybe two miles across, give or take—that floated in the sky. The heavily built citadel we'd seen on our arrival was positioned in the center, rising above all the other buildings.

"Who lives there?" I muttered to myself.

Damian took a seat next to me and handed me a leather water pouch that he must have bought. I was still salty about what had unfolded in the market, but my mouth was as dry as the Sahara, so I took the offering. The water was crisp and cool and tasted delightful.

As I drank, Damian turned and locked me with those brilliant green eyes. "Let's take a look at your back."

His anger seemed to have dissipated, replaced by an expression I couldn't discern. I felt his energy wash over me. Warm. Strong. Comforting. It dampened the residual anger I had from our fight, but that, too, made me uncomfortable. He'd killed that man. I couldn't forget that.

"I said it's just a scratch," I protested.

"I want to check on it anyway." His voice was rough, and I didn't feel like arguing.

I pulled my attention away from his hypnotic gaze and focused on the pain, then flinched as I shifted to let him inspect my back. The searing pain was spreading across my shoulders and down my spine.

"Okay," I muttered, "maybe it's not just a scratch."

I peeled my jacket off, careful not to move my right arm too much. I felt the sticky dampness where blood had caked into my white blouse. I was hoping Damian didn't expect me to take my shirt off *here*. The deck was empty, apart from a man who had fallen asleep on a bench across the way, but still...there was way too much chemistry between us for it not to be weird for me to get half naked.

Damian pulled free the book that was stashed in the back of my pants. "You went shopping?"

I shrugged. "It might be handy."

"Perhaps," he murmured as he inspected the gash. "This looks bad. The blade must have been tainted with magic. I need you to take off your shirt."

"Seriously?"

"Yes. We don't have much time—the magic is spreading."

Dang. The deck was still basically empty, and so I

pulled my shirt off as gingerly as possible. Damian helped, his touch gentle. My heart raced, and I clutched my shirt over my chest.

He put his hand on the wound, and I gasped as his magic pulsed through me. The healing energy was warm, and the heat between us was impossible to ignore. His magic flowed into me, creating a connection that lit up all my nerve endings. I leaned toward him slightly, my mind going foggy.

The pain gradually subsided, and I felt my skin knitting back together, leaving a tender, itchy sensation. Damian didn't remove his hand from my back. His warm energy continued to flow through me, and my skin erupted in goosebumps. I shivered, liking his touch far too much.

Please don't notice, I begged the universe.

Of course he did.

He made a low noise in his throat and removed his hand. I felt a pang of regret, longing for his touch.

What was wrong with me? This guy was dangerous, and I needed to stop swooning. It wasn't me.

"How did you do that?" I asked, clearing my mind.

"Despite what you may think, my magic isn't all bad."

I turned and looked into his eyes. They were a lighter shade of green than before, and I saw kindness in them. "So, you can heal. Is that part of your seeker magic, or...?"

"Angel. Most definitely."

"Huh."

There was a pause as he studied my face. "Ah...I see. You thought that since I was a *fallen* angel, it had to be something else." A smile ghosted across his face. He did look angelic. "I've done many things...good and bad. None of them were because of what I am. I own my choices."

Guilt tugged at me. Who was I to judge? I was half djinn, but that didn't mean I inherently had a dark side, did it? I'd never considered that...

Then again, he'd killed that man.

Uncertainty tugged at me.

"What's that tattoo?" Damian's eyes had shifted to my right arm.

I looked down and nearly choked.

An intricate design snaked around my forearm. It looked like a tattoo in white ink...but I didn't have a tattoo. *Sweet fates!*

I faltered. "Uh...my tattoo. I've had this for years. It's just a doodle I designed." I didn't know what it was or why it was there, but I didn't want to let on until I trusted him more.

"It's beautiful." He took my arm in his hand, gently turning it over. He traced the intricate pattern with his finger. It burned with heat where he touched. Good heat.

I looked at his face, feeling hypnotized. His lips were inviting.

Shit. Stop looking at his lips, I chided myself.

I pulled my hand away and took a clean shirt out of my bag. Fortunately, I had brought an extra set of clothes.

"Thanks. For the help." I needed to get away. I couldn't think clearly with him so close. It was like my mind and body were disjointed, each pulling me in a different direction.

I snatched my book from the bench and headed to the observation deck at the prow of the ship, glancing back despite myself.

Damian watched me closely with an expression I couldn't quite read.

I pulled my sleeve back and glanced at the underside of my forearm. The two spiral tendrils of white ink almost seemed like they had a life force of their own. I recalled the tingling sensation I'd felt after we planeswalked to the square. Was the tattoo tied to this place?

I looked out over the clouds, breathing deeply. The cool wind calmed my spirit. Time to focus on priorities.

Where was Rhia?

A couple or passengers jostled around me as I found a seat and opened the book, in which I was immediately engrossed. The breeze blew my hair back as I skimmed the index and found the section on djinn powers. I had to learn more about what I'd done to the thief with my magic. Unfortunately, the book wasn't an instruction manual— not that I'd gotten my hopes up. But it did speak of the djinn command over beings of air, the winds, and the storms.

As the hours passed, the other passengers retired below deck. The sky was a bright blue, and apart from a few thunderheads in the distance, there was nothing up or down—no land, no ships, no sign of civilization, just the sparse clouds and an occasional bird. An over-whelming sensation of freedom swept over me. The ship sailed at a steady clip, and I leaned over the railing, focusing my mind on the wind. The breeze quickened, and I opened my eyes.

I was hovering!

I lowered myself back onto the deck and gripped the railing. Oddly, I didn't recall speaking the name of the wind. Still, it would be a good idea to practice.

I spent the next half hour practicing until I was confident I could levitate on command. I couldn't zip about like a bird yet, but I was getting there.

Gradually, the winds strengthened and turned cold. I didn't notice at first, but it soon became difficult to hold position in the air. The sky darkened, and low rumblings echoed around us. The dampness cut to my bones. When thunder boomed, I scanned the sky. The thunderheads from earlier had moved closer. In fact, it looked like we were headed right towards them. The *Practical Guide* had mentioned the unpredictable ice storms that blew through the realm. They were strong and dangerous, and you didn't want to get caught in one.

Small chunks of ice floated around us.

Great.

As I turned to take shelter below deck, the ship suddenly shuddered, and I lurched against the rail.

"What the hell?" Had we hit something? No way, there was nothing out there.

Damian was suddenly at my side. I'd barely had time to wonder where he had come from when the ship quaked again, and I lost my footing. Damian caught me before I hit the deck. As he helped me to my feet, I felt the solid plane of his chest under his shirt.

I tried to ignore his grip around my waist, but heat zipped through me all the same. Fates. I needed to focus on what had just happened. "What did we hit?"

He let go of me and looked over the side of the ship. "I don't know. But we're turning."

There were shouts from the deck below. Several crew members were adjusting the sails.

"Ice!" one of the crew shouted.

There was a loud crash, and then another. I turned, following the origin of the sound. A large chunk of ice shot down from the sky and exploded across the deck, sending shards everywhere.

I grabbed Damian's arm. "Fates...is that *hail*? It's massive!"

The storm clouds enveloped us, darkening the sky.

The air grew colder by the second. Bolts of lightning flashed in the distance, and a deep rumble vibrated through the hull. Something moved below the observation deck just as another block of ice crashed onto the deck below.

"We need to take cover!" Damian gripped my arm, towing me toward the stairs.

"Wait." I peered over the railing, trying to get a better look. What was moving down there? Another ice ball plummeted from the clouds, this time landing a few feet from us.

I pointed. "There!"

A strange creature rose by the mast. Its form gleamed, tall and translucent, as if its body was hewn of ice.

Holy fates, it *was*.

Icy spikes protruded from its shoulders and back. The creature turned and looked up at us with two black hollows for eyes. Horns protruded from its temples. It held up a spear and gestured at us.

I gasped. "Ice devils?"

The deck of the *Jewel* shuddered again, and I ducked as ice fragments exploded around us. Screams sounded from below. We had to get inside before one of those projectiles hit us.

I started for the stairs, but Damian stopped me. I followed his gaze. The ice particles that were scattered across the deck in front of us were moving and pooling together.

"Oh, shit." Chills danced up my spine.

The pieces became one and began to grow, expanding until the thing was taller than I was. The devil morphed into its crystalline, bipedal form. I unsheathed my dagger and fell into a defensive stance, my knees slightly bent, alert and ready.

There was a thump behind us, and I pivoted. A

second ice devil had scaled the railing and was moving to engage.

Damian shifted between us, thrusting his hand out to his side. A dark purple smoke boiled forth from his palm and took the form of a radiant black sword.

Damn. That was a nice trick.

At that instant, something scraped behind me. I turned as an icy claw swished past my face. I deflected the monster's attack, and then another as he thrust in with an iron spear.

I dodged sideways and slashed his back with my dagger, slicing off a chunk of ice. He turned and whipped his spear in an arc. A blast of icy slush jetted from the tip of the spear and smashed into my chest.

Crap!

I staggered backward into the railing, my ribs throbbing.

The devil strode toward me, lifting his magic spear, ready to thrust it into my skull. I darted to my feet and leapt over the railing, dropping nearly ten feet to the deck below. I landed with a loud crunch, cracking the thin veneer of ice that now covered every surface of the ship, and barely maintained my footing.

This was going to be tricky.

Momentarily winded, I looked back up. The devil had turned his attention to Damian, who was now facing two of them. He extended his arm, and the first creature convulsed and flew over the side of the ship.

I was suddenly grateful for his magic, however sinister it seemed.

The other devil lunged toward Damian with his spear. He dodged it, but not in time. Damian shuddered as the point gouged his torso. He hissed in pain and looked down at the wound, then growled. With a powerful thrust, his black blade slammed through the devil's skull.

The beast shattered into a thousand fragments, and my breath caught in my throat. Would they reform like the gallu had in the museum a few days ago? When the shards remained immobile, relief flooded over me.

But the sensation didn't last long. I heard a clatter from above and looked up.

One of the devils was in the rigging, leering down at me. A second approached from my left flank.

I raced forward to amidships, hoping to get out of the trajectory of the one above. The creature to my left followed suit, glaring at me with those soulless eyes. His face was grizzled, and he stood at least a foot taller than the other devils.

"Man, you're ugly!" I yelled, and darted toward the mast.

He growled.

I slipped on the ice as I rounded the mast, colliding palms first into the wooden deck. My wrists throbbed, but I forced myself onto my knees just as Ugly came in for the kill. He didn't have a spear, but his razor-sharp fingers were just as deadly.

I rolled to my side as he lashed out. When I attempted to use my momentum to kick his legs out from under him, my foot collided with an immobile wall of ice. Swearing, I scrambled sideways, dodging his fist as it slammed into the deck. Splinters flew into the air, and I tried to ignore the pain radiating from my foot.

He swung again, and I instinctively reached up to guard my body. Suddenly, a blast of wind erupted from my palm, propelling the ice devil into the air. It landed with a thud on the deck, ten feet away but still upright and on its feet.

My arm tingled again, and I looked down at my hand. "Not bad," I muttered. "What else can you do?"

Ugly bounded across the deck toward me. He was fast.

I sprang into an offensive stance and sucked in the cold air, whispering the name of the wind. Currents of air rose around my arm. When I jabbed my fist forward, I felt the wind surge off me. A gust hit Ugly in the chest like an invisible fist. He was unfazed, but I was sure I could use this.

Ugly snapped his arm out at me. I dodged by instinct as two giant icicles slammed into the mast.

Fates. This got shitty quick.

I darted behind the mast as two more icicles shot

through the air, which brought me face to face with Ugly's brother. "Crap!" I ducked as he took a swing.

Damian must have heard my shout. He pulled a black bow from the ether and fired a burst of three matching arrows in rapid succession. One missed, but the other two flew home into the back of the ice devil lurching toward me. Each of the arrows exploded in radiant energy, and cracks cascaded through the ice devil's body. The creature exploded in a burst of ice shards. One grazed my forehead, burning my skin like dry ice.

The air behind me chilled, and I turned as Ugly's hand raked my shoulder. My jacket was thick, so his claws didn't break the skin. Nonetheless, a searing cold surged through my chest, and I gasped. My lungs felt like they were freezing solid. I staggered to the rail, almost out of control, and convulsed as shivers wracked my body and panic flooded me. I looked for somewhere to hide.

There was nowhere to run, however, and so I turned to face Ugly.

He stood about fifteen feet ahead, grinning maliciously, and raised his arm.

Oh, shit.

An icicle shot toward me with lightning speed. I crouched and lifted my forearm to block it, bracing for the impact.

But it didn't hit. The bolt of ice stopped midair.

An invisible force was pressing against my hand, and I stared at my palm, shocked. Was *I* doing this?

Intuitively, I flicked my wrist, and the icicle flew back to its origin. It impaled Ugly's shoulder, and he let out a rumbling groan.

Relief washed over me, but I was still shaking from the icy tremors. I had to move fast, but my body was sluggish. Gritting my teeth, I pooled my remaining energy and pummeled Ugly with three more wind punches. He staggered back, and I swept my arm through the air as if brushing something aside. The wind, moving at my command, knocked Ugly's feet out from under him and flipped him over the side of the ship.

"Oh, *hell* yeah," I crowed, and gazed down at my hands. These new powers would come in handy.

But I didn't have long to celebrate. A thick fog crept over the deck, dulling all noise. The quiet was bone chilling, and I tried to peer through the sudden cloud. Was the fog growing thicker? I could see a foot in front of me, maybe two. I shivered, and my lungs burned. My fingers were numb.

A thud vibrated through the deck, and then another from the bow. Or was it the stern? I was totally disoriented.

I inched forward, ready to strike.

Footsteps crunched on the ice-covered deck. They were nearby, but *where*?

A dark shadow loomed at the edge of my peripheral vision, and an icy claw slashed out. I jumped back, but it ripped into my torso. Cold shot through me. I twisted, wrenching myself from its icy grasp. Dropping, I crawled across the deck, feeling slow and disoriented. With any luck, the fog would conceal me from the devils...

Nope. An icicle embedded into the deck beside me with a jagged crunch.

They could see me. *Crap*!

"Nevaeh! Where are you?" Damian's voice sounded so far away.

I staggered to my feet and ran. Well, more like hopped. My ankle felt sprained, my lungs ached, and every step was like fighting through waist-deep water. The mist made it impossible to see, and I crashed into the deck railing, nearly toppling into the abyss below. I clung to the wood, panting as my heart jumped into my throat.

Where were the creatures? Where was Damian?

I shivered.

Out in the depths of the storm, a soft glow wove a path through the fog, as if searching for something. It turned and descended toward me.

I froze, mesmerized by the light. Something about it drew me forward. As it came close, I slowly raised my hand as if I were in a hypnotic trance. When the glow collided with my palm, it disappeared into my skin and sent warmth cascading through my body. The icy tremors stopped, and my lungs no longer burned. I drew in a deep breath with relief. Finally, I could breathe again.

What had just happened? Was this Damian's magic?

The floating light appeared once more, rising through my palm and into the air, bobbing as if it had a life of its own.

"What are you?" I asked in a hushed voice.

The light hovered in front of my face for a second before splitting into multiple sparks. They zipped off across the deck and burst within the fogbank, illuminating the forms of three ice devils.

"Gotcha." I summoned the wind to my palm and charged across the deck toward one of the glowing forms. Brightly illuminated by the strange sparks, they couldn't lurk in the fog now.

The devil heard me and spun, raking the air with his claws. But I had the drop on him, and I ducked low, slamming my hand into his side and releasing a violent surge of energy. The devil shattered in a cloud of ice, which whipped away from me as if caught in a tornado.

Only two left. Probably.

I scanned the deck. A faint light illuminated the area around me. Feeling the hairs on my neck rise, I glanced up to find a haloed ice devil looming over me in the rigging.

Before I could move, a bowstring twanged, and two

radiant arrows soared overhead. The devil exploded, raining tiny shards of ice down on me.

I glanced around but couldn't see Damian through the fog. It seemed he could see the glowing devils, too, though. Had he illuminated them with his magic? But if that had been his magic, why had it gone into me?

Could it be *my* magic?

No. Totally unlikely.

The third devil was far astern, locked in combat with Damian. I ran along the deck, trying not to slip on the ice.

I was about to call my magic when the hull of the ship creaked behind me, and I whirled around.

A dark form loomed. Ugly was back.

He lashed out, striking with wicked, icicle-like talons. I dodged and twisted as his claws cut through the air around me.

I wasn't sluggish anymore. The light had rejuvenated me...somehow. The thrill of combat surged through my veins, pushing me to move faster. I pulled my khanjar from its sheath at my hip. As Ugly struck out with his icy claw, I brought the curved dagger down. His wrist snapped with a crack, and he roared with rage.

I roared back, striking with my dagger, over and over, attacking recklessly. Seeing an opening, he drove his fist into my chest, and I flew backward. The blow knocked the wind out me, and the deadly chill returned.

"Okay, bud. Let's finish this," I growled, my breathing straining my frozen lungs.

He charged forward, eyes blazing.

I leapt, and the wind lifted me high into the air, unlike anything I'd managed before. I twisted and let myself drop onto his back, then plunged my khanjar into the base of his skull. His icy form exploded beneath me, but as I was hurled backward among the shards, I stopped myself in midair and slowly sank to the deck.

Silence reigned.

There were no more glowing forms, and the fog was still thick. Adrenaline pulsed through my veins. Or was it magic?

10

In a rage, I called the name of the wind, sending a gust outward from me in all directions to clear the fog away.

Damian stood near the helm, silhouetted against the retreating fog. He leapt down and crossed the deck in seconds. "Are you hurt?"

"I'm fine—thanks to you. You saved me back there." My arm tingled again.

"You were amazing." He cocked an eyebrow. "Are you certain you've never done this before?"

"I've always been able to fight. The wind powers, though...they give me a wicked edge."

Damian smiled. "You're a fast learner."

"Not a lot of options." I sheathed my blade, and gestured to his smoking sword. "That's a hell of a weapon. I needed to find a spell that will let me dismiss my khanjar like that."

With a snap of his wrist, Damian dismissed the blade into a ribbon of smoke. "I forged it. It's a part of me, for better or worse."

"You made it?"

Something flashed in his eyes, but I couldn't read it. He set his jaw and turned to stare out over the railing at the sky beyond. "I was a smith, once. A long time ago."

Well, that explained his physique.

Not much else.

Blood plastered his shirt to his side. "You're hurt. Can you heal yourself?"

He glanced down at his wound and frowned. "Their weapons must be poisoned. The spear tip is still inside."

So his magic had its limits. Noted.

I opened my mouth, but the captain burst onto the deck, cutting off my words. "Blessed winds! You've saved the ship." He took my hands in his. "Thank you, thank you. We wouldn't have survived the storm without your help. These foul ice raiders are a blight on the skies. Is there anything I can do to repay your kindness?"

I looked at Damian and back at the captain. "Do you have somewhere we can clean up?"

"Yes, yes. You will take my cabin. It's yours."

I nodded.

"When will we reach port?" Damian asked.

"Tomorrow morning. But we will dock early at a port in Capri. I'm afraid we can't risk going on to Azura like this." The captain gestured up at the sails. One of them was torn and whipped in the wind. "Capri is only a couple hours from Azura. I'm sure you can hire a boat to take you the rest of your journey."

The storm clouds were behind us now, and the sky was bright, the sun warm.

The captain led us to his cabin below. It was small but comfortable, with a single bed, a table, and a chair. Light streamed in through a pair of paned windows positioned at the stern.

"You must join me and the crew for dinner," he said as he turned to leave. "Join us in the mess hall when the watch changes."

"Thank you. We'll be there," I said.

Damian set his pack down and took off his jacket. He wore a black, fitted, long-sleeved shirt, which he pulled over his head in one quick motion.

Sweet fates, he was *gorgeous*.

His fair skin was smooth like sculpted marble. His muscles were...big. Not bodybuilder big, but chiseled to perfection. My eyes followed the indentations on his lower back. What were those called? Dimples of Venus? What a ridiculous name. Whatever they were, they invited my gaze as they disappeared under his belt.

He turned just then, noticing my stare. His eyes looked brighter now, an emerald green.

My cheeks blazed, and I crossed to a small table, filling a ceramic basin with water from a squat jug. I took a small towel, dipped it in the water, and tried to steady my emotions as I wrung it out. *Get a hold of your-self, Neve.*

Damian had pulled out a first aid kit from his pack and held a pair of tweezers.

"Let me do it," I said.

He paused, his expression serious, then handed me the tweezers.

I took them and bent to inspect the wound. The gash was deep, and the skin looked inflamed. I couldn't see the tip of the spear.

I looked up at him. "You ready?"

He nodded, observing me closely.

I put my hand on his torso to brace myself. He twitched at my touch, which sent goosebumps up my back.

Focus.

Carefully, I inserted the tweezers into the wound until I felt a clink. Damian didn't so much as flinch from the pain.

"There it is." I pinched the tip and pulled as steadily as I could manage under the circumstances. It probably wasn't the best way to get the damn thing out, but we weren't flush with options.

Damian's jaw tensed as the object came out. The tip was a good two inches long.

Still clamping it with the tweezers, I unlatched the window and threw it outside.

"Thanks," Damian said, his voice as smooth as

honey. The wound on his side slowly knit itself together until the skin was unblemished.

"Wow," I said, watching him heal. "That was fast."

Damian slowly stepped toward me, his eyes locked on mine. "Where are *you* hurt?"

"Umm..." I took a step back, bumped the table, and turned my focus to the pain in my body. "Everywhere."

He was only a few inches in front of me, and he radiated heat.

"Here?" He gently touched my forehead, where an ice shard had sliced me. Its sting faded under his magic.

I was suddenly aware of my breathing. My pulse raced, and my chest rose and fell rapidly. *Too* rapidly.

Damian, however, appeared as cool as a cucumber. He smiled and put his hand on the side of my torso. "Here?" His eyes didn't leave mine.

I nodded. A pulsing warmth flowed through his hands, and the throbbing of my bruised ribs subsided, only to be replaced by an aching heat in my lower belly.

"Better?"

Again, I nodded. My eyes fell to his lips. I wanted to taste him. Badly.

He leaned in but stopped short of my mouth. What was he waiting for?

My senses suddenly came flooding back like little alarm bells waking me up from a drunken stupor. My hand flew to his chest. It was solid and—

Stop that, Neve.

I pushed him back and scooted off the edge of the table. "We'd better go. It's time for dinner," was all I could manage.

Damn, I felt like a giddy schoolgirl. I had never been so flustered with a guy before, and I had seen my share of guys. What was it about him? His sinfully sexy body and gorgeous looks, obviously. But there was something else. Something deeper and less obvious. Maybe it was because he was off limits and extremely dangerous. A fallen angel, for fates' sake. Someone I couldn't get tangled up with—not without risking my career.

We cleaned up and headed to the mess deck. Damian secured the cabin door with a charm so nobody but us could enter.

A cheer erupted as we stepped into the room. The jovial crew sat around a long table. The captain stepped forward and handed us two mugs of what looked like a dark ale. I accepted one gratefully, needing something to take the edge off.

"Cheers!" the crew shouted.

I raised my glass. "Cheers!"

I took a swig. It was warm and malty, and if nothing else, it slaked my thirst. My drink of choice was gin, but this would do in a pinch.

We dined with the crew on a substantial meal consisting of steamed rice and some type of delicious spiced meat. The sailors were much more interested in me than in Damian, naturally. We shared stories of demons and devils, and they asked me about my life. Clearly, being a half djinn made me a curiosity. I had spent my life hiding my ancestry, yet these sailors knew just by looking at me—and *revered* me for it. It was liberating to let my guard down, if only in the realm, if only for a meal. My cheeks flushed. Was I glowing?

A few glanced at my new white tattoo. Did they know something I didn't?

And that wasn't the only thing they glanced at.

I caught Damian's gaze a few times throughout dinner. Was that jealousy I saw? I hid the slight smile that crept over my lips.

The hour grew late, and exhaustion tugged at me. I turned to Damian and nodded toward our cabin. We rose and bid farewell to our new friends, then made our way to the stern. Thank fates that there was a bed waiting for me.

Wait a second.

We would be sharing a room. With only one bed. A tiny bed. A flutter of nerves rose in my stomach.

Damian unlocked the security charm on the door and opened it for me. It was still bright outside—the sun never seemed to set—but he drew the curtains. "You take the bed. I'll sleep on the floor," he offered. His demeanor was in stark contrast to his earlier mood, when he couldn't seem to take his hands off me. I felt slightly dejected, but why? I hadn't wanted this...right?

"At least take a pillow and blanket," I said.

He accepted only the pillow. "Thanks, but I tend to run hot."

Suddenly, *I* was running hot.

I sat on the bed and unlaced my boots, trying to vanquish the image I'd conjured: me sitting on the table, him pressed against me, wrapping me in his arms. I swallowed hard. It wasn't working. I needed to change the subject, and *fast*.

"I meant to ask—how did you illuminate those ice devils?"

"What do you mean?" Damian raised an eyebrow.

"When we went into the fog bank, it got so hazy I couldn't see them. A floating light—like a little softly glowing spark—dropped down from the sky and lit the bastards up with a radiant halo. It seemed like your magic."

He looked confused, watching me closely. "That wasn't me, though I saw it, too. I thought it was something you did."

"Huh. Nope. That definitely wasn't *my* power." I didn't mention how the light had warmed and rejuvenated me. Apparently, there were a lot of things here that I didn't understand.

I climbed under the sheets and fell into a deep and fitful sleep. I dreamed of ice devils and of that strange glowing light, as well as the old bird-woman who taught me to fly.

And Damian.

We were standing on the stone square from yesterday. He faced me, his eyes darker than I'd ever seen them. The wind picked up and swirled around us. My hair tousled in the gusts. Terror shot through me, but...why?

I sensed his energy, and it felt dark. His aura flickered between a dark green glow and a fiery red.

Suddenly, I was paralyzed, locked into position. His gaze intensified, and I felt a crippling pain. I would have collapsed, but I was frozen in place.

My magic surged inside of me, as if amassing into a ball in my chest. I screamed but couldn't make a sound.

Damian reached his hand out, and I craned my neck in agony. I screamed again, and a terrible noise burst from my throat. It wasn't my voice, though. It was the energy inside, rushing out in a torrent and shooting upward in a blinding column.

Then it was gone, and I was left wasted.

Empty.

As my soul rose into the heavens, I saw Damian below, glowing with a new aura.

My aura.

11

I woke to Damian nudging my shoulder, and I jumped. "Neve. Wake up," he said. "You're having a nightmare."

I recoiled at his touch. I could still feel the dream. It was so vivid. So real.

"Yeah. Sorry, I just had a bad dream," I said, trying to shrug off the sick feeling in my stomach.

"Ice devils?"

"Uh...yeah." That was partially true. I got up and splashed some water on my face, but my thoughts remained foggy.

I opened the window for fresh air. A small speck of an island floated in the distance. Capri?

"We're about an hour away." Damian held up the piece of the lamp he was using to track the djinn with his seeker magic and gestured at the blue expanse. "I have a strong bearing now—the djinn is out there, somewhere close. Do you think you can fly for an hour or two? It would be better if we could take off from here and avoid Capri."

I thought for a second. *Could* I fly? I mean, I had practiced hovering. I had also levitated over the ice devil last night.

"Maybe?"

"Well, we'll try. If you run into trouble, I'll catch you." His perfect lips pulled up into a devilishly sinful smile. "But first, I'll find us some breakfast. We'll leave after that."

I nodded, and he left the room.

I couldn't kick the knot in the pit of my stomach. *It was just a dream.* But that image of Damian standing before me, paralyzing me with some unseen force, still haunted me. It was different than what he'd done to the thief in the market. This time, it was as if he'd been draining my power, wrenching the life force out of me.

I stared at the wooden slats on the floor. "It was just a dream."

Right?

Still, I couldn't stand around analyzing my dream all morning. I pulled out a clean shirt from my bag, but as I tugged my sleeve down, my eyes stopped short on my arm. "Again?" I muttered.

The translucent white design on my arm had grown. That must have been why my arm was tingling last night. This was definitely connected to this place—and my magic. I'd come a long way since we'd arrived yester-day. I could throw gusts of air, and I'd commanded the wind. I'd learned how to fly.

Well, to levitate.

What else could I do? Djinn supposedly had a vast array of powers, including the ability to control the weather and summon air spirits. But I was only half djinn. What were my limits?

At that moment, Damian came through the door bearing sustenance. My skin prickled as the haunting apprehension returned, but I forced a smile and shoved the dream toward the back of my mind. He was danger-ous. A killer. A fallen angel. It was probably just my subconscious telling me to be careful around him.

It was just a dream.

Thirty minutes later, we stood on the deck and bid our farewell to the crew. A few passengers had ventured out, but most were still shaken from the events of yesterday.

"Take this, Nevaeh." The captain handed me a rolled-up parchment. "It will aid you on your journey."

"Thank you for your kindness, Captain." I unrolled the document, revealing a detailed map. I recognized Madinat al-Nasim in the center. Around it was a network of smaller islands with distances marked between them. Among them, I spotted Tayir and Azura. Capri, too.

There were also notes in the margins warning of dangers. The island of Aeros had a red cross through it.

The captain gestured to the marks. "Whatever you do, avoid the red crosses. Those islands are overrun by monsters and miscreants. You'll only find trouble there."

"This is remarkable. Thank you again for your generosity," I replied, and handed the map to Damian.

He scanned the page for a second. Then, tapping his finger on the document, he said, "This is it. This is where we're headed."

Did seeker magic really work like that? I'd have to ask my friend, Nix. She was also a seeker. I glanced down to where Damian was pointing.

Aileth Islet.

Of course, it had a red cross through it.

"Be careful. I haven't been in those parts, but I've heard stories," the captain said.

I peered at him. "What kind of stories?"

"Some say the island is inhabited by dragons. Others have said that a dark force resides there. Ships that venture too close never return." The captain shuddered, then turned and headed for the steps. "May the winds bless your journey and keep you safe!"

My stomach sank as I thought of Rhiannon stuck on a dragon-infested island. I had to find her. Taking the map from Damian, I secured it in my backpack. "Ready?"

"The question is, are *you* ready?"

I balanced on the railing. "As ready as I'll ever be."

I stepped off into the void, and gravity pulled me downward. I feigned a scream and darted underneath the hull to hide, levitating on the wind.

Damian flew down in a blur, going too fast to notice me hiding under the ship. I smiled.

A minute passed, and he returned, hovering in front of me. My breath caught. His wings were stunning—broad and strong, and covered in iridescent black feathers that glittered in the sun. I guess I'd expected white wings, but black suited him well.

He looked slightly peeved, and I laughed. "Gotcha good."

He flapped his wings slowly, as if giving an annoyed slow clap. "Are you done?"

We took off into the blue sky.

I was far from graceful. While Damian flapped leisurely in the air, I had to push myself along with the wind. It was like playing volleyball with a balloon—I had to keep smacking myself with bursts of wind to stay aloft and correct my course. I definitely wasn't Wonder Woman. *Yet.* Every so often, I lost focus and dropped a few feet, which sent my stomach into a lurch.

This wide-open expanse was probably the best place to learn. There was no ground to serve as a crutch, or more importantly, no ground to splat me if I tumbled out of the sky.

Damian provided a few pointers, and slowly, I started sailing upon the wind instead of tumbling along like a ball pushed with the tip of a stick.

I dove and twisted in the air, the wind surging and swirling at my beck and call. When had I ever felt this free? This *alive*?

A cumulus cloud billowed below us, fluffy and white. I drifted downward and skimmed across its surface, dipping my hands into the mist. Tiny rainbows glistened in the air, and I dove through them, down into the fog. I couldn't wait to show Rhia my new powers. Idly, I wondered if I could use them back home.

Home. *Crap.* I'd texted Gretchen that I would be out for the day, but how much time had passed? Was time the same here? I bet she was having a fit. I'd have to—

Something huge careened in front of me. I pulled up fast, but the g-forces were too intense, and everything went black for a second.

I was falling, spinning like a skydiver caught in a parachute.

Blue sky. Clouds. Blue sky. Clouds.

My stomach lurched.

A dark shape drew close. I was whirling like a dervish and couldn't focus, but two arms latched onto me and slowed my spin.

I knew that strong embrace—Damian.

Thank fates.

He slowed my fall, and we hovered. He frowned, concern in his eyes. "You've got to take it easy, Nevaeh."

"There's something up there in the clouds!"

A piercing screech echoed in the distance.

"What *is* that?"

"Sounds like a bird," Damian said.

"Or a dragon? Didn't the captain say something about dragons in the area?"

"We better take cover in the clouds." Damian looked at me seriously. "Stay close. No more racing off."

"Fine." I was happy with that. I didn't want to come face to face with a dragon all by my lonesome.

We made a beeline for the clouds. At least we had some cover, though the mist made it difficult to see. I flew unsteadily, shaken by my fall, and Damian had to reach out and stabilize me a few times. "Are we getting close to the island?" I asked.

"We're almost there. Just a little bit farther."

The beating of wings reverberated around us.

"What's that?" I looked around wildly, trying to catch a glimpse of something moving in the clouds. My concentration faltered, and I dropped several feet before Damian steadied me.

We were just below the clouds now, and I scanned the sky.

"Dragon," Damian whispered, and I followed his gaze.

A massive white beast broke through the cloud bank. Its wings were covered in brilliant silver feathers, while its body was shielded by white reptilian plates. The creature beat its wings and spiraled through the air, its tail following like the ribbons on the end of a kite.

I stared, awed. "It's magnificent."

The dragon craned its neck upward in our direction. Uh-oh.

The beast wheeled around and shot toward us. Light glinted off its feathers, and its eyes gleamed a brilliant black. They narrowed on me.

I gaped in horror, floating paralyzed in the air.

"The clouds." Damian yanked me into the whiteness.

I heard the dragon as it flew closer, and then a *whoosh* of wind crashed into us. It slammed through me, sending me cartwheeling out of the clouds, but I flailed and managed to stop my fall.

Where was Damian?

Another screech pierced the heavens, and the beast broke through the mist.

Panic flared, and I whirled away, flying as fast as I could. Ahead, a large mass floated in the distance— Aileth Islet. We were close. I just needed to make it to the island.

I looked back. No sign of Damian.

Something rumbled, and a sudden burst of hot air hit me from above.

I looked up as the dragon swooped through the clouds.

Flying for my life, I darted to the side, but the dragon followed. With a frantic breath, I dove downward. The air rushed past me, pinning my arms to my side. Maybe I could lose him, I told myself.

Not a chance.

A white shape loomed in my periphery. The beast was far faster than I had imagined.

Still spiraling, I turned, despite the difficulty. A massive head appeared beside me. Ivory horns framed the creature's magnificent face. Its gray scales were offset by a glassy black eye that stared back at me, then blinked in a double-lidded reptilian way.

I clenched my teeth and pulled my torso up. My insides reeled, but I shot higher. I was getting good at this!

The dragon followed suit and was at my side. Again.

I careened left, silently begging it not to follow.

It did.

Its massive wings pounded the air beside me. Panic welled in my chest as turbulence whipped me around. There wasn't any way to outrun it. I was too slow. I would be dragon food any second—

Hold on a minute. I should be dead already.

I turned right, and the beast mirrored my movement.

Holy smokes. It's mimicking me.

The dragon turned its head and peered at me. Its pupils dilated as they focused on me, and then the creature bowed its head.

"Did you just nod at me?" I asked.

It abruptly turned and disappeared.

I slowed to a hover and watched it leave. There it was, beating its wings with an unparalleled slowness and grace as it rose into the clouds.

Damian appeared at my side, shaking his head. "I've never seen anything like that."

"I know. It was incredible." I stared almost longingly after the dragon's disappearing form. The moment had passed too quickly.

I hung there in the air, breathing heavily and feeling euphoric. I could fly. *With dragons.*

Finally, I caught my breath, and we continued onward to the island.

Every inch of my body ached. Flying drained me, consuming reserves of energy I hadn't known I had. "I hope we don't encounter any more visitors. I'm completely bushed."

Damian glanced at me, his jaw tense. "The island is surrounded by a ring of floating rocks. We'll take a breather on one and come up with a plan."

By the time we landed, I was quaking with exhaustion. "I don't know how much farther I could've flown."

"You did well back there."

I looked over at Damian. "You don't even seem winded."

He didn't answer, just strode to the edge of rock.

I rolled my eyes, pretending not to notice how magnificently angelic he looked against the backdrop of the blue sky.

The rock, one of many surrounding Aileth Islet, was about a hundred feet across and covered with sparse vegetation. Most of the masses in the Realm of Air were inhabited, but these rocks were probably too small to support a population.

I sighed in relief as I took a seat. As Damian pulled out a pair of binoculars from his bag, I remarked, "You're prepared for everything." Then again, when one was a professional bounty hunter and thief, one had to be.

Aileth Islet loomed in the distance, about a half mile away. A white citadel was positioned in its center, but we could only see its front half because our rock floated at a lower altitude. The citadel was actually more like a palace constructed of white marble that shone blindingly in the sunlight. Its plan was reminiscent of the Taj Mahal, with four domes offset from a central larger dome that towered over the others.

Damian scanned the enclosure with his binoculars. "Looks like we're going to have to find an open window. The gates are too heavily guarded."

"Figures."

"What do you mean?"

"Well, you *are* a criminal. I assume that sneaking through a back window is your specialty."

"I prefer the terms 'bounty hunter' and…'acquisitioner.' I have principles."

I raised my eyebrow. "Uh-huh. By whose standards?"

He ignored the gibe. "We need to reconnoiter the palace. Thankfully, there are a bunch of floating rocks to give us cover."

We flew from rock to rock, making our way around the side of the palace, slowly drawing closer. Fortunately, we were small enough that the guards didn't see us.

Billowing fog began to close in around the palace on all sides. I couldn't tell where the islet began or ended, but I saw the tips of smaller structures protruding from the mist. "Binoculars?" I whispered, and Damian passed them over.

Winged, hawk-faced guards were patrolling the sky and parapets. They were similar in form to some of the creatures we'd seen in Tayir and brandished long, barbed javelins. Rather than walking a perimeter wall, which would have been useless in the Realm of Air, they flew from point to point around the domed roofs.

"There's a pattern in their movements," I said.

Damian nodded. "We're going to have a tight window to slip in without getting noticed. They seem to be watching the sky, so we should come from below. Ready?"

Probably not.

I nodded.

"On my mark, follow me."

We dove off the rock, flying down beneath the level of the floating islet and taking cover in banks of mist along the way. To my astonishment, the bottom of the islet was a hanging garden. Vine-like growths with purple flowers dangled from the crags, and insects with long, iridescent wings darted from flower to flower. I hadn't expected such beauty to be hidden below, but I supposed it made sense, as the sun seemed to shine in all directions in this realm.

Damian motioned to me, and we began a slow ascent up the side of the floating crag. Concealing ourselves in the dense fog, we eventually found our way onto level ground, and I gingerly followed as Damian somehow led the way.

Suddenly, he reached out his arm and stopped me. "Hold on. We're here."

I appreciated the gesture, as I would have walked straight into the wall in front of us otherwise.

Damian was little more than a shadow in the fog beside me. "Stay here. I'm going to check things out," he whispered, then put his hand on my shoulder. "I'm serious this time. Stay here."

With that, he disappeared.

I reran the plan in my head. Get in. Find Rhia. Find

something precious to the djinn so we could bind him. Get out.

It was simple enough. The problem was, nothing had been simple since we'd arrived. I got the feeling that this wasn't going to be as easy as Damian hoped. What was his connection to all of this? Why did he want the djinn, and more importantly, what would he *do* with it? I had been so focused on finding Rhiannon that I hadn't really thought about Damian's motivations.

I jumped back as a massive shadow emerged from the fog, then realized it was Damian, with his wings out. As he came closer, the heat of his magic seared through my clothes. When was I going to get used to this?

"I found our way in. A window in the tower. We'll have to be quick."

His hand touched my shoulder again, and my stomach fluttered. "It wasn't locked?"

"It was sealed with a charm, but I broke it." His face appeared from the fog, just inches from mine. "Are you ready?"

I thought about Rhiannon trapped in this place. "Let's do it."

We launched up out of the fog. The bright sky was blinding, and it took my eyes a moment to adjust. I couldn't help but gasp in awe. The entire palace was a radiant white, every surface decorated with intricately carved latticework.

As I alighted on the windowsill, Damian pulled it open and gestured for me to enter. "Ladies first."

Coming from the guy who got kicked out of heaven.

The room was full of crates of food. Dates. Some type of dried meat and sacks of what looked like rice. Was that parmesan on the shelf? I loved a good parm.

Feeling peckish, I grabbed a wheel of cheese and shoved it my pack, then caught the smug smile pasted across Damian's face.

Ok, so maybe I was a *little* bit of a hypocrite.

"Strange," he said. "I can't sense the djinn or Rhiannon. This place must be protected by a disorientation spell of some kind."

"What are we gonna do?"

"We need to find an object that's precious to the djinn. Something to help with the binding spell."

My irritation flared. "Wait a sec. Our deal was to find Rhiannon first."

"We *will* find Rhiannon, I promise. But we'll need to depart as soon as we have her, so we need to get that object."

"Fine." I sighed. He was right—there was no way we'd be sneaking out of here. I pondered our predicament for a second. "The texts I've read claim that all djinn covet treasure and hide it in great hoards. I bet there's a vault somewhere in the palace. That's where we should look."

Damian's eyes momentarily grew dark. "We'll start there."

He turned to peer out the door, but I stopped him. "The texts also say that djinn protect their wealth fiercely and will hunt thieves to the ends of the world."

"We'd better not get caught, then." He shot me a wicked smile. "Good thing you're with a professional."

12

———

We slipped out of the room, and I followed Damian through the labyrinthine halls of the palace. From time to time, we heard footsteps or muffled voices reverberating along the corridors. We hid in the niched doorways, ready to strike, but encountered no one. Each hallway looked the same. I began to believe that the palace itself was playing tricks with my mind, and soon, I lost my sense of direction. "Do you have any specifics on what we're looking for?" I asked.

"I'm a seeker. I'll know it when I see it."

I shrugged, unsatisfied, but followed on.

Eventually, we came to a spiral staircase illuminated by glowing spheres. It descended into an ornate room decorated with Persian rugs. I peeked inside to find two people arguing within.

Damian pulled me back, shaking his head, and pressed me against the wall of the stairwell.

I held my breath as the two figures passed below. Their magic exuded scents of summer days, tea in the morning, and ripe oranges. One was a shifter, the other...I wasn't sure. Both had golden bands on their wrists.

Manacles.

"Prisoners. These must be some of the supes that were kidnapped. The djinn enslaved them," I whispered.

Damian nodded. "That would make sense."

Many genies sought subjects to enslave. Bastards. Was this my heritage? I almost didn't want to know.

"We have to free them. I can't leave them." I looked at Damian. "There must be a way to bring them with us."

"No." Damian reached for my wrist. "We can't let on that we're here. Not yet."

My anger flared, and I snatched my hand away. "How could you leave them?"

"Right now it's us or them. We need to keep a low profile."

I knew he was right, that there was so much more at stake, but it pained me. I thought of Rhiannon, bound like this and at the mercy of the djinn. I felt sick. "I'm coming back here to save them, I swear to fate."

"Fine. For now, let's go." He continued down the stairs, and I followed reluctantly.

We entered a colonnaded courtyard that encircled a garden resplendent with fountains and elegant statues.

"Wow," I murmured. This place was unreal.

Djinn were known for their extravagance. Feasts, sculpture, art, treasure—they ravenously sought the finer things in life.

I thought of my wardrobe. Okay, that checked out.

As I mulled that over, footsteps echoed across the courtyard. "Hide!" Damian growled, and we flattened our backs against a pair of pillars.

Once safely tucked away, I stole a glance. Two hawk-headed warriors escorted an ornately dressed man bound in manacles down the colonnaded corridor. The man carried an elaborate silver diadem. *Bingo.*

They passed without spotting us, and Damian motioned for me to follow them. "Fifty-fifty chance they're headed toward the treasury."

"Or the djinn," I muttered.

We got lucky, however, and they led us straight to the vault. There was just one problem: we had no idea how to get in.

We came around the corner as the last guard disappeared through a golden wall decorated with silver clouds. Approaching, Damian studied the wall. He moved his arm in an arc, tracing runes in the air. He'd done something similar in his office to access his vault, but this time, nothing happened.

His lips pressed together. "This will be complicated."

While I inspected the wall for some type of clue, the silver clouds shifted abruptly, joining to form a pattern on the wall. The air crackled, and Damian pulled me aside just as the two warriors reappeared.

They looked straight at me.

"Hi," I said, then summoned a surge of wind to my fist and decked one of them in the face. The gust magnified the impact, and the hawk-headed warrior slammed into the adjacent wall and fell unconscious. Damian had his partner down in seconds.

The man with manacles reappeared and stood stock-still, gaping. Slowly, he raised his hands in surrender.

"We're going in there," I told him, pointing at the wall. "How do we get in?"

"You have to make the clouds fit the pattern. It's magic. I...I can't do it." He gestured to his manacles, which must have been enchanted to block his magic.

I bet Rhia had a pair just like that. Bastard djinn.

"I think I got this," I replied, then reached out with my magic and pushed the clouds.

"Please don't! The djinn will kill us all," the man begged.

"We're going to figure out how to stop him and free everyone. Please help us."

He hesitated, then reluctantly showed me the pattern.

As soon as the secret portal turned translucent, the man turned and fled. I looked at Damian. "Should I go after him?"

"No. Our timer just started. We've got to move quickly." He grabbed my wrist and pulled me through the portal, which shut behind us.

We were in a small, dark antechamber. Two torches burst into flame as we entered, illuminating a second gilded door. Damian wove runes in the air, and the lock clicked open.

"You sure do know your way around a robbery, Mr. Malek," I said.

He raised an eyebrow. "You're a willing accomplice."

Fair point.

The door rumbled as it slid open, and torches flickered to life.

I gasped.

Unimaginable riches lay before us. Gold and silver furniture. Ornate statues. Piles upon piles of coins. Pearls. Boxes inlaid with gems. Persian rugs. Even a golden sarcophagus. How had the djinn accumulated this much wealth?

"Holy shit," I muttered, and glanced at Damian. He didn't say a word, but his eyes, now dark, burned with desire. "Hey!" I shoved him. "Let's get what we came for and find Rhiannon."

Damian shook his head as though freeing himself from a spell. He pointed straight ahead to a niche in the far back wall. "That."

A glowing gem was perched on a platinum pedestal. Its colors shifted in the flickering light as if it were at first a ruby, then an emerald.

"Dragon Heart," Damian whispered, his eyes fixed on the gem.

We scaled a heap of treasure to reach the stone. Scrooge McDuck made it look way easier. My feet sunk into the coins, and it was impossible to get a grip with my hands. It was an inglorious ascent, but finally, I made it.

I reached for the gem, but Damian grabbed my hand. "Are you crazy?" he demanded.

I looked at him, dumbfounded. "Isn't this what we're here for?"

"Yes. But you can't just take it."

"Oh, shit. Of *course,* it's booby-trapped." I tried to cover my embarrassment. "Sorry, it's been a while since I've seen Indiana Jones."

That was a lie. I *loved* Indiana Jones, and I'd watched it with Rhiannon last month—though I didn't support tomb raiding.

Damian inspected the pedestal from all angles. He muttered an incantation and pressed his fingers against six points in the wall. Each time, there was a little flash. With that task completed, he stood back, contemplating for a second, then announced, "Okay, I think it's safe."

He reached out and snatched the glowing gem, and I held my breath, waiting for something to come crashing down. Nothing did.

"Nice job," I said.

As we slid back down the mountain of coins, my boot dislodged something—an old, leather-bound book. I plucked it from the treasure and read the cover: *Secrets of the Djinn.*

"Look at this!" I cried.

Damian turned, aghast to find the book in my hands. "What happened to not touching anything?"

Coins clinked behind me.

Oh, fates! I turned as a giant serpent burst out of the treasure pile with a hiss. Its head loomed ten feet above me, and two savage white fangs dripped with venom. It must have been more than twenty feet long. The muscles under its skin rippled, and its head shot forward with lightning speed.

I jumped back, but I was too slow. Its fangs gashed my left arm. Agonizing pain racked my body, and I staggered back, stumbling on the coins.

Damian launched two icicles at the serpent, but it dodged them with ease.

Ice power? *That* was new.

The creature lashed out with its tail and slammed Damian into a pile of statues. He leapt to his feet and drew his black, radiant sword from the ether in a burst of purple smoke.

I trembled with delirium as I summoned my magic, but nothing came. In desperation, I pulled my khanjar from its sheath. My grip was weak, but I fell into my fighting stance.

Damian dodged and rolled, but the serpent was so fast. He spun through the air and brought his blade down, slashing through its tail. It didn't cut the snake, however, but rather passed straight through. The section he had severed dissipated in smoke.

The serpent lashed about. It was unbalanced now, and Damian had the upper hand. His wings burst from his back, and he vaulted into the air above the creature's flailing body. Damian dropped down onto the serpent's midsection, and I wondered what he could possibly be thinking.

The serpent shuddered as blue energy rippled through its body. It thrashed wildly at first, but then its movements slowed, then ceased altogether. It was frozen solid.

"Sweet fates," I muttered.

Damian slid down the pile of gold to my side, wings retracted, but I didn't have the wherewithal to appreciate the view. My head spun, and pain surged through my arm. When I looked down, I saw the problem: my arm was turning to gold.

Damian grabbed my wrist, and I felt his magic

course through me. Unlike the times before, this was agonizing. My back arched, and I clenched my teeth, trying to maintain consciousness.

Slowly, I felt the life returning to my arm. My vision cleared, and the pain subsided.

"Thank fates that worked," I mumbled, looking up at his angelic face. "I owe you big time."

"I'll keep that in mind." He looked me up and down to make sure I was all right. "Okay, Midas. Let's get out of here."

Was that a joke? I cocked my head. "Technically, Midas had a golden touch, not a golden arm."

He shook his head and helped me to my feet. "Lesson learned?"

"Ab-so-lutely. Is the snake dead?"

"Frozen for the moment."

"Good." I reached out and snapped up the book.

Damian stared. "Fair enough," he muttered, then grabbed an emerald necklace and some golden bangles and shoved them in his pack.

I looked back at the serpent, still frozen in place. "How did you do that?"

"That?" He paused. "Just something I picked up from the ice devils. Let's get out of here before he melts."

I nodded and rubbed my arm. *He picked that up quickly. Is he a mirror mage, too?*

The portal in the wall was locked. Thankfully, I recalled the proper configuration of the cloud pattern.

It only took two tries.

Pleased with myself, I led the way through, only to come face to face with half a dozen hawk-headed guards. Two had bows, while the rest leveled their barbed javelins at us.

"Not again," I groused, and shot a blast of wind that knocked them back into the wall. "Come on!"

We dashed down the hall. The guards clambered to their feet and charged after us, and those with bows took a couple of shots on the run. I pushed Damian to the side just as the arrows whipped by.

We turned a corner and skidded through an ornate doorway into another hall.

Footsteps echoed behind us. We were momentarily out of sight, so I made a split-second decision. I grabbed Damian's jacket. "Hold on and be quiet!" I ordered, then pulled him against my chest and called the wind. I flipped us into the air, pressing our bodies up against the corridor's high ceiling.

We hovered face to face, hidden by the low doorway. He was heavy, and his solid body pressed down on mine, causing a heat to rise in my belly. Damian looked like he was about to say something, so I pressed my fingers over his lips. They were soft and warm, distracting.

I pulled my attention to the corridor below and shot a sharp burst of wind at a door down the way. Luckily, it was not locked. The door slammed open just as the guards rounded the corner. I held my breath and buried my face in Damian's shoulder. We were sitting ducks if they looked up.

The guards slowed for a second and looked around. Thankfully, they took the bait and darted down the hall to the open door.

As soon as they were gone, I dropped us silently to the ground, and we hurried back around the corner, retracing our steps.

"I enjoyed that." A hint of a smile tugged at Damian's lips as we ran.

I forced back a smile, worried he would see how much I had enjoyed it, too. "They'll figure it out soon and come back this way looking for us. We need to lose them."

He gestured to an archway up the hall. "There's a stairwell this way—come on. I have a good feeling about this direction."

We raced down the stairs at top speed. I tripped, my feet thundering against the steps. Shit. So much for sneaking.

There were several arched doorways at the bottom. We ran through the central arch and barreled through a small antechamber, emerging into a large, colonnaded room with high ceilings. The walls were draped with tapestry and lit by the warm glow of burning braziers. A carefully laid banquet filled a long table on one side of the room—and there, in the middle of the room, stood Rhiannon, holding a tray with a tall silver teapot.

She gaped, and the tea set slipped from her grasp. The silver platter and pot crashed to the ground with a metallic clang that echoed off the walls.

Rhiannon looked at the disaster, then ran toward me. "Neve!" she cried, but before she could close the distance, her body jerked violently backward as something pulled her up short. She collapsed to the ground.

"Rhiannon!"

As I ran to her, she got to her knees, coughing, and tugged on a long sliver chain. It led from a collar at her neck to a point high on one of the columns. "Freaking chain!" she muttered, then yanked on it for good measure before embracing me.

I wrapped my arms around her. "Are you okay?"

"The bad news is I'm now a tea servant. The good news is that there's unlimited baklava. The other bad news is that I've gained half a stone since I've been here."

Despite the terror of the moment, I laughed. "Fates, I missed you. We're gonna get you out of here."

"You're insane to have come."

I stepped back to examine her. Rhiannon had golden cuffs around her wrists and ankles, as well as the golden collar and silver chain. She was dressed in exotic fabrics.

"You look damn sexy in all this gold," I said, "but I think we need to get you out of it."

"It's nice bling, but it blocks my magic. The chain's new. I've been, uh...less than cooperative."

Damn. Magicuffs.

I turned to Damian. "Can you get her out of these?"

He knelt by her feet. "I'll try."

Damian began to weave runes in the air. After a minute, there was a pop, and the ankle cuff dropped to the ground. "One down. Four to go."

At that instant, palace guards swarmed into the room.

I swung my left arm across my body, slashing outward with a sheet of wind. The guards flew back, but I knew more were coming.

Rhiannon clapped her hands together in joy. "Holy shit, Neve! You're blowing my mind."

"I learned some new tricks," I said, then turned to Damian, "Break her chain and collar first so we can run!"

"I can't. I've got to do the cuffs first. Everything is linked together."

"Triple shit." I unsheathed my dagger, ready to fight.

With a sudden burst, the air drained out of the room, and my ears popped. It was hard to breathe. The flames sank low and changed hue, filling the room with an eerie blue light. A rumble like low thunder rolled around us, and smoke poured into the room and took form.

The djinn.

My knees weakened.

The air vibrated, and waves of magic rose around him like an undulating desert mirage.

His power smelled of frankincense and left a dusty taste in my mouth. Something deep inside of me stirred. It was unnerving—I couldn't quite explain it. Not desire or any emotional connection, but something deeper. Something that drew me toward him like a moth to a flame.

The djinn sneered at Damian. "Good to see you again, dear friend. The last time we met, I let you be, out of pity. This time, you won't be so lucky."

I stared at Damian. They *knew* each other? What the hell had I signed up for?

The djinn turned to me, narrowing his topaz eyes. All the hair on my neck stood on end. "And you. A half-breed. Interesting. Where did you come from?"

The alarm bells inside me jangled, and my arms felt as if electricity was surging through them. I had never been so small.

The djinn towered over us, his skin a radiant blue. His eyes were lined with kohl, and his arms and chest were covered with intricate white tattoos, like calligraphy written across his body.

I looked down at my arm. My tattoo had grown

again. Would mine become like his? There was so much I didn't know about myself. As I studied his face, his eyes pulled me forward, step by step. Could he help me? Could he be the answer? I tried to summon the nerve to speak.

"Thieves!" he bellowed. His thunderous voice knocked sense into me. This djinn was no friend of mine. He threw his arms wide, and columns exploded around us in a cloud of dust and fragments. Flying marble chips sliced my face as I tumbled to the ground.

Damian struggled to his feet beside me but was blasted over with another explosion of stone.

Rhiannon was on her knees on the other side of the room. She fruitlessly tugged on her chain with bloody arms. "Get the hell out of here, Neve. Now!"

The force had knocked the wind out of me, and I strained to speak. "No."

With a slight wave of his hand, the djinn hurled her against the wall, then turned toward us. She crumpled at its base.

"Rhiannon!" I screamed.

Damian grabbed me by the arm and pulled me stumbling toward the door. The djinn casually waved his hand at us. I tried to block the incoming gust with a wall of air, but it was feeble compared to the might of the djinn. We flew head over feet through the doorway, and the guards were on us in a second. I sent a blast of wind at them, but they were prepared for my tricks now.

Three were able to dodge the gust, taking to the air using their feathered wings.

Damian leapt up and lashed out with magic, sending a burst of hail into their bodies. Feathers exploded through the chamber.

We dove underneath our airborne assailants and sped down the hall. Rounding the corner, Damian pulled me through a side door and locked it with a charm. The door shuddered as something heavy pounded against it.

"Can you hold the door with your magic?" Damian asked. "I need to unlock this window, but it'll take a minute."

I channeled wind at the door, pinning it shut, while Damian muttered an incantation behind me.

The pounding on the door stopped for a second— and then, an incredible blast of force ripped the door off its hinges. I pushed it back with a gust.

"Hurry!" My hand was shaking. I couldn't hold it much longer.

"Got it!" Damian shoved the window open. "Jump out."

"You first! I'm holding the door. I'll be right behind."

He paused but didn't argue, his expression torn. There was no time. He leapt out of the window.

A surge of energy overwhelmed me, and the door splintered into a thousand pieces.

The djinn loomed in the opening, wreathed in blue

smoke. Again, some nearly irresistible force drew me to him. I hated him, but we were connected in some way. I had never been so close to answers.

"You thought you could steal from me, little half-breed? You will make a nice addition to my collection of slaves."

Again, his cruel voice broke the spell. I needed to get out of there right away.

"Not today, asshole." I released my magic and flew out the window.

Damian hovered a few feet below.

A cyclone of power erupted from the window above us. Fragments of stone exploded into the air.

"Let's go, let's go, let's go!" I cried, and darted away, Damian following. We flew with all our strength.

The djinn dissipated and reformed into a massive whirlwind, driving down between us. The force hurled us apart.

"Damian!" I screamed.

He tumbled head over heels through the air. I fought against the magic wind with my own power, forcing my way toward him.

The voice of the djinn boomed. "I will destroy you! I will tear you apart, piece by piece."

I strained and reached out to grasp Damian's hand. He pulled me close, and I closed my eyes, bringing to mind images of home. My apartment. I summoned what strength I had, and we exploded through the ether.

The voice of the djinn thrummed in my ears. "You think you can escape? I know who you are, and I'm coming for you."

The cosmos wheeled around us. With a thump, we collapsed against a wooden floor. When I opened my eyes, everything was familiar. My apartment.

Clothes were strewn everywhere. It looked like a whirlwind had hit it.

Exactly the way I'd left it.

Oh, fates.

Damian scanned the room. "Is this—"

"Whoa!" I said, interrupting him. "Planes-walking sure makes a mess. It's like a tornado hit."

"And yet...the books and papers are so neatly stacked on the shelf."

"Huh." I died a little inside.

The euphoria of escaping ended quickly.

We didn't get Rhiannon. Didn't even have a chance.

Shit.

13

I was exhausted. Slightly mortified, I cleared a heap of clothes off a chair for Damian, then collapsed on the couch.

I glanced at my phone. 5 p.m. We'd been gone overnight and most of the day. So at least time in the Realm of Air worked much as it did at home.

Seeing that I had three messages from work, I groaned. I didn't want to face Gretchen right now. I'd just reenacted Twister with an angry djinn, and every muscle *ached*.

I shifted, trying to find a comfortable position. "What do we do now?"

Damian sat down across from me. "We can't stay here long. The djinn knows who we are now, and he'll find us sooner or later. He could come for you in your home, just as he did for Rhiannon."

I sighed. "I hadn't thought about that."

Damian reached into his bag and pulled out the pilfered gem. He stared at the object with a distant gaze, darkness flashing in his eyes.

"Damian?"

He jerked his head slightly and slipped the gem back into his pocket. "We have the Dragon Heart, and that's a start. The djinn enshrined it in a prominent place in his vault, which indicates to me that it's something he values deeply."

"So, what's it do for us?"

Damian looked up. "Before we set out, I spoke with a mage here in Magic Side. He can help us cast a powerful binding spell that will trap the djinn. Doing so requires three things. The first is an object precious to the target."

"The Dragon Heart?"

Damian nodded. "It will help us exert dominion over the djinn."

"Okay..."

"The second is an object strong enough to hold the djinn. Crafted purely of magic. That's our next objective."

"Hmm...and what's the last thing?"

"The binding spell." Damian got up and strode to the window. "Finding the object to trap him is going to be tricky, though. This is where your expertise as a researcher is essential. What is strong enough to hold a djinn?"

"Shit." I stared at the crack in my ceiling. "That's a tall order. Lemme think."

"You think, I'll heal your wounds." He came over and knelt in front of the couch.

I glanced down at my raw skin which looked like it'd been sandblasted with chunks of concrete.

"At least it was exfoliating," I muttered.

Dizziness flooded my head as Damian's magic poured over me. *Warm and tingly.* He placed his fingers on my forehead, and my cheeks burned. There was no way I could concentrate while he healed me. His touch left me euphoric. Wanting.

My mind raced as I tried to focus. "I don't know where to begin to look, but I have a friend in Magic's Bend who might be able to help. Nix Knight. She runs a shop called Ancient Magic with her sisters. They track down magic artifacts for a living. She's a bit of a bookworm, too."

Damian's eyes narrowed. "Good. Can you handle it on your own?"

"What? Why? I mean, yes, but what are you going to be doing?"

"I've got a mage to deal with if we want to get that binding spell."

I nodded. "Fair enough."

"Once you know where the object is, I'll help you get it. How soon can you leave?"

I grabbed my phone and started dialing. "I'll call Nix."

I tapped my foot as the phone pulsed, willing her to pick up. At last, a cheery voice greeted me. "Neve! My fates. It's been so long, how are you?"

"I'm afraid this isn't a social call, Nix. I'm in a bit of a bind, and I need your help."

I filled her in on the details of Rhiannon's kidnapping and the djinn. When I finished, she said, "Holy smokes! Of course I'll help you out. I don't know of any objects like that, but I know where we should start looking. Can you meet me at the library of Alexandria in the morning? 9 a.m. your time?"

"Yes! I've never been inside...it's been a dream. Can you really get us in?"

"Absolutely. I have killer credentials. You can use the Chicago portal and meet me in the entrance hall."

"Fantastic." Nix filled me in on the directions, and I hung up, brimming with excitement.

The library of Alexandria held the largest collection of magical texts known to supernatural kind. Much of its collection was ancient, consisting of magical scrolls and books. It was founded by the Ptolemies, who were relentless in acquiring knowledge. They "borrowed" books from around the ancient world but seldom returned them.

I looked at my own book collection and felt slightly

guilty for a moment. There were things I needed to bring back to the archives...once I got around to reading them.

I turned to Damian and briefed him on the plan. "Excellent," he said. "Once you identify the object, don't go looking for it without me."

I nodded. *Duh.*

"Moreover, you shouldn't stay here tonight. I'll put us up in a hotel downtown near the museum. While you're with Nix, I'll meet the mage."

I packed a bag, since I wasn't sure when I'd be back. My favorite shirt was caked with dried blood. Damn it— I'd need to find a laundromat with powerful magic to get that out.

An hour later, we were checking into the hotel, which was luxury at its finest. I had a corner room on the twelfth floor, and floor-to-ceiling windows provided an unparalleled view of the city and lake. The bed was huge and the bathroom to die for.

I was ravenous, but first, I needed a bath.

Ten minutes later, I sank back into the jacuzzi tub, the hot water soothing my sore muscles. The hotel room phone jolted me from sleep. I groaned, weighing whether I should answer.

Damian, perhaps?

Good. I had some questions I needed answered.

I pulled myself out of the bath and glanced at my watch. Yikes. 9 p.m. What would he want at this hour? My heartbeat quickened as I answered. "Hello?"

"I'm ordering room service," Damian said. "What do you want?"

Right. I was starving. "Um, a cheeseburger and fries, with a chocolate milkshake?"

There was pause on the other end of the line.

"Don't judge!"

"See you in a few," Damian said, then the line cut.

I pulled on the lush white robe that hung in the closet and stared into the mirror. Damian had just invited me over for dinner. And it wasn't a date. But also...it wasn't *not* a date. Because it totally wasn't necessary. I could have just as easily ordered room service on my own.

I sighed. *Get a hold of yourself, Neve.* Damian was dangerous, not to mention one of the Order's most wanted criminals.

Crap! The Order. I really needed to call work, let them know I was sick or something. Maybe after dinner.

I joined Damian in his room, which was nearly identical to mine. His gaze lingered briefly on the robe, but he said nothing and went to the minibar. "Beer?"

"Sounds divine." I'd drink my milkshake later.

Room service arrived, and we ate at the small table in the corner near the windows. I smiled. Damian ordered exactly what I had, minus the shake.

My stomach growled, and parched, I gulped down the beer. "I wanted to ask you something."

"Sure," he said.

"Back there at the palace, when the djinn arrived, he said something odd—as if he'd met you before."

"That's right." Damian took a swig of beer.

"How do you know him?"

He leaned back in his chair casually. "I've been hunting him. I met him only once before, but he got away."

"I see." I dug into my burger. *Fates*, it was good.

"Your tattoo has grown." His eyes were on my wrist. Trails of white ink snaked out from the robe. "I saw you rub your arm when the djinn appeared. Is it connected to him? And that place?"

So he'd caught that. No point in hiding it now. "I think so. It appeared after my fight with the thief. I mean, I think I felt it—forming?—when we arrived in the Realm of Air, but I didn't notice it until we were on the *Jewel*."

"May I see?"

I hesitated momentarily, then pulled the oversized sleeve up and turned my forearm over. Damian gently took my arm and inspected it closely. "It's remarkable. It must be tied to your powers—now that you've begun using them." He traced his fingers over the pattern, following it up where it disappeared beneath the robe. "Where else does it go?"

Warmth blazed through me. There was something between us, no question. He was dangerous and off limits, but...

I bit my lower lip and leaned back, letting my arm slide out from his grip.

Damian's eyes followed my movements. I saw a flash of something. Desire. Lust. Craving.

He abruptly pushed his chair back and stood, wrenching his eyes away and looking at the floor. "You should head back to your room." His voice was rough and disconnected. "It's late, and we'll have an early morning."

Confusion shot through me. Had I done something wrong? I rose abruptly. "Yeah. Of course."

Tension tightened between us like a wire pulled taught. Unsure of what had just happened, I turned and left.

"Nevaeh."

I stopped outside of the door and looked over my shoulder. Damian's jaw was tense, and he looked distraught. "Goodnight."

"Night, Damian." I headed back to my room and flopped on my bed, utterly confused.

My alarm beeped at 8 a.m., and I groaned. I was *so* not a morning person.

After a quick shower, I threw on my favorite pair of black leggings, a green silk blouse, and my boots. I recalled my "date" with Damian the night before and cringed. *So awkward.* I would have to shove that memory deep down into the recesses of my brain.

With half an hour before I was due to meet Nix, I tossed my jacket over my shoulder and raced to the hotel lobby. It was going to be tight.

Magic Side had several magical gateways—portals—that connected it to magical cities and places around the globe. The portal that gave access to the Library of Alexandria, however, was inside the Field Museum in Chicago proper. Luckily, Damian and I had stayed downtown in the Loop.

I dropped my overnight bag with the nice lady at the front desk. Damian would pick it up for me later, but I'd keep my backpack, which held a few books and my notebook.

There was a perfect cappuccino waiting for me.

Before I could wonder whether the desk clerk was a mind reader, she smiled and nodded, motioning behind me.

I turned and saw Damian across the way on his

phone. He was wearing tan trousers and a blue dress shirt that stretched across his broad shoulders.

I sighed, imagining how our night *could* have ended.

He caught my gaze and raised his coffee in acknowledgment as he stepped out the front doors, then disappeared into a black SUV that pulled away.

I grabbed the cappuccino and followed him out, where I found an identical black SUV. A man in a suit opened the back door and caught my eye. "Ms. Cross? This is for you. Courtesy of Mr. Malek."

I nodded my thanks and climbed in, muttering, "I could get used to this."

As we sped through the city, I considered calling in to work. By now, I'd missed a couple of days, and I was sure Gretchen was furious. Still, better to beg for forgiveness than have to explain and ask for more time off. Instead, I dialed my friend Ronnie, who worked at the Field Museum, and let him know I was running a little late.

I'd known Ronnie for half a decade, and we occasionally worked on research projects together. Although he was Magica, he lived outside the city and worked as a conservator, specializing in ceramics.

Ronnie was also in charge of the Field Museum's portal. He'd shown it to me several times, but I'd never had the credentials to use it before. I suspected that the librarians in Alexandria, who had a bit of a reputation, wanted to make it as hard as possible to visit. Luckily, Nix had connections and had sent me the passcode.

The driver dropped me in front of the Field Museum's monumental columned entrance. Ronnie had warned the museum guards that I would be arriving, and they let me pass through the staff-only doors. I ducked into the gift shop, and then, running a little late, darted downstairs.

The portal itself was located inside a 4,300-year-old ancient Egyptian chapel that once belonged to the royal chamberlain of Pharaoh Unas. It had been legally purchased by the museum at the turn of the twentieth century, when those sorts of acquisitions were permissible, and traveled by boat from Egypt to Chicago. Nowadays, the chapel was sealed up behind a wall in a break room, off limits to the public, but accessible to Magica with permission.

The break room was as one might expect—white walls, fluorescent lights, and a few tables—except along one side of the room was a pair of ten-foot-tall double doors.

Ronnie, a slender man with dark hair, stepped into view. "Neve!"

I hugged him. "Hi, Ron. Nice to see you. Working on anything good these days?"

"Oh, you know, the usual. I'm restoring some of the Chinese bowls from the twelfth-century Java Sea shipwreck."

"Coooool!" I loved shipwrecks. And so did Ronnie.

Ronnie unlocked the double doors and pulled them open, revealing the small limestone chapel inside. It was no bigger than an elevator, and its walls were elaborately decorated from floor to ceiling with carved hieroglyphs and scenes. Traces of original ochre and cerulean paint were still visible on some of the walls.

"Here you go," he said. "I have a meeting in five, so I have to split. Stop by when you get back. We'll grab a coffee."

"Sure thing, Ron. Thanks so much!" I waved and entered the chapel.

The floor was covered in sand from its original display in the museum's old location. The space was dimly lit by a pair of fluorescent bulbs along the base, and it was a good five degrees colder inside. The magic portal itself was a false door at the back of the chapel. False doors were common in Egyptian tombs, thresholds between the worlds of the living and dead through which spirits could pass. The side panels were covered in hieroglyphs, and the door was framed with moldings and lintels decorated with offering scenes.

I stood in front of the portal and nodded to the carved figure of Netjer-User, the tomb's owner and supposedly one of the sons of a pharoah.

"Hi, Netjer-User. Thanks for letting me pass."

He was seated on a throne, and ochre paint still colored parts of his skin.

I pressed a sequence of hieroglyphs Nix had texted me, each illuminating beneath my touch as I told the portal my destination.

I took a breath and stepped through. The limestone hieroglyphs dissolved around me, and I was sucked through the ether.

14

I emerged into a colonnaded library hall decorated with Greco-Roman statues and let out a sigh. "That's so much better than planes-walking."

Light streamed in through high windows, and dust motes drifted gently in the air. I was alone. Nix apparently hadn't arrived yet.

To pass the time, I strolled about the hall, studying the sculptures set into niches. Modern histories erroneously claimed that the library of Alexandria was burned to the ground. The truth was much sadder and more remarkable. During the Roman period, Egypt's overlords lost interest in the pursuit of knowledge, turning their attention instead to the pursuit of coin. Without powerful patrons, the library languished. The magic world, understanding what a resource it was, slowly moved it stone by stone and scroll by scroll into a pocket dimension, similar to that occupied by Magic Side.

Only Magica were allowed within the library, as we had curated the knowledge that the wider world ceased to value. It was the most ancient library in the world, and it was rumored that there were over four hundred million books and scrolls within its walls, dwarfing even the Library of Congress. You needed credentials to get in, and they were extremely hard to come by.

I huffed a silent laugh. So much for the freedom of knowledge.

Nix's voice echoed off the columns behind me. "Neve!"

I turned to see her hurrying toward me. "Hey!"

She gave me a warm hug. "It's been too long."

She wore jeans, boots, and a shirt with a print of a cartoon Egyptian cat on the front. "You look fabulous," I said, then held her at arm's length and inspected her outfit. "I love your shirt."

"Thanks. The ancient Egyptians adored cats. Their word for cat was *mau*. I wear this shirt every time I come here."

"I have a gift for you." I pulled out the wheel of parmesan-like cheese that I had picked up in the Realm of Air.

"Cheese!" Nix took it and breathed deeply. "Smells amazing. I can't wait to try it."

"I swiped it from the djinn's palace. It's vengeance cheese."

"That's the best type. Thanks so much" With a flick of the wrist, she pulled a satchel from the ether, dropped the cheese inside, and made the pack vanish again.

I grinned. "Thank you for coming to my rescue. I owe you a lot more than that. My world has turned on end in the last couple of days."

"Yeah, I know how that goes," Nix said with a sly wink. "Come on, let's roll our sleeves up and do some RESEARCH!"

We had to go through arcane security to get into the library proper. It was an unfortunate echo of the mundane world. Luckily, Nix had credentials and could get us both through.

A couple of guards went through our bags. They pulled two books out of my backpack and eyed them with interest. "These may be of use to the librarians," one said. "We'll borrow them."

Damn it. Bye-bye, books.

Nix raised her eyebrows. "Uh-oh, you brought books to the library of Alexandria? I hope you get them back."

I rolled my eyes and sighed. "I forgot they were in my bag. Should have left them in Chicago."

The methods of acquiring new books for the library had not changed in two millennia. Hopefully, the scribes just copied them and gave them back. I didn't want to lose them, but it wasn't like I had a choice. I had to get inside.

One of the guards pointed to a large sign beside the entryway and raised his brows. "Follow the rules, eh?"

The symbols indicated that no food, drink, cameras, weapons, or fire demons were allowed. I sighed and handed the guard my khanjar. "No drinks, I can understand, but I always bring my fire demon with me wherever I go."

Nix laughed. The guard did not.

They admitted us into the catalog room, where we came face to face with two dozen imps. Each was a couple of feet tall, but they crouched like gargoyles.

Nix gestured to the creatures sitting before us. "Meet the catalog."

I cocked my head. "No computers?

"Nope. No card catalogue either. Only imps. The Library of Alexandria had millions of books long before the invention of the computer. The librarians had to find an alternate solution to the problem of indexing everything, so the imps just memorize where everything is."

"That's incredible. I would kill to have a memory like that."

She grinned. "These imps were born from the magic of memories too strong to be forgotten. Their minds are so sharp, it's said that they can recall things they didn't even know yet. Each of the imps only knows part of the library, but together, they memorize everything in it.

Each collection is controlled by a different tribe, and they compete fiercely to find the best sources."

An imp with a hoary beard waddled forward on clawed feet. "How may we help our illustrious guests?"

Nix shook its extended claw. "Thank you, wise one. We're looking for magical artifacts. They cannot be owned by an individual or institution but must be lost to memory."

Two or three of the imps eagerly edged toward the archives' door.

"However, they have to be crafted from pure magic, and they must be containers that can be closed." Nix looked at me. "I think that's all, right?"

I nodded.

There was an explosion of dust and wings as all two dozen imps attempted to pass through the doorway at once.

I jumped back. Holy smokes.

Nix laughed. "They're *really* enthusiastic." She gestured for me to follow. "Let's find a place to wait."

A pair of clerks dressed in long brown robes led us to a reading alcove on the second floor with a beautiful view of the harbor. I watched the colorful fishing boats coming in with their fresh catches as we waited for our books to arrive. Around us, shelves covered every available wall, filled with every sort of printed material. Curious, I read the titles.

One was in Old English, The Ways of the Stone

Giants.

The one beside it was a book of recipes from medieval Estonia.

I frowned. "I don't think I get the organization here. What do the ways of the stone giants have to do with Estonian cuisine?"

Nix shrugged. "No one understands the filing system except for the imps. It's a tribal knowledge learned from youth and made as obscure as possible."

After a few minutes, several imps flew into the alcove bearing scrolls and books. They were smaller than the others, just youngsters.

Nix leaned close. "They're apprentices to the librarians and are still learning the ways of the library."

"That was fast," I muttered.

"The true art of scholarship in the library is not finding the books, but rather sifting through the strange tomes brought by the imps. Each is tangentially related to the subject of one's study." Nix held up a scroll. "I think this is in Chinese. Can you read it?"

"Nope." I pulled out one of the books in my stack and held it up. *The Mating Rituals of Werewolves*. "How is this even remotely related?"

Nix laughed. "Hey, lemme look at that."

"Not so fast, I'm not done with it yet."

I learned that part of the art of studying in the library was telling the imps when you had enough books. You needed to be gentle enough not to offend them, but strong enough that they would actually stop bringing volumes. We spent hours poring through texts, every once in a while accepting a new book as it was dropped off.

Deep into the day, I felt a gentle nudge against my leg and looked down. "Yes?"

It was a tiny imp, maybe only seven or eight inches tall. She held a scroll twice her length and too heavy for her to fly with.

I reached down and took it from her, then patted her on the head. "Thank you."

She awkwardly flew up to the shelves where a dozen other young imps were waiting, eager to see what we'd discover.

I would've set the parchment scroll aside, but she was too cute, so I examined it immediately. Dust dispersed into the air as I unrolled the fragile parchment.

I sneezed.

Nix peered at the scroll. "*Oh*...that looks like an old one. Can you read it?"

The text was in three languages: Greek, Coptic, and Arabic. My Greek was terrible, my Coptic iffy. I could read the Arabic, though.

"It looks like a letter written to the governor of Egypt in...886 AD."

"Wow! What does it say?"

I skimmed the document. "This is it! I think we

might have something here."

The small imp was immediately on the table beside me, studying the scroll with eager eyes.

"It seems that the governor was trying to recover a magical artifact from a hidden refuge in Bilad al-Rum."

"Where's that?"

"Land of the Romans. That's what the Islamic Caliphate called Turkey back then. The governor sent a raiding party to recover the object, along with an informant who knew the hidden passages in the refuge." I scanned the text. "Unfortunately, the informant was lost at sea when the ship was attacked by Byzantine pirates. The mercenaries proceeded on but couldn't find their way through the hidden chambers and wrote it off as a hopeless task."

Nix leaned in closer. "That sounds promising. What was the artifact?"

"A magic box capable of concealing any object inside from arcane detection."

"Do you know where the site is located?"

"Not yet. There are a few rough maps sketched on the back of the scroll. I'm gonna have to read the text a little more closely and look at some maps of the region." I turned to the little imp. "You've done a good job!"

According to Nix, it was customary to tip the imps when they found something useful. They didn't accept money, but they loved to collect things from the outside world that they could share with their clan.

I'd brought some souvenirs from the Field Museum's gift shop, just in case. Rummaging in my bag, I pulled a gold-plated ornament. It was a skeleton of a *Tyrannosaurus rex*—Sue, the museum's mascot. When I handed it to the imp, she held it above her head in triumph as her companions gathered around to inspect the gift.

"I won't forget this," I said.

The little imp beamed. Clutching the gold-plated dinosaur to her chest, she took off and flew down the hallway.

"I'll have the imps bring us some maps of Turkey," Nix said and ducked out of the alcove.

Once the maps arrived, Nix worked on pinpointing the location while I translated and transcribed the scroll into my notebook. I was just finishing my translation when the hairs on the back of my neck stood on end. I turned and looked around the alcove, but nothing was there. "Do you have a funny feeling, Nix?" I asked. "Or is it just me?"

Nix stopped what she was doing. "Now that you mention it...yeah."

Something grabbed my shirt from behind, choking me. I screamed as I was lifted into the air and hurled against the wall. The impact drove the breath from my lungs and sent pain rippling through my back.

I was on my knees, coughing. Holy fates, what just happened?

"Neve!" Nix burst to her feet and conjured a dagger. She frantically scanned the room for my attacker, but the room was empty. "Are you okay?"

I staggered to my feet, gasping and clearing my throat. "Yeah. I'll live. What the hell was—"

Pain exploded through my chest as an invisible wrecking ball threw me onto the table, knocking the scroll and maps across the floor.

As panic pushed down the pain, I wildly searched about for my attacker. Something grabbed my foot and pulled me off the table, dragging me out of the alcove. Fresh pain surged through my ankle.

Out of desperation, I shot a burst of wind toward my raised foot. The force released my foot, and there was a loud crash as something slammed into a nearby bookshelf.

"Shit!" I cried, "these bastards are invisible!"

Nix ran closer. "Holy fates! You can shoot wind? When did you learn that?"

I leapt up, ignoring the agony in my foot. "It's a long st—"

The invisible force grabbed my hair and dragged me backward. Pain flared through my scalp as I thrashed to escape.

Nix leapt forward and lashed out with her dagger. A scream like the howling wind echoed through the hall. My invisible assailant let go, and I darted to the side, dropping into a defensive stance. My hand dropped to my belt, where my khanjar normally was, but I had checked it with security at the front. Shit. Too bad I couldn't pull weapons from the ether like Damian and Nix.

At least I had the wind.

Nix backed toward me, slashing blindly with her outthrust dagger at the air in front of her. "Are you okay?"

"Probably. These bastards pack a mean punch."

A gust of wind slammed into us, and we toppled backward into the stacks. I cracked my skull on a shelf, then silently swore. Our assailants had wind power, too.

I pushed aside some books that had fallen on top of me. "How do we fight these guys?"

"I've got an idea." Nix leapt to her feet, and with a wave, she conjured a bag of all-purpose flour.

"I like where you're going with this."

She ripped it open. "Okay, blast wind around the room."

I raised my hands and shot a gust in the approximate direction of our unseen assailants. Nix shook the bag, and flour exploded outward across the room. The burst coated two figures who loomed in front of us.

"Hell, yeah!" Nix jumped the one on the right, slicing it with precision. The demon wailed and flew into the air, shooting a jet of wind downward. Nix dashed to the side, avoiding the onslaught.

The creature in front of me raced forward. I braced

my feet and crouched as it barreled into me, then used its momentum to heave it overhead and send it toppling into the adjacent bookshelf.

I cringed as books crashed down. Holy fates, this was a disaster.

Nix plunged her dagger into the chest of the demon she was engaged with. "Take that, airhead!"

The creature dissipated with a roar of wind that hurt my ears, like diving too deep in the water.

I grappled with the one I was fighting. It was like trying to catch the air, and I couldn't get a grip on it. The demon slipped through my fingers like a ghost.

I summoned a raging vortex of wind around my fist and hammered the miniature cyclone into my opponent. The beast spun head over feet and crashed back into the shelves, and I pinned it down with a continuous stream.

Nix pressed her dagger against its flour-covered chest. "Who sent you?"

The demon cackled. "He's coming for you."

My chest tightened, realizing who "he" was. "Kill it."

Nix nodded and thrust the dagger into the demon's chest. There was a whoosh of air as the creature disappeared, returning to its hell.

Nix rose. "What *was* that?"

"Wind demons. Sent by the djinn to hunt me down." I stared at where the demon had been. "It seems he can find me anywhere. I'm not gonna be safe until I put an end to him."

"Okay, well, first thing, we'd better get a concealment charm for you. I don't like invisible monsters."

I surveyed the wreckage around us as I stretched my aching body. "Holy shit. What have we done?"

Books and scrolls lay in tatters, shelves had collapsed, and everything was covered in flour.

Nix cocked her head at me. "Neve, you need to get more sun. You're looking too pale these days."

We were both covered head to toe in flour. I giggled, and soon, we couldn't stop laughing. Then the librarian showed up.

Holding my breath, I tried to tamp down the laughter and maintain some form of composure, but he looked as horrified as if I'd set fire to a bag of puppies. "What on earth have you done?" he screeched.

I was going to explain everything. Truly. But then I looked at Nix. The expression on her face showed she was trying desperately to hold back a full meltdown. I lost it, and she followed suit, and soon, we were laughing uncontrollably.

The librarian went apoplectic. His face turned bright red, and he released a stream of curses that would make a sailor blush. The look on his face, and the outdated curses, made our laughter even worse.

Two surprisingly strong clerks ushered us out of the library post-haste. While they returned my books and dagger, they hung onto Nix's credentials for "further consideration."

I was banned for life. That kind of killed the buzz.

A wave of guilt washed over me. This was one of the most important resources in the world. Even on Order business, I had been refused access. I had led the wind demons here, destroyed countless books, and blown it for both of us. What if we couldn't find the box? What if we needed to do more research?

"I'm so sorry, Nix," I began once we'd been shown the door. "I had no idea—"

She grinned ear to ear, totally unfazed. "Do you think this is the first time I've been barred from the library? They're a bunch of prudes. Like any of this was our fault. How did the demons get past security? Invisible intruders should be at the top list of things they look out for, not cheese wheels and paperbacks. I'll get my creds back, and I'll get a set for you, too. It usually only takes a rare book or two as a bribe." She winked and put a hand on my shoulder. "Now, you're coming back with me to Magic's Bend. We'll have Connor make you a concealment charm. We can't have a bunch of invisible airheads hunting you all over the planet."

I nodded. I hadn't been back to Magic's Bend in a few years, but this would be a good opportunity to decompress.

Nix dialed in the coordinates, and we were whooshed through the ether.

15

The portal dumped us out in the Museum of Magical History in Magic's Bend, Oregon. The moment we stepped through, our phones exploded with texts, emails, and calls from robo-dialers.

The library of Alexandria took blocking cell phones to the extreme. Not only did its magic wards block reception, but phones didn't even work while inside. The librarians were real sticklers for "keep quiet" and "no photos allowed."

My phone showed 8:17 pm Oregon time, which meant we'd spent 13 hours studying. No wonder my stomach was growling.

Nix called Connor to let him know we were on the way, and I had two texts from Damian, plus a few from work. Bruised and battered, and recently expelled from one of the most important research institutions in the world, I wasn't prepared to face my colleagues' questions at the moment. Instead, I dialed Damian while following Nix to the parking lot.

"Success?" Damian asked.

"Yup. I found a lead on an object in Cappadocia. Turkey. Looks perfect. I'm still working the details."

"Excellent."

"Also, we got attacked by wind demons and were permanently banned from the library. It's been a hell of a long day already. I have to wash half a bag of flour out of my hair and"—I examined my filthy skin and clothing—"well, frankly, everywhere."

"I wish I could be there to help."

I blinked. "What?"

Damian cleared his throat on the other line. "I meant with the wind demons. In the library. Not the…"

My cheeks burned, and I glanced at Nix. "Right. So, did you get the spell?"

"Not quite. I spoke with the mage. We'll need to go see him once we have the object."

"Okay. I'm gonna get a concealment potion from an alchemist in Magic's Bend. Which is where I am now." Fates, now I was tripping over words. Maybe *I* was thinking about him lathering my hair in the shower. Maybe I wasn't. Okay, I definitely was. "How do we get to Turkey?"

"We'll take my jet. I'll pick you up there."

"Holy shit, you have a *jet*?" Yup. I was literally blurting out whatever came to my mind at this point.

"Yes."

"Neat."

There was an awkward pause.

Damian broke the silence. "I'll be there as soon as I can. Where are you headed?"

I repeated the question to Nix, who shot me a wry grin. She had totally been eavesdropping on my half of the conversation. With a wink, she said, "Well, we're headed to Potions & Pastilles. You can crash at my place tonight...unless you have other plans..."

I turned back around to conceal another blush. "Potions & Pastilles. I can crash with Nix. Can you pick me up in the morning?"

"I can pick you up tonight. We should move quickly. I'll head straight to the airport, and I can be there in around five hours."

"Uh...okay."

"The jet has a shower and a bed. You can clean up and get some rest while we fly."

"Good, because I really am going to need both of those things."

"I'll collect your weekend bag from the hotel and text you an arrival time once we get off the ground."

"Sounds like a plan. Cool. Bye." I hung up abruptly, which was super-awkward.

Nix was still smiling. "So...this mysterious man is your new guy, huh? Tell me all about him."

"It's not like that." I gave her a gentle nudge and then a wink. "But holy fates, he has a jet! With a shower! And a bed!"

"Bow-chika-wow-wow," Nix teased.

I blushed deeply and shook my head. "No, no, *no*. Put that out of your mind. Let's just get to the alchemist. I need a concealment charm. Like now. I'm turning into a beet."

It didn't take long to get to Potions & Pastilles. Magic's Bend, Oregon wasn't nearly as crowded as Magic Side, Chicago. Still, it had grown since I'd been there last, and I didn't recognize much.

Potions & Pastilles turned out to be a rather cute bar and coffee shop. Nix said they served excellent pastries in the morning and Cornish pasties at lunch and dinner.

I would be the judge of that.

Nix held the door open for me. "Here we go. Get ready for a great drink and what's almost certain to be a foul-tasting potion."

"Let's start with the drink."

The cozy interior was lit by warm lights hanging in mason jars. Several patrons sat at the bar, and a few couples crowded around short, round tables. An impressive selection of whiskey bottles glittered under the lights behind the bar, but I hoped that they also had a few good gins. I needed a cold drink after spending the day in the dusty tomes.

Nix held the door for me and waved at the bartender. "Hi, Connor!"

The bartender, caught in the middle of shaking a cocktail, nodded. "Hey, Nix! Be right there."

I thought I picked up just a hint of an accent. British?

His longish dark hair was messy, his grin devastatingly sexy. Broad shoulders pulled at his dark T-shirt, which bore the name of a band I didn't recognize. He had the beauty of a poet or artist, and my brows shot up.

I leaned in close to Nix. "What's his specialty, love potions?"

She snorted. A girl at the bar arched a brow at me. Whoops. That came out louder than I'd intended. I blushed and hoped Connor hadn't heard me over the rattling ice.

To hide my embarrassment, I inspected the paintings on the wall, pictures of fluorescent pink and yellow fish on a neon green background. Each had a little label off to the side. They were, well, horrific.

"Are these..." I looked at Nix, unsure of how to finish.

"A favor for a friend," a man said.

I turned back. The bartender had come to our end of the bar, and I blushed again. "I'm sorry, I didn't mean..."

"We have a monthly rotation of artists. Only two more weeks on these." He looked around and shrugged. "At least they add a little color to the place."

Nix grabbed him by the arm. "Connor, this is my friend, Nevaeh. We worked together on a couple of projects at the Museum of Magical History. Neve, this is Connor. He makes amazing drinks, coffee, and pastry."

Connor chuckled. "Well, any friend of Nix's is a friend of mine. How about we start with a drink? You two look like you already had a violent run-in with pastry. Why are you covered in flour?"

"Long story." Nix sighed. "Neve, what do you want?"

"Nice to meet you, Connor. Could you make me something with gin? Bartender's choice?"

"Sure, let's see what's fresh." He turned back to the bar, picking some leaves from a bunch of herbs and selecting a lemon from a hanging basket.

Nix indicated the woman who had overheard me talking about Connor's hotness earlier. "Neve, this is Sora, a new friend of ours. Sora, Neve."

Sora smelled of lilac, but I couldn't get any sense of her magic. I was sure she had it, though. Weird.

"Hi," I said as I pulled up to the bar.

"Hi." She pointed to my white-dusted T-shirt. "Looks like you two have been doing some baking." She had a mild British accent.

I shrugged. "I was doing some light reading, actually, but my plans went a-rye."

Nothing.

"Thank goodness it's happy flour now."

Blank stare. Dang it. I was terrible at puns. Rhia was

great with them. Well...perhaps not *that* great, but she used them a lot. And she always laughed at my attempts, no matter how pathetic they were. My stomach sank as I pictured her in magicuffs in the djinn's palace. Or worse.

The clink of a glass on the counter pulled me from my reverie, and Connor smiled as I looked up. "Basil smash. Lemons are good this time of year."

The translucent yellow cocktail sloshed in a short glass with a sugar rim. Lemon wedges bobbed in the bottom of the glass, floating among muddled bits of basil.

I took a sip. "It tastes divine."

"Thanks. It's hard to make a bad drink with fresh ingredients." He was lying, of course. I had been to plenty of hipster bars with drinks made from fresh, organic ingredients that made you want to scrape your tongue off. Connor had talent.

"Man, I needed this," I said, and clinked glasses with Nix.

Connor leaned closer. "I gather there's something else you need me to make, eh?"

"Yes! A Cornish pasty," I quipped. Nix had told me all about the half moon shaped savory pasty that was Connor's specialty. Then, thinking better of it, I said, "Sorry. Nix told me they were great. Actually, I need a potion."

He laughed. "Well, you're in luck. We have pasties

ready to go, and I'm closing at eleven tonight. Then I can make your potion. Is that all right?"

"Yeah, of course. I could sit here and drink these all day."

Nix leaned closer. "I recommend the cheese and onion pasty."

I looked at Connor. "Two, please."

"Make it three," Sora said.

"Coming right up." Connor grinned at Sora, and the warmth in his smile made it immediately evident that they were dating.

A few minutes later, he brought us the half moon–shaped treats that he'd reheated. The flaky, buttery crust contained a savory mixture of cheese and onions that smelled and tasted divine.

I chewed and swallowed. "These are amazing."

Sora nodded. "Connor brought the recipes for these over from Cornwall when he and his sister moved here years ago."

The wait gave me some time to catch up with Nix and get to know Sora, who was also cool as hell. The drinks kept coming, and the conversation flowed easily —just the break I needed. I couldn't help but worry about Rhia, though.

Finally, Connor closed up. "Ready to get started on that potion?"

"Ready." I stood, and Nix joined me.

Sora waved us on. "I'll wait out here."

Connor led us through the narrow kitchen to a crowded workshop in the back. The tables and shelves were stacked with hundreds of bottles of ingredients and tools of all varieties. While Nix and I tucked ourselves out of the way against the wall, Connor lit the fire under a small cauldron that sat on the table. "Nix said you needed a concealment charm."

"Two, if you can manage it. My friend and I got sideways with a djinn. He sent some air demons to hunt me down at the library of Alexandria. They were invisible, hence the flour."

"Hmmm. Djinn are bad news. Insanely powerful. I'll make the potion stronger than normal, but it won't last as long. Perhaps just a few days."

I gave a thumbs-up. "Okay, that would be great. We really appreciate it."

"I'll need a bit of your hair. It helps to make the potion specific to you."

He handed me tiny scissors, which I passed to Nix. "Make me look fabulous. I've been needing a new look."

She laughed and snipped off a few strands.

I beamed and patted my hair. "I love it already. Very fresh."

"Do you have anything belonging to your colleague?" Connor asked.

I thought for a second, then pulled out Damian's business card.

He shrugged. "That's not quite what I need, but worth a shot."

"Sorry."

"No matter. We'll make do." Connor took my hair and set it aside in a little silver dish. Then he began rummaging through the cabinets, pulling out various ingredients and weighing them. Soon, he had the cauldron bubbling. The combination of things in the pot gave off an awful stench.

Connor saw my expression. "Yeah. Potion making isn't always glamorous. Also, this is why we have a laboratory separate from the kitchen."

It was well after midnight by the time the potion was done. Connor put it into two vials, then handed me one.

I frowned. "Is it gonna be bad?"

He poured a shot of peppermint schnapps and passed it over. "Yes. You'll need a chaser."

Oh, fates.

I took the vial and slugged it back. "Oh, that is *awful!*" I said, trying not to gag, then slammed the chaser. "Ugh. Also, not a good combo."

Nix patted me on the back. I shook my head and coughed, acutely missing the taste of the pasties. "Man, this is going on my Yelp review. 'Friendly atmosphere. Great bar. Amazing pasties. Avoid the bottled worm poop.'"

Connor laughed. "Please don't. People would just start ordering it out of sheer curiosity."

I thanked Connor a dozen times in leaving. He gave me a few pasties for the flight—which was how I knew he was a divinely good person—and Nix drove me to the airport. I was exhausted, still covered in flour, and a bit nauseous.

Nix looked at me as we got out. "Are you sure you don't want to shower at my place?"

"No, it's okay. Damian is bringing me fresh clothes. And the jet has a shower."

"So, are you two...you know, a thing?"

"Not a chance." I said it too quickly, and it sounded like I was covering. "I mean, there's something definitely there. But..." I paused, unsure if it was my place to reveal that he was one of the Fallen. "I don't trust him yet. He's a criminal. The sort I help lock up. If the Order found out I was consorting with him, they'd fire me. Or worse..."

"Hmm. Well, maybe you should give it a spin, anyway," she said thoughtfully, then winked. "I mean, it's going to be a long flight."

"Cut it out!" I stretched my arms. "Hell, it is going to be a long flight, isn't it? Twelve hours? Sixteen hours? I don't even know. Do we have layovers?"

"Keep an open mind," Nix teased. "There are only so many in-flight movies you can watch."

Damian's flight arrived a short time later, and security escorted us out to the sleek, white jet parked in the middle of the tarmac. MALEK was emblazoned on its side in giant black letters. Damn. Part of me hadn't believed it was real.

Damian stood on the stairs, waiting. Damn. Part of me hadn't believed *he* was real. Connor was handsome, but this guy was my type. Dark. Gorgeous. Full of riddles and contradictions, like a good mystery novel.

My heart spun up like a jet engine.

Then it spun right back down as I remembered that I looked like I had just lost *The Great British Baking Show*. Oh, fates.

Damian pretended not to notice. "Ready?"

"Yup. Here I am. Totally prepared for adventure." I stopped being an idiot and remembered my companion. "This is my friend, Nix, by the way. She got me into the library and helped fight off the demons."

Damian shook her hand, and something flashed across his face. "We're in your debt. Thank you."

"Sure! Glad I could help. Good luck with part two." Her voice was cheerful, but I could tell something about her expression was troubled, though she hid it well.

Nix gave me one last hug before I headed up the stairway. She squeezed me tightly and whispered in my ear. "Neve, I think I was wrong. Be wary of this man."

"What? Why?"

"I just...have a feeling. I can't tell you why. Just be careful. Keep your wits about you when you're with him."

Well, if that didn't just kill the mood. What put her

off? His magic had a dark aura. Did she sense he was one of the Fallen? Or was it something else?

"I will." I squeezed her hands. "You take care, too."

With some trepidation, I turned to the jet and slowly climbed the stairs to the open door, where Damian was waiting. I could smell his magic and see his aura about him, green and red.

I remembered the dream I had of him on the *Jewel* after our battle with the ice devils. Damian's aura had been green and red then, too. Right before it changed... right before—

I gave an involuntary shudder and shook my head.

16

On the plane, I leaned back in the white leather recliner, savoring the moment. I'd never been in a private jet before.

A stewardess in a black pantsuit served me a glass of lemon water and a bowl of salted almonds. "Can I get you anything to drink?" she asked.

"A gin and tonic, please." Boy, I could get used to this. She quickly returned with my cocktail, and I gave it a test sip. *Damn*, it was good.

At the front of the plane, Damian spoke to the captain. Did he always travel like this? When he finished, he took the seat across from me. "You look like you've had a long day."

"Wind demons. *Invisible* wind demons. Speaking of which..." I reached into my bag and pulled out the vial of Connor's concealment charm. "Drink this. The wind demons were sent by the djinn. This will hopefully prevent a repeat of today."

Damian took the vial. "I thought it was possible, but how'd they get into the library?"

I shrugged. "I guess they slipped through security."

He popped the cork off and smelled the potion. "You drank this?"

I nodded.

He shot it back and grimaced.

I leaned forward. "What do you think it tastes like?"

"I have no idea." He grabbed the water from my table and chugged it down.

"Okay, let me put this into your mind." I waited until he had recovered. "Cucumbers and earthworms. *Right*?"

Damian blanched.

"Not that I've ever eaten worms before, but it's how I imagine them to taste," I added.

He narrowed his eyes and watched me closely. "You are a strange one, Neve."

I shrugged.

"There's a shower in the aft cabin, if you want to clean up." He handed me my overnighter from the hotel.

I caught a glance of my disheveled form in the reflection on the glass divider behind him.

Holy moly.

I nonchalantly rubbed a smudge of flour on my forehead, desperately hoping it would come off.

Damian smiled. "Did he send the Pillsbury Doughboy after you, too?"

Another joke?

We had reached cruising altitude, so I grabbed my bag and headed into the cabin at the back. The room was small but comfortable. It was like an airport sleeping pod but more tastefully decorated, and almost filled by a double bed. *Hmm.*

The shower felt heavenly, and I definitely needed to wash my hair. My scalp still ached after the wind demon had dragged me around like a rag doll. Running my fingers through my damp hair, I peered out the small window, but there was nothing to see but moonlit clouds. I gazed down at the tattoo on my right arm, tracing the intricate pattern with my fingers. It was beautiful. Had it grown? I frowned. Maybe a little.

I recalled what Nix had said at the airport and shivered. *Be wary of this man.*

Once out of the shower, I pulled on a clean pair of skinny blue jeans and a cream-colored sweater to ward off the chilly air. I stepped out and saw Damian writing in a journal. He looked up and closed it. "Hungry?"

"Always."

He gestured to the other side of the plane, where the stewardess had prepared a table for two with a white tablecloth and flameless flickering candles. The cabin lights dimmed as I took a seat, and my gaze met his. "So, how'd your visit with the mage go?" I said, breaking the silence.

"Fine actually. Matthias—the mage—will help us with the binding spell once we have the object."

"Great. How do you know him?"

Mixed emotions played across Damian's eyes for a brief moment. "We worked together, long ago, but we've mostly drifted apart. Different objectives. Different ways of seeing the world."

The stewardess brought us a feast of steak, green beans, and roasted sweet potatoes. It was an odd hour to have dinner, but I was starving.

"What kind of mage is he?" I asked, shoving a piece of steak and sweet potato into my mouth.

"Iron mage."

"I assume that's why he's so good at forging binding spells, huh?" I'd never met an iron mage before. They were experts at binding and bonding spells, as well as alchemy and enchanting metal items.

Damian nodded. "He's something else, too, but I haven't prodded. He likes his privacy."

I could understand that. Damian undoubtedly did as well. He hadn't exactly announced that he was a fallen angel. I eyed him intensely. What else was he hiding from me? There was something, for sure.

"Tell me more about this place in Cappadocia where we're headed," he said.

I filled him in on the details I had learned at the

library. "From what I can tell, the box is hidden somewhere in the underground city of Gizli Tepe. I'm hoping that you'll be able to track it, being a seeker and all." I pulled out my notebook. "These are the coordinates, according to Soviet military maps."

"This lost city was recorded on Soviet maps?"

"Yup. The only good thing that came out of colonial efforts in the region were the maps. They recorded everything on the ground. Roads, hills, archaeological sites. Gizli Tepe still exists. But nobody has explored the city yet because the whole region of Cappadocia is honeycombed with underground cities."

"Why?" Damian plugged the coordinates into his handheld GPS unit.

"Well, the region was once the frontier between the Byzantine and Islamic empires. Yearly raids and skirmishes by the Muslim armies required the Cappadocians to hide. And what better way than to build underground cities in the chalky substrate, totally invisible to outsiders?"

"Wow, that's fascinating. And you learned all this... today?" Damian looked surprised.

I smiled and nodded.

Lie. I was a total nerd and had previously taken some deep dives into the history of Turkey. The ancient lost city and the magical box were the only new additions. But if he wanted to believe I was a super sleuth and walking encyclopedia, I wasn't going to stop him.

We finished dinner, and I opened *Secrets of the Djinn*. I flipped to the section on summoning air elementals. There was a lot of good info in there. No wonder the djinn had it hidden away in his treasure vault.

Damian had offered me the bed in the stern cabin, and I happily obliged. I sank into the pillowtop mattress and recounted the day. The portal, the library, the imps, the great flour battle, Potions & Pastilles...Damian. Those broad shoulders and rigid muscles. His perfect jaw. Those deep, mysterious eyes. I drifted off into slumber, thinking of him.

I dreamed again. This time, they were good dreams.

I woke as the plane began its final descent to Kayseri Erkilet Airport.

The low, sonorous sound of Damian's voice greeted me. "Good morning."

I groaned and pulled the pillow over my head. This was how I normally greeted the day. Also, I wasn't sure what state I was in. My mouth was dry. Hopefully, I hadn't drooled.

"I have a cappuccino."

That changed things. Normally, the morning didn't greet me so kindly. I sat up, pulling the sheet around me, and let my red hair drop forward as he passed me the cup.

"Thanks," I mumbled. "Mm. It's nice and hot."

So is he, my traitorous libido reminded me.

Damian flashed an unexpectedly disarming smile. "We aim to please when you fly Malek Air."

I blinked. Was the ice angel starting to open up?

I maneuvered the sheets, trying to manage them and the coffee. Clearly, he was enjoying this.

"What time is it?"

"Just before dawn. You slept through the refuel."

He was sitting on the side of the bed. The way his torso was turned pulled his shirt taut against his solid chest. Was he doing that on purpose? It was getting quite hot beneath the comforter. Thankfully, my lower leg slipped out of the sheets and into the cool air. Damian did not fail to notice.

Was he really looking at me like this? Fallen or not, with his angelic form, he could have anyone he wanted.

The captain's voice came on the loudspeaker. "Beginning final descent. Buckle up, sir."

Thank fates.

Damian headed forward, and I bolted to the bathroom to wash the sleep off my face. What was it about him that turned my stomach into knots? The cold water brought me back to my senses. I rested my hands on the vanity and inspected my reflection. Not bad after an international flight.

The world outside was dark, and the lights of

Kayseri flew by as we touched down. Gizli Tepe was only about an hour and a half's drive from here.

As I wondered how we'd make the trip, I spotted a black Range Rover parked on the tarmac. The driver stepped out wearing a black suit.

Damian was prepared for everything. The nice stewardess handed me a breakfast sandwich on the way out of the plane, and I scarfed it down while we walked to the car.

Damian greeted the driver with a hug, and they exchanged a few words in Turkish. He turned and gestured toward me. "Selim, this is Neve. Neve, Selim."

I nodded and smiled. Selim opened the car door for me, and we set off.

While the car wove along the winding road that cut through the high steppe, I made myself comfortable in the back. "You speak Turkish?"

Damian looked up from his GPS and nodded. "A little. It helps to be multilingual in my line of business."

This guy was full of surprises.

The landscape was surreal, almost alien as dawn crept over the world. The chalk hills were broken by bizarre spires of rock, some of which towered a hundred feet in the air. Guidebooks referred to the spires as "Fairy Chimneys." Some were thin spindles, while others looked like rows of pointed tents. I was traveling through another world as strange and alien as the Realm of Air, with its floating islands and cloud palaces.

We passed by a few villages incorporated into the Fairy Chimneys. The soft rock was easy to work, so over the millennia, villagers had carved houses and structures into the bases of these rock formations. The countryside was honeycombed with such caves, comprising homes, monasteries, churches, and even entire underground cities.

As we rumbled over the washboard roads, I watched several colorful hot air balloons drifting through the sky in the distance as the sun rose. I longed to drift upward through the clouds again. "I've always wanted to try a hot air balloon flight," I murmured.

"Well, now you can fly all on your own," Damian said.

"Maybe. I haven't tried flying since we returned from the Realm of Air." A part of me was scared to even attempt it. What if I could only fly in the Realm of Air, and not here?

I turned and met Damian's gaze. His green eyes searched mine.

"My control over the wind in the library of Alexandria was nowhere near as strong as it was in the Realm of Air." I'd be crushed if I was grounded, no longer able to lift myself off the earth. I looked out the windows, longing for the power and courage to chase after the balloons.

Damian reached over and took my hand. "Give yourself a break, Nevaeh. It's only been a few days since you learned to fly. You've come a long way since your first flight in that square in Tayir."

How many times had I hit the pavement?

I glanced at Damian, whose lips were pulled up in a smile. I started laughing, and he shook his head.

"There it is." Selim's voice interrupted the moment. He gestured to a large hill in the distance that towered over the surrounding mounds. Grasses and a few scrubby trees covered the surface.

I shook off the hypnosis of travel and looked around. "Not a village in sight. That's good." We could be in and out without anyone ever knowing.

The car dropped us off at the base of the hill. Damian muttered something unintelligible to Selim, and the car drove off. "He'll be back in a couple of hours. I don't want to attract attention with him parked here."

I nodded, adjusting the laces of my boots so they were snug. I couldn't risk twisting an ankle.

"Where's the entrance?" he asked.

"Good question." I inspected the hill. It rose several hundred feet and was narrower than it was tall. It sort of looked like a massive Fairy Chimney, minus the pointy top. "My guess is that the entrance is on the north side."

"Your *guess*?"

We started up the hill. "More like an educated guess. The entrance wasn't marked on the map. We should be able to find it. I reason that the prevailing wind is from the north. If I built an underground city, I'd want a breeze blowing through the front door."

"Clever thinking. Let's see if it holds water."

"Shouldn't be too hard to spot it."

Famous last words. It turned out that finding the entrance wasn't hard—it was impossible. We searched among the rocks for half an hour, slowly spiraling around the formation. It wasn't on the north side, or the east, or the south or west.

We worked our way down the hill. It was hot, dusty work, and I was hot, dusty, and tired. "How is it that every spire around here is literally honeycombed with holes," I groused, "but thi—"

"Quiet. I see something." Damian grabbed my wrist and pulled me down behind a shrub, pointing to something on the slope above. A murmur of voices carried on the wind.

I peeked around the bush. Two short figures stood about fifteen feet upslope at the entrance of what appeared to be a rock overhang. One of the figures raised his hands in exclamation. They were arguing.

"Dwarves," Damian whispered.

I'd never met a dwarf before. They inhabited cave systems and were prolific in the Realm of Earth—not to be mistaken with the real world. They weren't typically benevolent, but they weren't necessarily evil. If the dwarves lived here, they must know something about the underground city.

I stood and tromped up the slope toward them. "*Neve*," Damian whispered after me, but I ignored him.

The dwarves were so engrossed in whatever they were arguing about that they didn't notice me approaching until I was a few feet away. "Hi!" I said, startling them.

The dwarves stopped mid-sentence and turned to me, otherwise frozen with shock. I guessed they weren't used to visitors. They wore dirty trousers and tunics cinched around their round midsections by leather belts. Their braided mustaches hung down a good six inches. Though I'd never seen a dwarf before, these were pretty much what I imagined.

Damian appeared at my side. One look at him, and the dwarfs scuttled into the space under the rock overhang.

"Hey! Wait!" I shot after them, but they were gone. I felt around the rocks hopelessly, looking for a door, but there was nothing there.

Well, crap.

17

As I castigated myself, Damian stepped forward and swept his hand in front of the back wall. The air rippled like a mirage, and then the glowing outline of a doorway appeared in the rock face.

His lips pulled up in a smile. "Perfect."

"How do you do that?" I demanded. "Is it a seeker thing?"

"It's a detection spell. It only works for a very limited area." He motioned for me to take his hand, and I obeyed. It was warm and soft.

The door hadn't opened, but the rock had become translucent. It reminded me of Damian's secret vault in his office. We stepped through the rock door together and appeared in a dark, damp chamber. The air was stale and heavy and smelled of dust. Damian flicked on a flashlight.

"Can you teach me to do that?" I asked.

He handed me another flashlight. "No. It's seeker magic."

I sighed and inspected the chamber. It was worth a shot. "Sometimes, I just wish I could absorb other people's magic, you know?"

Damian frowned. "You shouldn't." He paused, as if lost in thought, then continued. "You've been blessed with your own talents."

"Easy for you to say. I've spent most of my life mostly powerless and afraid of what little I can do."

"Not anymore. You were incredible in the Realm of Air. You did things I've never seen before." He stepped forward, closing the distance between us, and looked down at me. "I bet we haven't discovered half of what you can do."

The way he said it made my breath catch. I didn't dare let it out. My gaze flicked to his lips. He could kiss me at any moment.

Did I even want that? I *had* that night in his hotel room. But now...I had no idea. I slipped around him but let my fingers linger for a moment on his side. "So, what next?" I asked with forced nonchalance.

The bare room was hewn from the chalk bedrock typical to the region. The walls were incised with ancient chisel marks left from when the space was carved out of the earth. Two passageways veered off in different directions, one continuing down a set of four stairs.

I eyed Damian playfully. "Should we split up?"

"No. We stick together."

"Thank fates. Because splitting up is how everyone dies in the movies. Can you use your seeker skills to find the box?"

"Not from here. I can sense it, but the signature is too vague to say which way will lead to it."

"Alrighty. Then let's take this one." I motioned to the corridor on the right and led the way down the stairs.

Conveniently, humans had constructed the city, not dwarves. The ceilings of the passages and chambers were tall enough that we didn't constantly bump our heads, though Damian had to stoop, and the space was pretty constricting. The darkness didn't help. Walking carefully, I shone my light on the floor ahead.

"Careful." I motioned to a hole at the base of the side wall, shining my light down into the bottomless abyss. "Don't want to fall in there."

"Any particular reason you chose this way?"

"Not really. It looked less creepy." I usually relied on my gut instinct. Often, it was wrong, but sometimes —*sometimes*—it was right.

"Look at this," said Damian.

I turned and found him standing in front of a niche in the wall, looking at a small ceramic object perched on the ledge. There were lots of nooks and crannies in the walls. Some were storage cubbies, while others were nothing more than hollowed-out cavities.

I recognized the object immediately. "A lamp! Must've been left here ages ago."

I'd seen lamps like this in museums but never in their original location. Soot stains covered the nozzle where the flame once burned, and a molded design of a cross decorated its surface.

Damian reached out to take it, but I slapped his hand away. "No! Don't touch it."

"Why? It's not a trap. I'd probably sense it if it were."

"It's an artifact, and this is a heritage site. We shouldn't be disturbing or taking things."

Damian looked at me skeptically. "Aren't we here to steal a box?"

"A magic box. One created by Magica. Plus, it's an emergency." I pointed to the lamp. "*That* is not an emergency."

Pebbles fell from the ceiling down the way, and Damian flashed his light around. "I'd hate to be in here during an earthquake."

"Yeah, this is not exactly the place you'd want to build an underground city."

He paused. "What do you mean?"

"It's at the junction of the Arabian and Eurasian plates, so it's prone to earthquakes."

"Great. So it's a death trap. Good thing I'm not claustrophobic."

Unfortunately, I was. Or, more accurately, having taken a moment to contemplate the immediate consequences of global tectonic drift, I had suddenly become claustrophobic.

"Let's get a move on." I marched on at a faster pace.

The air grew moist and stagnant as we descended into the mountain. It wasn't a steep drop, but the floor was definitely declining at a gradual angle. A few rooms opened before us, but they led nowhere and appeared to be storage space.

Vivid thoughts of being buried alive kept me moving. I turned a corner and bumped into something. I'd have toppled over if Damian hadn't grabbed my shoulder.

A muffled grunt sounded below me.

Heart racing, I shone my light toward the sound.

A dwarf stared up at me, wide-eyed and gaping. His attire matched that of the dwarves we'd ambushed outside, but unlike them, this fellow had a long beard interwoven with gray crystals. The short man took two steps back and pulled a hammer out of his belt, holding it menacingly above his head.

Damian stepped in front of me, raising his arm in a non-threatening gesture. His other hand appeared at his side, revealing a marble-sized purple gem that flickered under the flashlight. "Easy...we're looking for something. Can you help us?"

The dwarf's eyes narrowed on the gem, and he lowered his hammer. "Slag!"

It appeared to be a curse.

"Don't you know sneaking up on a dwarf can be deadly? You're lucky I'm the kind type. What do you want?"

"Sorry to intrude, but we're looking for a magic box that was hidden here many centuries ago. Do you know where it might be?" I asked.

The dwarf scrunched his face and raised his hand, demanding payment first. Damian dropped the shiny gem into the dwarf's chubby palm. "I don't know of such a thing. But...if you are right and such a thing is here, then it might be in the sunken pits. Our people do not go down there."

The sunken pits? *Nope*, I decided, *we aren't going there.*

"And where might those be?" Damian reached in his pocket, probably for another gem.

The dwarf pointed down the passageway. "Straight ahead, turn left at the junction, right twice and follow the way down. You're not in your right mind to go down there."

"Why's that?" I asked.

The dwarf shook his head. "You won't come back."

Damian handed the dwarf another gemstone, this time yellow. "Thanks for your help, friend."

The dwarf pocketed the gems and muttered something unintelligible, shaking his head as we continued forward.

"There's *got* to be another way," I said.

"I don't think so."

We followed the dwarf's directions down the narrow passage, winding deeper into the bowels of the mountain.

"Straight. Left. Right and then left," I muttered to myself. "Or wait. Was it right and then right? Crap." I had incredible recall for images, but speech, not so much.

"I think we head this way." Damian pointed to the corridor to our right. "I can sense the box now."

The passage grew steeper, and water began seeping out of the walls and dripping from the ceiling. I wiped the wetness from my forehead and rolled up my sleeves. It was more humid than Aquaman at a disco.

"We're getting close," Damian said.

A faint breeze cooled my damp skin as we stepped into a wide chamber, larger than the rest we'd encountered.

My heart sank.

The corridor continued at the opposite end of the room. One problem, though: the corridor was flooded.

Little waterfalls drained from the porous rock, and the muddy brown water rose to a foot below the ceiling.

Damian took off his jacket and stored it in his backpack, tightening the straps to ensure a snug fit. Speaking of snug fit...did he just tailor his shirts to show off his perfect form? "I hope you can swim."

"Why, are you hoping to see my breaststroke?" *Damn it*, I thought, aghast, *did I really just say that?*

Damian shot me a wicked grin. "I bet it's spectacular."

My cheeks flushed, and I suddenly felt uncomfortably hot. That's it. I was having a heatstroke or something.

Damian strode into the water, peering down the flooded corridor that provided our only way through. "It looks like the passage isn't fully submerged. We might be able to wade through."

Things were looking up. A little.

I hopped in and let out a gasp as the cool, dark water enveloped my body. I cringed at the thought of what sort of creatures might be lurking in the muddy abyss. The water lapped at my chest as I waded forward, trying my best to focus only on Damian's form ahead of me.

Something solid brushed against my leg.

"Shit!" I jumped onto Damian's back. "There's something in the water."

If there was one thing I hated, it was murky water

and the things in it. Damian shifted, wrapping a strong arm around me, holding me up.

The surface of the water was glassy, but I looked about wildly, half expecting a monster to come bursting out.

"It's probably just a fish," he soothed. "Let's keep moving. I can see light up ahead. Looks like another chamber."

His words weren't reassuring, but I loosened my grip and climbed out of his grasp. I wanted out of this water ASAP. We hastened our pace, but it wasn't exactly easy.

Suddenly, Damian came to an abrupt stop and stared ahead.

I tensed. "What? What is it?"

Silence.

My heart thundered in my ears, and all the little warning bells in my body went off. "Damian?"

A small ripple appeared, and a black fin broke the surface of the water.

"Not sure," he said. "Let's go. Pick up the pace."

Shit. Shit. Shiii—

Something slimy wrapped around my calf and pulled me under. I kicked my legs as hard as I could, but the pressure on my calf only tightened, causing my muscles to spasm. I began flailing, and my lungs burned something fierce as I twisted and writhed in vain. Desperate for release, I grabbed my khanjar from its sheath and whipped my upper body forward, slashing the dark water, but my dagger found no target. I flipped onto my stomach and clawed at the stone floor as I was dragged backward. The ache in my chest grew, my movements slowed, and a peaceful darkness began to tug me into the abyss. I knew I should fight to free myself, but the darkness beckoned. It would be so easy to drift off...

The peaceful euphoria ended abruptly as something firm grabbed my bicep. Was that a hand? My oxygen-depleted brain moved slowly.

The grip on my calf loosened as two powerful arms wrenched me free, and then my head broke the surface. Gasping and choking, I gulped in as much air as my wheezing lungs could handle. I clung to Damian's chest as he plowed through the water, and my senses slowly returned.

The submerged passage opened into a giant space illuminated by a single column of sunshine that pierced through a hole in the ceiling.

Damian lifted me out of the water onto the muddy ledge. I lay on my back, staring at the light. My mind was still foggy, but my pulse and breathing had slowed. I turned my head and watched as Damian braced his hands on the ledge to pull himself up.

With a splash, he disappeared into the placid water. *No!*

I shot upright and looked around for something that might help, but the room was bare. Without warning, the water surged, and Damian burst upward, clutching a black reptilian body. He was dragged under again, and the water swelled with thrashing movement from below.

Then it stopped.

I peered into the dark waters, now calm. "Damian!"

No response.

Oh, hell.

18

Where had Damian gone? Did he need my help? Fear chilled my skin, but I climbed back into the water anyway. Every inch of me cringed. How the hell was I going to help him when I couldn't even see him?

With a gasp and a splash, Damian popped his head up several feet from where he went under. I scrambled back onto the ledge as he hauled himself out of the water.

He smiled as he dripped on the rock. "Were you worried?"

"Of course! I don't want to be down here alone." It was only a half-truth. I *had* been worried for him. "What was that thing? A snake?"

"Not exactly. More like a newt. A giant one." He pulled his shirt off and wrung it out, his chest speckled with gleaming water.

That cleared my head real *fast*. I turned to give him privacy, but mainly so he couldn't see my flushed cheeks. I was shivering, so I couldn't blame the heat for my sudden coloring. "Did you get it?"

"Yes. But I can't promise there aren't more. We'd best find another way out. Maybe we can squeeze through that crack." He motioned to the opening in the ceiling where light poured through. We would need to fly up because it was a good fifty feet above us. I desperately hoped I could make it.

"Sign me up if it means we're out of that water for good." I looked down at the soggy clothes revealingly plastered to my skin. *This* was inconvenient.

"Take my jacket. You're shivering." Damian pulled his jacket out of his backpack. It was still dry. His backpack was apparently waterproof. Of course.

I took it. "Thanks. But what about you?"

"I told you, I run hot."

My cheeks flamed. I zipped the oversized jacket up and scanned the room as he pulled his damp shirt back on.

The space was barren apart from a bench and staircase that had been hewn into the rock. Strange black stains dripped from the upper walls. *Guano?*

I climbed the stairs, which led to a doorway and another passage, draped in shadow. I could just barely make out boulders littering the floor and obscuring a section of the corridor down the way. "Crap. Might be collapsed up ahead. I can't see much. I'm afraid I dropped my light in the water."

Damian pulled another from his bag and tossed it to me. "Always bring spares."

"Thanks." I flicked it on.

He squeezed past me into the passage. "Let's hope it's not blocked. My tracking sense is ringing. We can't be far now."

I followed along behind. Black stains coated the walls of the passage, too. Except they weren't stains. More like...secretions.

Damian noticed me inspecting the stuff. "Mineral deposits of some kind?"

I pinched a piece of the sticky substance off the wall. It smelled putrid, not mineral. "Maybe some kind of cave lichen? I've never seen anything like it." Maybe I should bring a sample back to the Field Museum. They had a collection of lichens from around the world and always welcomed new samples.

A crash of tumbling rocks startled me. I whipped my light toward the source of the noise and spotted Damian heaving boulders off an old collapse that blocked our path. *You could have warned me*, I started to say, then paused. Sure, I could help him, but I was enjoying the view. His shoulders flexed beneath his damp shirt with each heave.

Was it getting warmer in here again?

The rocks were piled up to the ceiling, with a narrow

gap at one end. I shone my flashlight through. "Looks like it's open on the other side."

"Think we can fit?" Damian pulled another rock off the collapse.

"Me, maybe. It might be tight for you." I handed Damian his jacket, afraid to accidentally snag it on the rocks. Clenching the flashlight in my teeth, I crawled up the rockfall and squeezed into the narrow gap. It was a tight fit, even for me, and I had to inch forward on my stomach. I moved gingerly, careful not to catch my clothes on the sharp rubble. The rockfall was about ten feet deep, and from what I could tell, the passage was clear up ahead.

"How are you doing?" Damian asked.

"Good. But you're definitely not gonna fit," I mumbled through my clenched teeth. I stuck my head out of the gap. All clear. The passage curved up ahead.

I carefully pulled my body out of the rockfall and dusted off my front. My damp clothes were coated with streaks of mud.

"What do you see?" Damian sounded concerned. "Are you all right?"

"It looks clear. There's a bend up ahead. I'm gonna go check it out."

"Be careful."

I rounded the corner, then another. The passage continued, but fifty feet ahead, it opened into a side room. Damian's muffled voice echoed behind me. And then...something else.

I turned my head to pinpoint the origin of the strange noise, listening carefully. It sounded like scuttling. But scuttling *what*? I didn't want to wait and find out.

I jogged forward, eager to find the damn box. Slowing, I flashed my light into the side room.

Vibrant but crumbling frescoes covered the white plastered walls. Winged creatures. A knight in chain mail. An angel holding a cross. They were remarkable.

I swept the room with my light. It was no bigger than my bedroom. Several dusty rugs were neatly rolled and stacked in one corner. Beside them were two wooden chests and at least a dozen long ceramic jars with narrow necks and two handles. I recalled those from a Nat Geo episode on ancient shipwrecks. What were they called?

Scratching noises echoed down the hall.

I paused, my pulse quickening. What *was* that?

Heart pounding, I bolted to the chests and flipped the lid off one. It was filled with embroidered textiles and several metal jugs decorated with filigree designs. No box, though.

Shit. Where was it?

The letter said it was a box. Or was it a chest? The Arabic word could be translated either way. Heart pounding, I began searching frantically.

Could it be one of these chests? How would we get a chest out of here?

My mind raced. I flipped open the other chest, but it was full of silver coins and glass bangles.

"Damn it!" The box wasn't in it either.

Pushing past them, I searched the rugs, unfolding each one. But there was nothing there. I pulled the ceramic jars out, one by one. Maybe it was hidden behind one of them. But no.

My heart sank as I scanned the other side of the room. Besides a small rockfall, it was bare.

I walked over to the rubble and slumped to the floor, resting my flashlight in my lap. We'd made it all this way for nothing. I thought of Rhiannon and felt sick. Frustrated, I leaned my back against the cool wall and gripped a piece of rubble that had fallen from the ceiling. Maybe the box was in another room. We would just have to keep looking.

I took a breath and sighed, releasing my grip on the rock. My hand brushed something smooth and cool. Curious, I glanced down and caught a glint of metal buried beneath the rubble, illuminated by my flashlight. My pulse surging, I pushed the rocks aside and...*sweet fates!*

A brass box.

It was small, maybe six inches all around, and it stood on four short legs. Ornate floral and vegetal designs decorated its dusty surface. I pulled the box forward, and its magic reverberated off my fingertips.

"Yes!" This was definitely it. I clutched the box and rose, turning to leave.

A giant spider filled the doorway. Horror shot through me, and I stopped short.

Its legs were as thick as mine and covered with gray bristles. Eight glassy black eyes stared back at me, and I saw my reflection in each of them. Two pincers clicked as they opened and closed, and black slime dripped from the corners of its mouth—the same stuff we'd seen on the walls. Definitely not lichen, but why did it need to be spiders?

More scuttling reverberated from the passage.

Oh, crap. There's more of them.

I took a breath and whispered the name of the wind. Energy surged down my arm and into my palm, but it wasn't as strong as it had been in the Realm of Air. I focused on drawing it together and forced a blast of wind at the spider. It wasn't a powerful gust, but it shoved the creature into the wall of the passage, giving me just enough time to dart by.

I raced down the corridor, wheeling around one corner and then another. The scratching noise behind me grew faster...and louder. I spotted the rockfall ahead.

"Damian, I'm coming through!" I glanced behind me, and panic swelled. Two spiders were closing in, *fast*. I tripped on a rock, and my flashlight flew out of my hand, but there was no time to grab it. I ran through the darkness, my free arm outstretched in case I ran into a wall. A soft glow appeared ahead, lighting the path.

What the...?

Was it the same light that had illuminated the ice devils on the ship? It had to be, and thank fates—I needed all the help I could get. I scrabbled down the hallway as quickly as I could.

As I came around the corner, the beam of Damian's flashlight shone through the rockfall. My lungs burned, but I quickened my pace. *Almost there.*

Scrambling up the boulders, I dove into the gap, grasping the box with my outstretched arm. I heard the spiders skittering behind me.

"I'm coming through, and I've got friends!"

Using my free hand, I pulled myself forward on the jagged rocks, kicking my feet for momentum.

Something clawed at my foot, and my heart leapt into my throat. *Shit.*

Damian shoved his arm into the gap, reaching for me. "Give me your hand!"

Instead, I shoved the box at him. "Take this!"

He pulled it through. With my second hand now free, I moved faster. The spiders clawed at my feet, making my skin crawl.

Damian reappeared and grabbed my hands, hauling me out of the crack. Pain shot through my stomach and thighs as rocks raked my body. He caught me and set me down, gripping my arms. "Are you hurt?"

I shook my head, lungs heaving as I tried to catch my breath.

He shoved the box into his backpack. "Let's get out of here."

We rose and jogged into the illuminated room ahead. The glowing light beside me was gone now. *Weird.*

Behind us, the spiders clawed at the rockfall, beginning to break through.

Damian stopped abruptly at the top of the stairs. I joined him and stared down into the room. A giant spider looked up, while two more scurried along the walls toward us.

"Time to get the hell out. Can you fly?" Damian pointed up at the opening in the ceiling.

"I freaking hope so." I closed my eyes and focused.

Nothing.

Damian hovered in front of me, his wings glinting in the beam of sunlight. A crash sounded behind me, and I turned. Two spiders scuttled down the passage toward us, their bodies filling the narrow space almost entirely. They must have broken through the rockfall. With no time to spare, I leapt into the air, my arms reaching for Damian.

Except, he didn't catch me—I was flying! Well, more

like hovering, but I'd take it. Damian steadied me, and we darted upward.

The hole was a few feet in diameter, much too small for Damian's wings.

"Go! I'll follow you." Damian latched onto the rock overhang and his wings disappeared. He began climbing up through the hole, except one of the spiders was crawling along the ceiling, headed right toward him. It would be on him in seconds.

I dropped back down and directed a burst of air at the spider, but only a faint breeze shot forward, not nearly strong enough to affect it. Whipping out my khanjar, I flew myself onto the spider's hairy back. Its bristles scratched my arms, but my power had dissipated, so I clung on with all my strength. The spider craned its head backward. chomping its pincers in an attempt to knock me off.

Clenching my legs and tightening my grip, I raised my dagger and sunk it into the creature's back. It screeched and dropped from the ceiling. I jumped, using my feet to propel me away from the spider as we plummeted.

Out of the corner of my eye, I spotted Damian surging toward me, his powerful wings flashing as he tried to catch me before I hit the ground. Heart racing, I summoned all my remaining power and channeled it outward. I stopped ten feet from the ground, just as Damian reached me. The spider landed on its feet and scurried away.

"Let's get out of here," I said. "For real, this time."

Damian nodded, and we flew toward the ceiling. There were no spiders to stop us, thank fates, and I darted up and out, the sunlight momentarily blinding me. Damian climbed out a moment later.

We stood on the opposite side of the hill from where we had entered, about three-quarters of the way down. I sprinted away, and Damian followed. I was fairly certain the spiders wouldn't leave the cavern, but I didn't want to take any chances.

We hurried down the hillside, but I stopped short. The car wasn't there.

I looked at Damian. "How long were we in there? Seems like hours."

"A couple of hours." He pressed his cell phone to his ear and spoke a few words of Turkish, then hung up and met my gaze. "Selim will be here in ten."

"Thank fates." I bent over, hands on my knees, panting. I wasn't used to all of this running and flying. I'd need to start working out more.

"Here." Damian handed me a water bottle. "Thanks for saving me back there."

I chugged the water, not realizing how thirsty I was. "We'll call it even. You slayed the newt."

"When you put it that way, it doesn't sound that impressive. It really was more like an alligator."

"Yeah, I can see it now. Damian Dundee... newt wrestler."

He chuckled, and we sat in companionable silence for a moment, breathing hard and soaked to the bone.

The Range Rover appeared around a bend. Silently, I thanked the fates...I was ready for a cushy seat.

19

Despite the luxurious plane, I didn't sleep well on the flight back to Chicago. Fitful dreams of winding tunnels, spiders, and Damian left me exhausted and restless.

A driver met us at the airport. It was early evening, and the city drifted by in a blur as we sped back to Magic Side.

Thoughts of my apartment flooded me. My bed. My wardrobe and clothes. "I wish we could go back to my flat, just to get a few things."

"It's just not safe. The concealment charm may hide our locations from the djinn, but that doesn't mean he can't hunt us down. Remember, he laid a trap for your friend in her apartment. I'd be willing to bet he's set one in yours, too. Hell, perhaps he could even get into mine. Their power is incalculable."

I sighed.

Damian absently tapped on the limo window with his knuckles. "But I assume that you'll need new clothes. I certainly do."

Somehow, Damian still looked dashing, despite the overnight flight. Meanwhile, I was in shambles. By now, everything in my weekender bag had been slept in, rumpled by air travel, caked by mud, soaked with newt water, or covered in flour, and it was jumbled together in a disgusting wad. I would kill for three minutes with my wardrobe—or for any article of clothing not covered in newt juice.

Damian tapped on his phone. "We'll have the hotel wash everything tonight. I'll have my assistant Jeanette pick up an extra outfit or two for you and have them sent up. Here's her contact. Tell her what you want— brand, size, style—and she'll run out and get it for you."

My phone pinged. "Wow...I mean, I can just wait for the laundry."

I wasn't used to this lifestyle.

Damian absently waved his hand. "You should have something on hand tonight in case we have to run for it. Don't worry, Jeanette has good taste. It's on me—a business expense."

I winked. "Well, all right then, you've twisted my arm."

Suddenly awake, I spent the rest of the car ride sending Jeanette my sizes and a list of a few of my favorite stores. Some of them were...well, not stores at which I would normally splurge...but I knew a good opportunity when I saw one. Sending Jeanette links to a few designer dresses, I murmured, "Go big or go home."

"What?" Damian turned to me.

"What?"

"You said something."

"Nope."

"Okay," he said suspiciously.

"Okay." I buried my face in the phone.

Despite the silence, the air between us vibrated with tension. Damian sat so close that I could feel the heat from his body. His scent wrapped around me, a combination of juniper and the sea.

I peeked over the top of my phone, taking him in while he gazed out the window. The city lights flashed behind him, illuminating his profile—he was so damn handsome, it was distracting.

Damian turned again and caught my eyes. My face flushed, and he shot me a devilish grin as we pulled up to the hotel.

I forced myself out of the car. A dull throb rose from the small of my back to my shoulders, but I barely had the energy to acknowledge it.

Damian accompanied me up to my room, then started to follow me in. "And what do you think you're doing?" I asked, torn between playfulness and exhaustion.

But he was all business. "I'll weave some protective

charms on the doors and windows. The other half of being a thief, as you would have it, is being able to keep other people out."

"Thanks."

He drew glowing runes in the air over each of the exits. "This should keep anyone out. It will also trip an alarm if anyone attempts to break the spells."

"Even you?"

"Nope."

"Good to know. Thanks. Now, let a girl get some sleep." I leaned back on the open door, and as he passed through, his eyes lingered on my body for a second. Heat shot right through me, and then I caught sight of my reflection in the mirror on the opposite wall.

Fates be damned!

My hair was a rat's nest, my clothes were rumpled, and I had raccoon eyes. I silently cringed, even though Damian didn't seem to have a problem with it.

Damian turned and tapped his watch. "Remember, we have a meeting with the mage at 9:30 tomorrow morning. Let's meet up at 8:30 for breakfast. Set your alarm."

"Got it."

"Night, Neve."

"Night." I closed the door, still slightly mortified.

The hotel room was probably nice, but I was too tired to notice.

I peeled the loathsome clothes from my body like a

half-drunk lizard and staggered into the shower. It roared to life, scouring me with hot, purifying water. Delight swept across my skin. Rather than a shower in a jet, this was a real shower *with* jets.

Thank fates.

I took a *really* long shower. My skin was raw and rosy by the time I finally stepped out and toweled off, but as I dripped on the plush bathmat, someone knocked at the door.

Damian?

I quickly draped my wet hair over my shoulder and wrapped myself with a towel. Slipping on the plush bedroom slippers that had been set out, I caught my reflection in the bathroom mirror—*major* improvement.

I cracked the door slightly and peeked out. My visitor was a bellman. Too bad.

"One sec." Feeling slightly dejected that it wasn't Damian, I shut the door. It *would* have been a fine opportunity to scold him for disturbing my shower.

Wait a second—what the heck was I thinking?

I clearly couldn't trust my better judgement when it came to Damian. I recalled the urges I'd had recently... in the cabin on the airship while he healed me.

Oh gods, and in the tunnel in Cappadoccia. Had he *actually* wanted to kiss me then, or was I just fantasizing it all?

Crap.

One thing was certain—I needed to reign in this sex-crazed weirdness. A-stat.

I grabbed a robe from the closet then peered out the door. "Hi. Can I help you?"

"Hello, Ms. Cross. I have a cheeseburger and a milkshake for you. May I?"

I nodded and stepped aside, though I hadn't ordered food.

The bellman wheeled in a cart covered with a white tablecloth and one of those silver plates with a domed cover. A vase with three red carnations sat beside a tall milkshake. My stomach grumbled.

"There is one more thing. Err...actually, several more things," he said, ducking back into the hall.

"Huh?"

A small troupe of bellboys wheeled five racks of clothes into the room. "A woman dropped these off on behalf of Mr. Malek."

"Fates...Jeanette wasn't kidding around." I sat on the edge of the bed as they maneuvered the racks of clothing about the room, trying to find space for everything. "Thanks. Do I need to sign for all this?"

"Mr. Malek took care of that. The tip as well. Good evening, Ms. Cross." The bellman nodded and shut the door behind him.

Of course he did.

Cheeseburger in hand, I stared at the racks for a long moment. As my excitement thrummed, I stood up and investigated the outfits, careful not to get any ketchup on them. There was denim and leather, but also linen and cashmere and silk. Everything was insanely nice. The price tags were still on, and my brows rose. Yep, way out of my usual price range. I spotted a pair of jeans I'd been eyeing for months. "Score."

There was also a blue silk negligee that I hadn't ordered. Hmm...I glanced at the tag. Fleur du Mal. This certainly wasn't on my list, but I loved it.

Thirty minutes later, I had tried on all the clothes and chosen a few amazing outfits. I was a saint for not choosing them all, I decided, but then again, maybe I'd double-check my selections in the morning, once I could see straight. The clothing-inspired surge of adrenaline had worn off as a food coma kicked in, and the crisp, clean bedsheets called out to me in a siren song. *Sleeeep.*

I sighed as I slumped onto the soft mattress. It was a real bed, it wasn't moving, and right now, it was more beautiful than all the clothes in the world. I made it about halfway under the covers before passing out.

A loud pounding on the door dragged me from the abyss of sleep. Every muscle ached slightly, and I realized I hadn't moved an inch since falling into bed. Groggy, I glanced at my watch.

8:45. *Shit!*

"Neve. Are you awake?" Damian's voice echoed through the door.

"I'll be just a minute!"

Total lie.

"How long do you need? Honest estimate."

"Uh." I looked at the stacks of new outfits. "About three hours."

"Can you do twenty minutes?"

"Yes." I crossed my fingers.

"Good. I'll call Matthias and let him know we're running late. I'll have pastries and coffee."

"Okay. Thanks so much!"

"Twenty minutes."

"I'll be there."

Trying to sort out my clothes, I ran frantically around the room. Wooziness rushed over me. *Ugh, settle down, Neve.* I was holding my breath from the stress. Great goblins, was this how Rhiannon felt all the time? She was always late.

Somehow, I managed to put myself together. The new jeans were perfect. I paired them with a mustard-yellow blouse. As I was about to pull it on, I caught sight of my tattoo in the mirror. It had grown again, though I couldn't remember when I had looked at it last. That was...troublesome.

I drew in a deep breath and shoved down the worry. The tattoo was a future me problem.

I met Damian outside my room at precisely 9:05. He looked me up and down with interest and handed me a coffee and a stuffed croissant. "Nice outfit. Were you pleased with Jeanette's selection?"

"A-plus." I nodded between mouthfuls of croissant. "Jeanette did great. Though she did pick up something that I, uh...wasn't expecting."

I recalled the way the silk negligee hugged my body in all the right places.

Damian glanced at me as we hurried down the hall, a faint smile ghosting his lips.

I coughed as a piece of croissant lodged in my throat. Could he read my thoughts or something?

He held open the elevator door and motioned for me to enter. A man in a gray suit stepped to the corner to make room.

Damian raised an eyebrow. "I take it you like it?"

Holy fates. Had *he* picked out that expensive lingerie? *No.*

Still chewing, I nodded discreetly. "Mm-hmm. Fit great."

"I can only imagine." There was the faintest roughness to his voice, and a shiver ran down my spine.

The elevator ride took a century. Tension sparked the air between us until my skin felt too tight for my body. As soon as the doors opened, I was out and heading through the lobby. *Just a bit of fresh air*, I told myself, *that's all I need.*

Damian followed, and we slid into the limo waiting outside. I moved over to make space for him, staring at my coffee like it held the answers to the meaning of life.

Right. It was time to stop blushing and get down to business. I took a long sip of coffee, the nectar of consciousness, which dragged me out of that elevator and back into the car. "So, how much do you know about this mage?"

"Not much."

I eyed him. He wasn't being forthcoming.

Grudgingly, he continued, "We have mutual interests from time to time. He seems to know a little about everything, but he acts like he knows a lot about everything."

Sounds familiar, I almost retorted, then bit my tongue.

The limo arrived at the Gaslight District, a decadent historic neighborhood with large trees shading the street. The mage's house looked like it had been built in the nineteenth century. A peaked roof topped the brightly painted three-story building. Decorated in bold reds, yellows, and browns, it stood out from its more subtly colored neighbors. The Gaslight District was one of the few places you could find wooden houses in Magic Side—after the Great Chicago Fire of 1871, most buildings had been built of brick.

The driver dropped us off and pulled around the corner to park. The mage's lot was surrounded by an unconventionally tall iron fence topped with ornate, sharp spikes. The narrow ironwork gate buzzed and automatically opened when we approached, revealing a brick walkway lined with yellow and violet flowers that led to a welcoming porch.

Damian mounted the stairs and knocked on the front door. It swung in with a slow creak, and there was a metallic clank as a massive, armor-plated knight stepped up to occupy the doorway.

I stumbled backward. "Holy shit!"

Damian smiled. "Don't worry. It's just his doorman."

20

The knight in Matthias's doorway silently gestured for us to enter.

Something was off about it. I squinted to see through the eye holes in the helmet. There was no one in the armor. It was entirely empty.

"Armor golem," Damian said nonchalantly, and made his way in.

"What?"

"Golems are magical constructs usually created to be servants or bodyguards. They can be made out of a variety of substances, like clay or stone. Or, as in this case, a suit of armor."

"Ah." I followed cautiously behind, peeking inside the armor when I passed. It was probably rude, but curiosity got the better of me.

Yep—completely hollow. So cool.

The golem closed the door behind me and led us to a study in the back.

The mage sat behind a large desk. He was shuffling through a stack of notes and turning pages of an open book.

His magic hit me like a landslide. Smoke. Steam. The scent of hot iron. There was something else there, too, that felt like a fire hidden beneath the coals. Why had I been sensing so many weird auras lately? Damian. Sora. Matthias. Even Nix, when I thought about it.

The mage didn't look up. "I'll be with you in a minute."

We waited. I shifted awkwardly, but Damian looked calm and composed. The walls of the room were lined with thousands of books, neatly organized. Unable to resist, I started browsing.

Phenomenology and the Thousandfold Self.

Identity, Id, and Ennui.

The Denouement of Myth in the Modern Age.

The laborious titles continued book after book, shelf after shelf. *Fates.* I seldom ran into a book I didn't want to read, but this room was literally packed with them. It was like Matthias had googled the most pretentious books ever written and added them to his Amazon cart.

"Please have a seat." He waved his hand, and two bare metal chairs appeared in a flash of steam.

Annoyance tugged at the corners of Damian's smile.

He was not used to being kept waiting. But there was something more there too. Rivalry? Not quite.

The mage—Matthias—had slick dark hair, a square jaw, and thick, black-framed glasses. Fifty bucks said those were fake.

We sat, and Matthias didn't bother with introductions. "I gather you have had a successful trip?"

Damian pulled the ornate box from his bag, placing it on the desk.

The mage made a show of switching glasses and examined the metal box. "Very fine work," he muttered. "Looks like eighth-century patterns. Or perhaps ninth. Hmm...simultaneously crafted from brass and magic by a very skilled artisan. Perhaps Syrian?" He popped it open and looked inside. "My, my, I wish I could add this to my private collection, I do so love high-quality Islamic metalwork. You found it in Turkey?" He raised his eyes to mine, and I nodded. "Then it must have been booty from a raid on the Levantine coast. Maybe late ninth century."

Okay, so *maybe* this guy knew a thing or two.

He closed the box and placed it back in front of us. "Damian, I am pleased. You have the other item I requested?"

Damian produced the Dragon Heart, which flickered between emerald and ruby. Something about that tugged at the back of my mind...something I just couldn't put my finger on.

"Yes. Hopefully, this will do. Clearly valuable. But did the djinn treasure it?" Matthias took the gem, inspecting it closely. He closed his eyes and placed his hands on either side of it.

I wasn't sure what he was doing, but I held my breath anyway.

After a moment, Matthias smiled. "Yes. It was indeed valuable to the djinn. Very good."

"Of course it's valuable!" I snorted. "It's a gem the size of an egg. I've never seen anything like it in my life."

Matthias turned my way as if seeing me for the first time. It was a deliberate, condescending look, meant to make me feel invisible. And it worked.

Damian shot the mage a look that froze the marrow in my bones.

The mage cleared his throat. "My apologies. It's not surprising that you haven't seen one before. Dragon Hearts are extremely scarce. Their size and rarity are not what makes them valuable, however. They can be used to control dragons. Sadly, the spell will destroy it." He placed the gem on the table and continued. "Still, that is not what is valuable to us. For our binding spell to work, we need an object that is precious to him, something that was part of his identity. It makes the spell individualized. You understand?"

I inclined my head ever so slightly.

Matthias turned the gem over in his hands. "Binding magic is all about the bonds we make with the world around us. Part of my magic is seeing those bonds. I believe your djinn valued this object because it would allow him to command a dragon. For some djinn, the world can be very binary. Rule, or be ruled. He was trapped for God knows how long. Since he has been freed, it sounds like he has sought to capture and dominate all those around him. That is his dream. Retribution. Exhibition of power."

I sat back. "Well, that's heavy."

"Very." The mage folded his hands in front of him.

Damian leaned forward. "Do you have the spell that will enchant the object?"

"Yes. Do you have my payment?"

Damian pulled out his phone and swiped the screen a few times. "It's been released into your account."

The mage popped open his laptop to check. After a moment, he snapped it shut and stood. "Excellent. All is in order. Now, I will need your help to cast the spell. It will require all of our strength. Follow me."

I scanned the bookshelves as we left and revised my opinion of the man. He was still someone who deliberately ordered the most pretentious books he could find, but he had probably read them all and was eager to remind you of it, if given the chance.

The mage led us to a brickwork carriage house in the backyard. The interior of the building had been gutted, and the floor was paved with large slabs of basalt, each with a single rune carved in its face.

"Welcome to my laboratory." Matthias positioned the box carefully on a rune-marked stone in the middle of the room. He indicated a separate stone for Damian. "Stand here." Next, he indicated a rune-marked stone to my left. "And you, stand here."

"Hi, I'm Neve," I said cheekily.

"Hello, Neve. Stand there." He gave a slip of paper to each of us. "This is the incantation of binding. Memorize it now. You will chant it with me as I work the spell. As the magic rises, you will feel your energy drawn out of you. Don't worry, that is part of the process." He gave us a moment to look over the incantation, then asked, "Ready?"

We nodded.

Even though daylight streamed in through the windows, the mage lit candles mounted in the corners of the room. He also ignited some incense and placed it by the box. "We begin," he said, then snapped his arms out, and the sunlight vanished. All around, the candle flames turned green. He raised the gem in his left hand and began to chant, marking sigils in the air with his right. After a moment, I mastered the rhythm and began to follow along. I had never worked magic in that way before, though parts of it distantly reminded me of the Sumerian spell I had used to bind the gallu.

The words filled the room, pushing outward on the boundaries of reality. It was like space itself twisted around the little brass box. I felt my power pull out of me and begin to circle around the room, like water spiraling a drain. My magic mixed with Damian's and the mage's, and I sensed their magic much more clearly now. Something terrified me about it, but I kept chanting.

Everything warped. Magic pulled the world inward toward the gem in Matthias's hand. It began to glow with white light—faintly at first, but soon it became white hot and radiant. Matthias stepped forward and placed it in the box as he continued the chant.

A roar soon filled the room, like a hurricane rushing inward. The box shook and began to glow. Thunder clapped, and the lid snapped shut.

Suddenly, the carriage house returned to normal. Sunlight beamed through the windows, and dust drifted lazily in the wind.

My legs went weak, but Damian caught me. I gasped, gripping his shoulders and meeting his dark eyes. "You're fast," I mumbled.

One corner of his mouth quirked up in a devastatingly sexy half smile. He pulled me up, supporting me with strong arms.

"I'm fine."

"Of course you're not," the mage scoffed. "Powerful magic takes its toll. Power demands sacrifice. I, myself, feel like crap."

Despite my intention to dislike the man, a chuckle

escaped. Yeah, I felt like crap, too. The lousy end of being drunk.

Matthias picked up the box. "Follow me."

He led us to a bright kitchen trimmed with white shelves and cupboards, then produced three glasses and pulled a pitcher from the fridge. "Fresh lemonade. Literally the perfect antidote for all that is magical."

I downed mine and poured a refill. It was ice cold, sweet and tart, with bits of mint. A glass and a half in, I was nearly restored. "Fates, this is good."

"We're lucky. Lemons are good this time of year," the mage said absently.

Damian leaned forward. "So, how do we work this? Just show up and open the box?"

"Right in principle. Wrong in execution." Matthias set the brass box on the table and opened it. The magic had consumed the gem, leaving only a burn mark on the inside of the box. He indicated the lid. "First, you must get very close to the djinn, within thirty feet. Second, you open the box and chant the phrase I taught you to initiate the spell. Third, chant until the djinn is sucked into the box. I don't know how long this will take. Maybe only a few recitations. Maybe minutes." Matthias snapped the lid shut. "Then you close the box once the djinn has been drawn inside. Do *not* open it again. Lock it or seal it if you can. The bonds may take time to set. Honestly, it's a simple process. The trick is to cast the spell while only thirty feet from the djinn...and to keep chanting the whole time. Don't stop, or you'll have to begin the process again."

"That's going to be difficult," Damian said, eyeing me.

"Absolutely." The mage looked at the two of us. "My money is on the djinn." He slid the box across the table. "Good luck."

The limo sped away from the mage's house.

I turned to Damian. "Woof. He's a total dickweasel."

"Yes. And expensive. But he's the best at what he does."

I leaned back into the seat with a sigh. "He makes good lemonade, though. I'll give him that."

"That's very generous of you."

"I know." I studied the shadows lining Damian's face. "You know him better than you're letting on."

His jaw tensed. A confirmation.

I raised my eyebrows.

"Fine. I know Matthias well—knew him well. It was long ago. We were allies once, before going our own ways. I would be dead many times over, if not for him. But he is, as you say, mostly a dickweasel." Damian turned to face me, more serious now. "I assume we'll need to use the *Atlas of the Planes* to return to the Realm of Air?"

He was changing the subject but also right. Our journey wasn't over.

I had been entirely focused on the library, then the potion, then Cappadocia, and finally the spell. But it was all leading up to a moment when we would have to face the djinn once and for all.

Dread slowly began to creep through my veins. "I think we need to use the *Atlas*. I'm not sure I can put us directly on the spot. Last time, I dropped us in the middle of nowhere, remember?"

"Don't be hard on yourself. You were channeling your powers for the first time, using an artifact you had only encountered minutes before. Temper your expectations. Using magic the first time is always difficult."

My mind flashed back to Rhiannon in the djinn's palace, bloody and bound. Frustration surged. "I appreciate the sentiment. But when is the last time *you* had to learn new powers on the spot?"

Damian tensed, a shadow flashing across his face. I frowned. Something I said hit a sore spot. But what? Either way, I was out of line. He was just being supportive and trying to boost my confidence.

"Sorry. I'm just agitated. I could have killed us that first time. Jumping and not knowing what I was doing... we were lucky I remembered the island from the book."

"We'll go to my office and get the manual."

Soon, we left the Gaslight District behind, heading back downtown to the Rhombus. Traffic wasn't bad, and it took only about fifteen minutes to get to Damian's office. I glared at the secretary as we walked in. She smiled and waved at me enthusiastically.

Once he had locked the door behind us, Damian pulled the *Atlas* from his vault. I opened it, and the scent of old leather and parchment wafted upward as I turned the pages. "I don't think we should jump directly to the djinn's island," I said. "I could pop us in the middle of his dining room without meaning to."

"Good thinking. I suspect he may have warded his palace against teleportation anyway, especially since he knows you're a planes-walker. Could you get us to one of those small rocks nearby?"

I considered for a moment. From our last experience, planes-walking into thin air was extremely disorienting and dangerous. "No. Too much risk. I want a big target. If I missed a rock, we'd be just dropping through the infinity of space with no idea of which direction to go."

"Okay, where?"

"Capri. It's here on the map, and only a few hours from the djinn's palace. We made a similar flight last time. We can do it again...it'll just be a little longer."

"Great. Ready when you are." He studied me intensely, perfectly composed.

I took a deep breath. The memory of us spinning and plummeting through the sky flashed into my mind, and a lump formed in my throat. "Okay, then. Hold on tight."

Damian wrapped his strong arms around me, pulling me against his chest. I breathed in his fresh scent and steeled myself for the impending whirlwind through the ether.

My eyes fell to the book, and I noticed the islands and the sky begin to move, drawing close. I pinpointed Capri as its ink outline zoomed up to meet me.

Then we jumped.

21

Magic tore through us. The first time, I hadn't been prepared. This time, I knew what was coming, and that was far worse. Or it would have been, but I could feel Damian holding me, his strength unrelenting, even as we dissolved into the cosmos.

The vortex consumed us, transporting us atom by atom into a realm on the other side of reality.

I calmed my mind. *It's just a whirlwind.* I was born of wind.

Thinking of Capri, I reached out with my mind and pulled the image of the island close.

A single breath later, our feet slammed into the pavement. The impact surged though my body, along with a rush of triumph. It was the impact of an arrow sinking into a bullseye. I didn't even need to look around to know that I had found my mark.

"Hell, yes!" I yelled.

This dramatic outburst startled the local populace. A few avians fluttered their wings and moved away.

We were in the middle of a square, somewhat similar to the one in Tayir. I had felt drawn to this point. Perhaps these squares were designated landing pads for far travelers.

Whereas Tayir had been urban, Capri was much less developed. We stood on top of a hill. Vineyards and terraced gardens dotted the slopes, a postcard of idyllic loveliness. I took in the landscape, breathing deeply from the rich air. "It's beautiful."

"Yes." Damian said distantly. "But I'm afraid we shouldn't linger. I have food in my pack. Are you ready to fly? Or do you need rest?"

The jump had exhausted one part of my being. But just standing here, amid the floating islands, I felt another part of my soul refreshed. I wanted to leap into the sky, but the coming battle would require every bit of my strength.

"Just give me a second to catch my breath," I replied.

We stood next to a vendor's stall, and Damian turned to the man. He bought a few strange fruits and handed one to me.

"Thanks." I bit into one of the tart red fruits and collapsed onto a nearby bench. I'd sit, but just for a minute. Just until my legs stopped shaking. I stared out at the verdant fields that disappeared into open sky. "I'm scared."

He watched me closely, then pulled a flask from his bag. "Here."

"Liquid courage?" I asked, tossing it back. To my surprise, it was pure, cold water. "I was expecting booze."

"It's just water. There's no need to be afraid."

"*I* think there is. We're going to face a djinn. A creature with unrivaled cosmic powers. I recall someone saying a djinn could crush me with a wink."

"True. But I have a good feeling."

"Why?"

"Well, I have a half djinn with untold power at my side."

I scoffed. "How did you find me in the first place?"

"I'm a seeker. I told you."

"What, you just asked the universe for the nearest available planes-walker?"

He looked at me for a moment and turned away, his eyes dark. "I asked the universe for someone who could help me defeat the djinn."

I was unsure how I should feel about that. "Why did you take this job?"

Damian shifted his shoulders back and forth. "I've done a lot of things for money. Others out of boredom or habit or even revenge. This, I'm doing because it needs to be done."

"Very noble for a thief, I'm sure. Who's your client?"

"Someone who made a well-intentioned mistake." He shrugged. "Now I'm stuck cleaning up their mess...as are you."

"Go on..."

"I don't discuss my clients. Or my collaborators." He turned and gave me a wink. "Thieves' code."

The tart fruit, cool water, and momentary rest did the trick. My legs stopped shaking, and soon I felt the itch to get moving. "I'm ready."

Damian unfurled his wide wings and leapt into the air.

I chased after him. It was so much easier to fly in this realm. I certainly hadn't mastered the technique, but I felt twice as strong as I did back on earth. I pushed to keep up with Damian, though I suspected he could have gone faster.

Joy vibrated through me as we flew.

For a time, we were alone, but soon we began attracting wind sprites, who played and dove around us like dolphins at the bow of a ship. I had seen a few on our first voyage. The sprites left trails of mist streaming in the air behind them, like jet contrails across the face of the sky. Soon, there were a dozen, and we raced in the air, turning and twisting as we flew on toward our destination.

A sprite came close, matching my flight. She laughed. "Who taught you to fly? A bird?"

"Yes," I said, beaming.

The little sprite frowned. "You're joking."

"I'm not. It was a raven."

Her jaw dropped as she slowed to a hover. The other sprites stopped one by one, and, unsure of what was happening, we did, too.

"You learned to fly...from a bird?" the sprite inquired.

"Yes."

"But birds can't fly!" cried a male sprite, clearly aghast.

"Of course birds can fly," I said. "That's what they do. They're birds!"

The sprites looked at each other, completely dumbfounded by what I was saying.

What didn't make sense here? Birds. Fly.

The friendly sprite drew close and spoke hesitantly, as if explaining a principle to a small child or a foolish friend who should know better. "Birds can't fly. That's why they have wings. To help them fly." She pointed to Damian. "He can't fly. That's why he has wings. Because he can't fly."

My brain squealed in pain. "I don't understand."

The sprite was clearly frustrated and unsure of how to proceed. "How do you fly now?"

"I just call the wind and push myself along."

A dozen wind sprites gaped at me, utterly horrified. "You *what*?"

"I use lift?" I responded, completely at a loss.

The sprite came close, and spoke in calm, reassuring tones, as if to a very stupid person. "You are a djinn. You are like us. You are like the wind. The wind doesn't need lift. The wind doesn't have wings. The wind *is*."

I was exasperated. "Fine. So how does the wind go where it wants to go?"

"The wind decides where it wants to go and goes. It is the wind. This is the wind's world."

"You're going to have to explain."

The sprite flitted around me. "Where do you want to go? Just choose."

I picked a point in the sky and strained my muscles. Nothing happened.

"Well?" The sprite raised her eyebrows.

"I'm trying!"

"Decide what you want. Reach out. Draw it to you."

I thought of the sky. Then I thought of Rhiannon. Of the palace. Of the isle.

Reaching forth with something inside of me, I pulled. The world came rushing toward me, and I exploded through the sky. The air shook as I passed, and I pulled as hard as I could. Shock waves curled around me. I was alone at first, and then surrounded by sprites, spiraling in a celestial dance.

Reaching out to my right, I pulled again, turning at an impossible speed. I should have blacked out, but I was unfazed. The sprites followed, a second behind.

I am of this realm.

I'd been told that when I'd arrived, but now I understood. I was the wind. This whole time, I had been fighting against myself, yet my body was the sky. I was limitless.

Looking back, Damian was a distant speck. Any farther, and I would lose sight of him forever. I turned back and pulled, soaring in a rage of turbulence. I overshot and had to try again, slowing myself as I approached.

"Hell," he said, otherwise speechless.

I was electrified. Flying before had drained me. *This* filled me with power, and I felt as if I could explode.

"Not bad for a girl who thought she was a bird." The sprites whirled around me. They laughed, and with a burst, they flew off into the cloudless sky.

We took off at a steady clip, keeping a slight distance from each other so we didn't collide. Damian's wingspan was at least ten feet.

After another hour of travel, dark clouds rose in the distance. Cool drafts of wind converged around us, raising goosebumps on my skin. "We're headed toward a storm," I said. "Which way should we go to get around it?"

Damian gestured to the brewing thunderheads. "That's where we're headed—we're close."

"What? The palace is in *there*? The storm is over the island?"

He shook his head. "I don't think that's a natural storm. I think the djinn has made a wall around the island. To keep intruders like us out."

Great. We were expected, then.

As we drew close, the billowing clouds filled the expanse of the sky. The outer edges roiled as wind currents stirred the air, creating new white puffs of fog. Every few minutes, dull flashes of lighting burst within the massive gray storm wall.

My pulse quickened. "We really need to go in there?"

"That's where Rhiannon is. And the djinn. It's going to be hard to see in there. Stay close and watch out for updrafts. There might be some turbulence."

"Turbulence?" We'd flown through smaller cumulus clouds in the past, and I'd never had any issues.

"A lot of it."

I swallowed. Turbulence was the worst part of flying internationally. Now, instead of being trapped in a nice, safe, flying tuna can, I was going to be completely exposed to the raging elements—and I didn't have so much as a seatbelt.

We broke through the wall of clouds. The gray mist choked out the light, and it soon became hard to see. The air was dense and wet, highly unstable. Gusts of wind surged around me. Suddenly, I dropped a few feet, my stomach lurching. It took every ounce of will I had not to cry out.

Breathe. Just fly.

The wind buffeted my clothes as we pushed forward, and my stomach whirled every time I dropped. The nagging voice in the back of my head reminded me that this was why airplanes didn't fly into thunderheads.

A column of air shot us upward several hundred feet, knocking the breath from my lungs. Seconds later, a downdraft sent me spiraling out of control, and I screamed.

Damian soared down beside me and clasped my hand. "You can do this!"

No, I can't.

I closed my eyes. Frustration surged through my veins, and I pulled my hand away. *I should be able to master this*, I told myself. *I am like the wind. This is my domain.*

I lashed out and fought the wind with all my strength, bending downdrafts and updrafts away from us, creating a slightly smoother pocket of air. The thunderhead still rumbled around us, and invisible currents still shook my body, but we kept pushing ahead.

My breath was heaving by the time we burst through the clouds and into clear sky.

Like a hurricane, the storm was hollow, creating a formidable barrier around the small island that floated in its center. It was much larger than the islet I remembered. Waterfalls spilled over the island's edges, pouring into the sky. Gusts of wind shot spray into the air, and tiny rainbows glinted where the sunlight shone through the clouds above.

I wouldn't have believed this was Aileth Islet, except the djinn's palace still lay at the heart of the island, shrouded with fog. *Had the palace grown larger as well?* I could barely make out the cloud-colored towers.

I swooped in close to Damian. "Where is Rhiannon?"

"In there." Damian pointed toward the palace. Lighting struck, and patches of fog began to part as if the storm itself were acknowledging our arrival.

I gasped.

The sprawling palace had not only grown, but now it was surrounded by a strangely patterned garden. Twisting vines and hedges curved around the main building, protecting it. Barring it.

A maze. And everything was so much *bigger*. "Where did all this come from?"

"The djinn's power is growing," said Damian. "And so is his dominion."

I shook my head. "I don't understand. Why put a maze around a palace in the Realm of Air? It seems that everybody here can fly."

"Look at the way the light shimmers over the palace and the maze. There's some kind of magical dome—I think the djinn has been planning ahead since our last visit. The only way in now is through the garden."

The fog continued to clear, almost inviting us

forward. The maze bridged the vast lake of water that spilled over the island's edges and led right up to the palace's front door.

I groaned. "I hate mazes. Why did it have to be a maze?"

"In a world where everyone flies, make your enemies walk."

My throat tightened. "How the heck are we going find our way through? Do you think there's a back door we could fly to?"

Damian pointed to the glowing clouds in the distance. "It's too dangerous to fly through the lighting storm above the palace. We also can't risk getting spotted by the guards."

"Well, I hope you're good at puzzles, because I'm the worst."

Damian pulled something out of his backpack. "I find that hard to believe. You've solved most of our problems quite well."

"Problems, maybe—mazes, no. Ask me to tell you about the corn maze at the Illinois State Fair when we're not so busy."

He held up a silver square case. "Well, lucky for you, I have a magic compass."

My eyebrows shot up, and a little spark of hope flickered in my chest. "You mean *that* can navigate us through..." I turned and motioned at the maze. "*That?*"

"Theoretically. I haven't tested it before. Bought it from an art dealer in Sicily."

"Let's try it, then." I looked back at the maze and spotted hawk-faced guards patrolling the air above the island. "Damn. It'll be hard to get in."

Several of the guards arced in our direction, monitoring the outer circuit of the thundercloud barrier. Though they were birdlike, there was something unnervingly human about them—probably the fact that they were five feet tall and wore leather breastplates and red tunics.

Damian and I ducked into the thunderhead for cover. We were just a few feet inside when the patrol darted by, barely visible as shadows against the mist.

My shoulders relaxed. "They didn't see us."

We let a few minutes pass before emerging again into the light.

I racked my brain for another route. "Are you sure I can't planes-walk us in? I can remember what some of the rooms look like."

Damian's brow furrowed. "I don't think it would be possible. Do you feel the magic sparking in the air?"

I nodded, feeling it prickle against my skin.

"That's a protection spell. The dome probably wards against teleportation and flight. Many magical places have similar defenses, though this is quite large. We're going to have to go through the maze."

Well, shit.

22

We darted down toward the maze, ducking in and out of the clouds to avoid being spotted by the flying patrols. Dozens of hawk-headed guards circled the perimeter of the storm, but the island was so large that they often remained specks in the distance.

We shot for a wide bank of fog tumbling off the edge of the isle, then landed silently on damp moss in all shades of green. Strange budding plants shrank away as we picked our way toward the maze's entrance, just inside the magical dome.

Just to be sure, I tried levitating. And it *worked*. I was hovering several feet off the ground. "Damian! Maybe we can fly in here after all."

I flew upward to see if I could get a view over the mist and the top of the maze, when I slammed into an invisible barrier that zapped my skin. Electricity shot through me and I dropped.

Damian caught me before I landed. I gazed up at him as my vision cleared. His jaw was set, and worry flashed across his face. "Are you alright?"

He set me down, and I wasn't sure if it was the electric shock or Damian's magic that had my skin tingling. "Yeah. Just got a little jolt of energy. I'm fine."

"Strange." Damian looked up. "It doesn't seem to be an anti-flight spell."

"No. Just a don't-fly-above-ten-feet spell." I glared up at the invisible barrier—*stupid magic dome*—and resigned myself to walking.

As we progressed, the mist dissipated, revealing a cobblestone path that wound its way into the verdant labyrinth ahead. Two giant, perfectly trimmed hedge creatures flanked the entry. One was a vulture-like bird with outstretched wings and an open beak. Opposite it was a giant griffin, rearing back on its hind quarters, its mouth agape in a silent shriek.

I grabbed Damian's arm. "What's the chance that these are *just* hedge sculptures?"

"Slim to none. Feel the magic in the air?"

I nodded, not liking the prickling sensation, and pulled my khanjar from its sheath. Its reverberating ring was always reassuring, reminding me that *I* was in control. "Well, I hope you brought garden shears. These hedges need a trim."

Damian summoned his blade. "Lead the way, Livingstone."

When he wasn't being dark and mysterious, Damian *actually* had a sense of humor. As we inched forward toward the gate, weapons bared, I wondered what else he was hiding under that lethal façade.

The massive hedge sculptures loomed over us, motionless, patiently waiting to strike. We moved back to back as we passed between them...and then we were through.

The sculptures hadn't moved an inch.

Damian frowned, shifting his sword to his off hand, and summoned a smoking black dagger from the ether. He hurled it at the hedge vulture, and it sank into the leaves. No response.

He turned in a slow circle, warily searching the area around us. "That protective magic is coming from somewhere."

I searched but could see nothing out of the ordinary. An unknown threat, just waiting to strike.

Great. Let the mind games begin.

As we passed through the gateway, a thick fog rolled in, obscuring the path ahead. Fortunately, it concealed us from the eyes above.

Unfortunately, it made us vulnerable to ambush.

The cobblestone path was damp, devoid of the mossy growth that covered the rest of the island's surface. Hedges towered fifteen feet tall on either side of us, draped in thick vines that sprouted large red flowers. They were beautiful but grim. Five thick petals cradled a ring of teeth-like stamens. As we passed by, the flowers shifted forward, and the petals opened wide, releasing a putrid rotten odor.

I scrunched my nose. "Ugh. Do you smell that?"

"Be careful, they're—"

Before he could finish, one of the flowers shot toward me. Damian lunged, smacking the flower and pulling me out of the way. In the scuffle, the compass flew out of his hand. The flower caught it, chomped it once, then spat it out. Quickly, he sliced off the flower as it shot toward us again.

Panting, I gripped Damian's arm, my senses on high alert as I searched the other flowers for signs of attack. "Holy crap. What was that?"

"Death lily." Damian looked me over for a bite, then stepped back. "One with an unusually long stem."

"It's carnivorous, isn't it?"

"They'll take off a finger if you give them the chance."

"Like Audrey in *Little Shop of Horrors*?" I stopped short, recalling the plant that ate people. The rancid stink of the air suddenly made me nauseous, and I swallowed sharply.

Damian stared at me blankly. "I haven't been to that store. Is it in Magic Side?"

I blinked several times. *Seriously?*

He grabbed the compass off the ground, and shook it. "It's broken. They're strong bastards."

"Let's see what's ahead, then." I walked onward, warily watching for death lilies with extra-long stems.

A short while later, the path ended.

"Dead end," said Damian.

"Did we miss a turn?" I didn't recall seeing one, but maybe I had been so focused on the flesh-eating plants that I'd completely overlooked it.

I turned. A wall of fog rolled toward us, blocking the path we'd just come along. I raised my hand and issued a steady, light breeze. It was easy to use my magic here, not like in Cappadocia. I shuddered. *Maybe* this was better than giant spiders.

The fog rolled back, and a gap appeared in a section of hedge we'd just passed. "Bingo."

Damian slashed through vines and flowers that reached too close as we pushed along the winding path.

I dodged a biting flower. "This isn't so bad."

"You say that. Just wait till one of those nips you."

Then the fog parted, and another dead end blocked our path. I kicked myself for speaking too soon. "What the heck? I'm sure we didn't pass an opening."

"We didn't."

I looked behind us, spotting the hedge as it shifted ever so slightly. "Did you see that?"

Damian looked puzzled. "See what?"

"The hedge...it moved." I pointed to a gap that appeared. "See! This was—"

Vines reached out, wrapping around my limbs and yanking me into a hole in the hedge.

Damian shot forward, but the bushes closed in around me, squeezing and scratching my body. I screamed, and the mass of branches constricted, crushing my chest and driving the air from my lungs. They pulled me backward, deeper and deeper into the thick hedge.

Heart racing, I released a surge of energy from my hands. It ripped through the branches, leaving two empty cavities.

Whoa.

Vines hurled me through the air, expelling me onto the cold stone pavement with a painful thud. My khanjar clattered across the ground.

Apparently, the hedge didn't like me blasting it apart. "What did you expect?" I snapped at the hedge.

It didn't respond, of course, but I was too pissed to be embarrassed about talking to a plant.

Elbows and tailbone aching, I climbed to my feet. The hole where the hedge had spit me out was slowly reshaping, knitting itself together.

"Damian?" I rushed toward the hole and peered in.

A hollow growl reverberated through the hedge, and the hole closed fully.

Oh, *fates*. This was bad.

I reached for my dagger and scanned my surroundings. The path opened in two directions. I chose the option on my left, following my gut.

I rounded a corner and—*holy shit*!

Wrong choice.

Up ahead, a giant stone creature stood in the middle of the cobbled path like a massive statue...except it was alive and mobile. It crouched, its back facing me, apparently eating something. The creature was probably a gargoyle, but I wasn't going to get close enough to check.

Suddenly, its long, gray ears twitched toward me, and the sound of chewing stopped.

Oh, crappity crap.

I froze and held my breath, desperately trying to slow my pounding heart. Gargoyles had excellent hearing, and it would be only a matter of seconds before it sensed me. Sure, I could fight it, but as I'd learned the hard way, where there's one monster, there's usually *more*.

Slowly, I stepped backward, retracing my steps toward the corner. If I could just get out of sight, maybe it wouldn't notice me.

A piercing screech echoed from up ahead, on the other side of the gargoyle.

Aaand there it was. The gargoyle had a buddy. The creature shot to its feet and bounded down the path toward the cry, and I gave a brief thanks that it wasn't after me.

I ducked around the corner and sprinted in the direction I'd come. Once I was certain I'd put enough distance between myself and the gargoyle, I slowed. Had I already been down this way before? It looked the same, but I was suddenly disoriented.

I freaking *hated* mazes.

I pushed onward, letting my gut guide me. Where was Damian? How much time had passed since we'd been separated? Hours? Minutes? Was my sense of time as warped as my sense of direction? I wanted to shout for him, but I wasn't going to risk alerting the gargoyles or something worse.

I paused at each corner, peeking around to make sure I didn't bump into any unexpected creatures. But there were none.

Another junction appeared out of the fog ahead. I walked and walked but had no way to gauge my progress. Everything looked the same. Was I going in circles?

Then I hit a dead end.

A dense fog bank floated several feet above me, obscuring the top of the maze. Could I fly up enough to get a hint about where to go next?

I recalled the electric shock I'd gotten the last time I tried this, but it was worth a shot. I *hated* mazes and at the rate I was going, I'd starve before I cracked this one. I pushed off the ground and glided into the thick fog above. The tops of the hedges were taller than I'd expected, and the white vapor obscured my vision.

Damn.

I floated higher, hoping I might get above the fog and steal a view, but my movement came to a jarring halt. I was jerked backward by something sharp that had wrapped around my ankle, cutting into my skin.

"What the—"

Another violent jolt pulled me down. I surged upward with all my strength, but the harder I pushed, the stronger it pulled. Several vines lashed out toward my face.

Fear iced my skin. Gripping my khanjar, I slashed the vine that held me, severing it before ducking from another. More grasped for me, so I shot toward the ground, but a particularly nasty one constricted around my torso, pulling me back. I reached behind and sliced it cleanly, then dropped below the fog bank and landed.

Rubbing my stinging ankle, I glanced up. Several vines twisted through the fog above, then disappeared.

I definitely wouldn't try that again.

Where the heck was Damian?

I gazed down at my khanjar. I needed help.

Ask for it.

I remembered the book I'd stolen from the djinn's vault, *Secrets of the Djinn*—in particular, the section on summoning air elementals. I wasn't sure exactly how it'd work or who I'd summon, but at this point, I was ready to try anything.

"Help," I said, feeling awkward. "I could use some help?"

I waited, but no one appeared, and I sighed. *The maze it is, I guess.*

A *buzz* whipped through the air, and then another. I shot to my feet, looking around wildly. Where had it gone?

The air vibrated behind me. I turned, my hand clutching the khanjar a little too tightly.

A tiny sprite hung in the air before me. Whereas the sprites I'd met previously had been vaguely formed, this one had a woman's body, and her skin was faintly tinted green. She was no bigger than my hand and wore a dress made from a leaf.

I found my voice. "Hi, there."

The little sprite smiled and flitted in front of me, hovering a few inches from my face. She moved like a hummingbird, swiftly and erratically, but didn't speak. Instead, she beckoned me with a wave of her hand.

"You want me to follow you?"

She nodded, then led me through the maze, around corners and bends. The little thing seemed to know where she was going, and we didn't encounter any more impasses.

Quickly, she zipped ahead and out of sight.

"Hey! Wait!" I ran after her, but she was gone.

The maze opened into a giant courtyard dotted with trees and a structure partially concealed by clouds. I called upon the wind and pushed the fog away, revealing a domed conservatory. Its glass windows were opaque with grime, and the inside was filled with bushes and trees and ferns.

What the heck was this place?

There was no door to the structure, just an arched opening. I stepped inside, breathing the warm, fragrant air. Alluring—though it made my head spin. The little sprite appeared again.

"There you are." I hurried toward her.

She hovered for a second, then zipped down a flag-stone path shrouded in giant ferns and hanging flowers. Unlike the death lilies, these smelled aromatic and invit-ing. The scents were intoxicating, clouding my mind, and numbing my senses.

I followed cautiously, carefully avoiding the plants that snaked onto the stones. The flowers seemed to inch closer to me, though I couldn't tell if it was real or just my paranoia. I could taste the air, which had grown more perfumed. Honeysuckle...

Something tugged at the edge of my consciousness, but my thoughts moved like molasses. I reached out to touch a fern, missing it by a mile and nearly stumbling. I took a seat on a stone beside the path. I was so tired, and this was the first safe place I had found in the maze. *Just a little rest*, I told myself, and sucked in the sweet aroma. What *was* it? I could almost taste it. The air was warm, comforting, like a warm blanket and good book on a cold winter's day. Was this heaven? Just peacefulness and...*scones.*

Wait. *What?*

There it was again, a thought trying to form. It felt like a distant memory, ever so faint but there.

The sprite appeared again. She was so beautiful. And so kind to have brought me to such a marvelous place.

"Hello, again," I mumbled.

The tiny woman flitted onto my hand and pried open my fingers. She reached up to a flower that hung above, tilted it sideways, and poured a viscous liquid into my hand.

"Honey!" I stared at it with glee. This was definitely a little heaven. Scooping up a blob with my index finger, I raised my hand to my mouth.

STOP. DANGER.

The nagging thought burst through my foggy consciousness like a torrent breaking through a dam.

Danger. Run.

I jerked my hand back, smearing the gooey honey onto the moss below.

Get out. Now.

I stumbled to my feet, trying to gain control of my clumsy movements. A deep fog permeated every corner of my mind. Terror shot through me. What if I forgot what I was I doing? What I needed to do?

Got to get out of this conservatory...

Over and over, I repeated it in my head.

The sprite swooped down in front of me with outstretched arms and snarled, baring a set of tiny jagged teeth.

Holy shit. I'd summoned a demon sprite. An evil, wicked, little fairy devil...

Focus. Got to get out of here.

I drew my energy into my palm. It was sluggish, but I felt it surge through my body. Swiping my arm drunkenly, I shot a burst of wind at the little demon sprite, sending her head over heels into the bushes.

Panic rising, I pushed through the plants that twisted around me. I swept my arms out in an arc and blew them back with a blast.

Got to get out of here.

My legs were so heavy...

I saw the opening up ahead and plowed forward. Come on. Almost there.

I burst out into the foggy courtyard and sucked in the cool, fresh air, clearing my mind. My senses returned, but I kept moving, desperate to get as far away from that damned conservatory as I could.

The courtyard ended at a path that headed into another set of hedges.

"Damn it!" I shouted. At least my head was clear, and the horrible drugged sensation was fading. I sighed in relief. That was close. I'd have to be more careful and less trusting. Not everyone was a friend.

I blew the fog away and scanned the courtyard. There weren't any other options, so I headed into the hedges. Death lilies draped over the manicured bushes. I chopped a few flowers down that reached toward me. Screw this place.

Branches twisted and cracked behind me. I stopped and turned. The hedge rustled, then gyrated fiercely.

Here we go again. I crouched, holding my khanjar loosely, ready to strike.

When the hedge split open, Damian strode out, two daggers in his hands and a grimace on his face. His torn shirt stretched across his broad shoulders, and his tousled hair gleamed in a ray of sun that cut through the fog. Gods, he was perfect.

We locked eyes, and he dismissed the daggers into smoke with a flick of his wrist.

I don't know why, but I leapt into his arms. "Thank fates you're okay."

"I've been looking for you," he whispered, pulling me close.

A moment passed—an eternity that I never wanted to end—and we peeled ourselves apart. He set me down, and I turned away, my face burning with heat. "What took you so long?"

"I got jumped by two gargoyles." He brushed aside a strand of hair from my face. "What happened to you? Your hair is full of leaves and petals."

"Several arguments with a hedge."

He traced his thumb along the line of my jaw, and his warm magic trickled across my skin. I winced at first, but then sweet relief flooded through my face. He soothed the forgotten aches in my forehead and cheekbones. My headache departed. I shivered beneath his touch, swaying toward him. "You're supposed to go down the paths, not through the hedges."

"*Now* you tell me," I joked. "How'd you find me?"

His scratches were already healing themselves. His shirt was still ripped, though, and his skin looked tantalizing beneath the tattered fabric. Heat washed over me, and my heart fluttered.

"I tracked you." His voice was rough and sexy, and it sent shivers up my legs. "I would've found you sooner if it weren't for those gargoyles. And those carnivorous vines. Not to mention a nest of giant wasps. And that damned hedge that keeps shifting."

My mind started working again. "But how? You don't have anything of mine...do you?"

Damian had returned my opal necklace after our first trip to the Realm of Air.

"I don't need anything to track you." Damian took a

half step closer, his mouth within striking distance of mine. "I can sense you. Feel you."

My breath caught in my throat. His heat washed over me in full force, and I inhaled the heady scent of his magic—windswept juniper forests by a raging sea. I ached for his touch and longed to feel his skin against mine.

Danger.

Warning bells pinged in my mind, Nix's warning. I should heed it.

But Damian pressed his hand to the small of my back, pulling me closer and making my mind fog. His fingers slipped beneath my shirt, grazing the base of my spine. Shivers radiated from his touch, and my skin erupted in goosebumps.

His dark green eyes, full of secrets and stories untold, penetrated mine as if searching my soul.

"Neve." My name sounded like a prayer on his lips.

Heart racing, resistance crumbling, I wrapped my arms around his neck and rose on tiptoes. A low groan tore from his throat, and he swept me upward, his strong arms around my back. His lips met mine, devouring.

Time stopped.

His lips moved skillfully, parting mine to kiss me more deeply. I drank him in, pressing myself closer to the hard plane of his chest. Pleasure flooded me, and I arched my back, wanting no space between us. Wanting to feel all of him. He groaned and pulled me closer, kissing me like it was the end of the world.

This...*this* was heaven.

A deafening crash resounded through the hedge behind us. We jumped apart, my head spinning and heart racing, to find a gargoyle fifty paces in front of us, growling and snarling.

Holy shit.

The beast shot forward at lightning speed.

Damian pulled two black, smoking daggers from the ether and hurled them through the air. The gargoyle deflected one, but the other lodged into his shoulder with a hiss. He let out a thunderous roar but didn't slow.

His first attack stymied, Damian stepped forward and raised his hand. The gargoyle abruptly staggered, clutched its chest, and crashed sideways into the hedge. I turned to Damian. His eyes had gone black, radiating a dark light.

What the heck sort of magic was *this*?

I backed away as he strode menacingly toward the gargoyle. It struggled against the force of his magic but could not rise. Damian slowly clenched his fist. The creature quaked, then exploded into a flurry of rocks and dust, as if crushed from the inside out.

It was the same thing that he'd done to the thief in the market on Tayir. My legs shook. While we had both dispatched many demons with our weapons and magic, there was something awful about this power. Something savage.

He turned away from the disintegrated gargoyle and walked back toward me, coming close again. He raised his hand as if to place it on the small of my back. "Where were we?"

I pulled back, unable to take my gaze from his hand —*that hand* could extinguish life just as easily as extinguishing a candle. *That hand* could kill without remorse. What had I gotten myself into? This man was destruction incarnate. Was I ready to be entangled with one of the Fallen?

I looked up and met his eyes, catching the surprise there. "You don't need to be afraid of me, Neve," he murmured.

"I know." *Did I?* I was not ready for this. "We were on our way to the palace. To save Rhiannon. To trap the djinn. That's where we were."

Damian's expression hardened, regretful, as if he knew the moment was gone. "Right. We better get moving."

We stood just short of an intersection in the labyrinth. Damian strode forward and looked around the corner of the hedge, checking both directions. "Right or left?"

I shrugged. "Right hand rule?"

"Right it is," he said, and stepped out.

In an explosion of leaves and grass, long brass claws

erupted from the earth. I screamed, stumbling backward. The claws closed around Damian and dragged him into the ground, leaving nothing but a cavernous black hole in their wake.

Panting, I stared at the pit, horror opening a chasm in my chest.

Damian was gone.

23

I scrambled forward, clawing at the dirt where Damian had disappeared. With a grating noise, a brass plate slowly closed over the top. I tried to stop it, pulling at the metal lip, but my muscles gave out, and the plates ground closed.

I staggered to my feet, heart pounding and mind racing.

"Damn labyrinth!" I hissed, wanting to shriek it to the heavens. But I didn't need to bring another gargoyle down on my head.

There was no response from Damian or the hedge.

It was a trap. Perhaps there was another.

I began searching the ground nearby. As I brushed away the grass, my hand encountered a sharp metal point protruding from the dirt—the tip of a claw. There were others nearby.

Same trap, most likely. Perhaps it went to the same place…

My options weren't great. I could either continue wandering along through the maze, or—and this was a really terrible idea—I could try to follow Damian down.

It was dangerous, but I was done running into dead ends.

Screw this maze, I thought, and stepped deliberately into the middle of the trap. The brass claws erupted around me, raking my skin and tearing my jacket. With a sudden lurch, they tightened and dragged me into the dark earth.

I rocketed downward, choking on the soil as it cascaded around me.

Pain streaked through me as I collided against a hard metal framework. Blinded by darkness but with my feet dangling free, I scrabbled for purchase and began feeling around.

Holy fates. My stomach pitched. I was in some kind of metal cage, swinging back and forth in the air.

"Damian," I whispered.

Nothing. I tried a bit louder. "Damian!"

"I'm here. Are you all right?"

"Yeah." Everything was pitch back. "Where are we?"

"Not sure. We're locked up in cages. Or at least I am."

"I thought I had lost you."

"No, I'm just hanging around." He paused. "Do an experiment for me. Try to summon your magic."

I tried to call the wind. Nothing. I tried blasting a gust from my hand. Nothing. I tugged, but it just wasn't there. Heck, I even tried to planes-walk. It didn't work. "I've got zilch."

"As I thought. We're in an anti-magic room. You can feel it in the air."

I slowed my breathing and sensed the air. It was thick, heavy, and *wrong*.

Well, *this* was a predicament.

I looked down into the darkness. "I wish I could see."

There was a flash, and a soft glowing light popped into view. It split into three small sparks that floated aimlessly around the room, like motes in the sunlight.

The light didn't travel far, but I could see a little at least.

"I thought you couldn't do magic," Damian said.

"It's not me." I paused. "It's like the lights on the ship when the ice devils attacked. Maybe it's some kind of creature native to this realm?"

One of the sparks drifted over and illuminated Damian's cage in soft light. It dangled over the black, cavernous space. Damian's wings were visible.

"Damian, your wings..."

They were too large for the cage and poked through the brass bars.

"I know." He shifted them awkwardly. "They're always there—I just normally banish them with magic."

"How the heck are we gonna get out of here?"

"I'm working on it." He pulled out what appeared to be a lock picking kit from his bag and started fiddling with the large padlock on the door. "Give me a moment."

I peered into the darkness and shuddered. "Fates. I wonder what's down there?"

As I said it, one of the bobbing lights began slowly dropping downward.

There was no bottom to the chamber, just a roiling bank of fog. The spark drifted over the clouds. Were there dark shapes writhing below? Maybe it was just a trick of the light. Maybe it was snakes.

With our luck, my money was on snakes.

"Damian?"

"What?"

"Don't drop the picks."

"Noted."

An abrupt clang reverberated through the room as a brightly lit doorway opened in the side of the chamber above.

Two hawk-headed avians burst forth, carried aloft by their broad wings. Each wielded a long pike with a sharp point and a sinister hook.

"We've got company!" I shouted.

"Can't stop, almost there."

The avians surged through the air, closing the distance between us. One thrust his pike through the bars of Damian's cage, piercing his wing. He braced and grunted in pain but didn't stop working the lock.

Dread crept up my spine as the guard pulled his blood-soaked pike free for a second thrust. We were in an anti-magic room. Damian couldn't heal here.

A screech echoed above me, and I spun. The second avian rocketed downward and jammed his pike through the bars of my cage. I drew my khanjar, using the hooked blade to deflect the blow. He tried to catch my arm with the pike's wicked hook, but I dove right, avoiding it.

"Got it. Hold on!" Damian reached to pull the padlock free, but the hawk-headed guard thrust his pike through the bars, aiming for Damian's chest. He dodged to the side and grasped the shaft as it grazed him. Pulling the pike forward, he grabbed the guard by a tuft of feathers and viciously slammed its head against the brass cage, over and over, until it lost consciousness and tumbled into the mist below.

In an instant, Damian bolted to the door of the cage and flung the padlock off. Pike in hand, he burst into the air, his iridescent black wings shimmering in the dim light.

The other guard dodged my blade and withdrew his pike. He spun to strike Damian, who dodged inside the guard's reach. They came together in a violent flurry of wings and tumbled in free fall into the mist.

I jumped forward, clutching the brass bars of my

cage. "Damian!"

There was a moment of stillness, then Damian came hurtling up out of the roiling clouds below. A black tentacle lashed at his feet, but he rocketed up. Its quarry out of reach, it slipped slowly back into the mist.

My skin chilled. "What the heck was that?"

Damian alighted against my cage, causing it to sway gently at the end of the chain. He held on with a single hand, leaned back casually, and smiled. "Don't go down there."

"Noted."

He pulled the lock picks out of his pocket and set to work. Blood stained his shirt, leaking from several grievous wounds. "Are you okay?" I asked.

"I'll be fine once we get out of this room. Are you hurt?"

"A few minor cuts and scratches. Get me out of here, and I'll be just dandy."

"Almost there..." The padlock opened with a click, and he tossed it into the abyss below.

"I can't fly in here. Not without my magic." I eyed his bloody wounds and torn wings, doubtful of his strength. "Can you carry me?"

"Of course."

Without warning, he scooped me up in a single arm and leapt into the air. I yelped as we hurtled through the darkness. I was used to flying by now, but only under my own power and control. Not like this.

Sensing my concern, Damian tightened his grip, his muscles flexing beneath his bloody shirt, his wings surging power. The anti-magic room had stripped away the scent of his magic, leaving me with only the scent of him. Sandalwood and sweat. It unleashed a storm within me, and heat flared in my center.

Shit, no.

This was *not* happening.

We flew through the air to the open doorway in the side of the chamber, landing on a narrow ledge over-hanging the abyss.

Shoving back my desire, I looked over the ledge. Dark tentacles writhed in the mist below. Then the chamber went black as the little lights drifted out of sight through the walls.

"You can let go now," Damian said.

Right. I was still clinging to him like a horny koala. Releasing him, I stepped back, mortified at how my body was reacting. "Thanks. I wasn't fond of being a canary."

Finally, I felt some control over my body. I glanced at Damian's bloody shirt. "Your wounds."

"I'll be fine once my magic starts working again." He poked at his side. "I didn't need my spleen, anyway."

A huff escaped me. "A fallen angel with a sense of humor?"

I was actually getting used to it. And truth be told, I liked it.

"When you've been kicked out of heaven, everything seems to be a bit of a cruel joke." He turned, clearly unwilling to say more.

I hadn't thought of it that way.

"Come on." He gestured me forward, and I followed.

We entered a small antechamber, apparently where the guards had been lurking. The air buzzed as we crossed the boundary of the anti-magic field. My spine tingled, and my powers came rushing back. I breathed in deeply, as if I could draw the magic straight out of the air. I called a light breeze to dance around me, just to feel its presence again.

Damian's wounds slowly knit together. The process was probably painful, but he didn't show it.

"Can you feel the djinn or Rhiannon?" I asked.

"I can't sense the djinn at the moment—he keeps going in and out of range. Perhaps only part of the palace is shielded from detection." His eyes focused on the opal necklace around my neck—the one Rhia had given me. "I can sense Rhiannon again though. She's not far off."

Rhiannon. My pulse quickened. I couldn't wait to see her. I was going to hug her and never let go. "Are we inside the palace, then?"

He nodded. "I think so—the dungeons."

Better than the maze.

Damian led us down the corridor, holding his black, smoking blade in case we encountered more of the hawk-headed soldiers. But the palace was empty. In fact, it was a little *too* empty, considering all the guards we'd spotted outside.

I shifted, wariness prickling at the nape of my neck.

Damian knew exactly which stairs to take and which corner to turn, almost like he was being pulled forward by an invisible force. I still didn't quite understand how he did that. He paused by a door. "She's not far now."

He quietly swung the door open, and sunlight flooded over us. I shielded my eyes, blinking until my vision cleared. We stood at the edge of a vast, open-air garden in the middle of the palace. Beds of blue and white flowers ringed pomegranate trees bursting with fruit. A large, ornately tiled fountain burbled in the middle of the garden, feeding small ponds full of waterlilies and bright red fish.

In a different circumstance, I would have lingered for hours.

"I can feel Rhiannon just across the way, on the other side of the garden," Damian said. I stepped forward, but he restrained me, pointing to the sky. Though there were few guards in the halls, they were still patrolling overhead.

We crept around the edge of the garden, moving stealthily along the path bordering the green space. We slipped through a pair of oak doors, then entered a vast room surrounded by an arched colonnade. It reminded me of the ornate Islamic palaces around Cordoba, with pink marble floors and carved geometric designs decorating the space.

"Is it just me, or does it seem quiet in here?" I whispered.

"Too quiet." Damian's muscles tensed, and his eyes narrowed on the door at the far end of the room. "Rhiannon's in there."

My pulse skipped at the thought of Rhiannon so close. "Let's go."

We moved quietly along the perimeter of the room. The columns weren't thick enough to hide behind and did little to obscure our movement, but the rest of the room seemed still. This was getting creepy. Where were the palace guards?

Damian crossed to the pair of doors and undid the lock while I guarded his back. We cautiously slipped into a room filled with fragrant steam that smelled of cinnamon and peppermint. I could only make out amorphous shadows and was beginning to develop a strong distaste for steam, fog, clouds, and mist—really, any form of diffuse airborne water. With an impatient wave of my hand, I blew it away.

The ornate walls of what appeared to be a bathhouse rose around us. Steam wafted from a raised octagonal pool in the middle of the room.

But the room was empty.

Where was Rhiannon?

24

Damian took a moment to magically lock the door behind us, and we quietly explored the chamber, tiptoeing over the wet tile. Sneaking had become habit rather than intentional.

"Look." I pointed to the wall. A silver chain ran from the ceiling and into a nearby alcove. "Rhiannon?" I whispered.

She poked her head around the corner.

Her jaw dropped. "Neve? What are you doing here? Are you insane?" She paused. "You look like hell."

I crossed the room and hugged her with all my might.

"Ouch," she squeaked.

Oops. Too tight.

She pulled a leaf from my hair. "Seriously, you look a little worse for wear."

"I got into a fight with a hedge. Someone put a stupid labyrinth outside. Remember the state fair? Worse."

"Oh, *fates*. I am a-*mazed* you made it through."

I grinned at her, grateful to find her spirits intact.

Damian dropped to his knees and began breaking the magical locks on her magicuffs.

Rhiannon squeezed my hand. "Neve, in all seriousness—I'm infinitely thankful, but you shouldn't have come."

"No way I wouldn't."

"This whole place is a trap. After you left, the djinn went into a rage and rebuilt it to catch you." She put her hands on my shoulders and looked me in the eye. "Neve, I'm bait. There is no way he doesn't know you're here."

"Don't worry. We've got a trap of our own. Are you up for helping us catch a djinn?"

Rhiannon beamed. "Do burgers love bacon?"

Man, I'd missed her.

In moments, Damian had the magicuffs off and started working on Rhiannon's collar. She stood stock still, but impatience glinted in her eyes. The door to the bathhouse started rattling.

"Oh, shit, hurry up," I muttered, clutching my khanjar and positioning myself between them and the door.

Damian finally broke the enchantment on the collar, and it parted with a clack. Rhiannon sucked in a full breath. "Thank fates. And thank you, Mr. Big Hunk. It's good to breathe again."

"Name's Damian. Let's get out of here."

"The servants' passage. That'll be our best bet. We might be able to free some of the others along the way." Rhiannon dashed over to a small door in the alcove and opened it. "This way!"

I followed her into the narrow corridor, while Damian locked the door behind us and brought up the rear.

She led us down the labyrinthian servants' passages. After Cappadocia, the maze, and this, I was pretty damn sick of endless winding corridors, but in this case, they worked to our advantage. Rhiannon knew where the other captives were working. We could pop out, grab them, and break their bonds in the safety of the corridor.

Our first stop was the kitchen, where a shifter was preparing some delicate pastries. I scarfed two down while Damian broke her bonds, grateful for the sugar rush. I'd need all the energy I could get. We then fled back down the hidden passages to a workroom where a young alchemist was brewing potions. Finally, we grabbed two others who were sleeping in the servants' quarters.

Rhiannon gestured to the group. "That's everyone. The rest are all his minions or collaborators."

I examined the motley crew. They were by no means

a battle-hardened gang. Terrified and beaten down, they looked like a stiff wind would blow them over.

I huddled up with Damian and Rhiannon. "We need a new plan. If we take these folks into battle, we're going to spend all our time keeping them alive."

Damian nodded. "I agree."

Rhiannon pointed down the hall. "These passages are as safe as anywhere in the palace. The servants know them far better than the guards do."

Damian motioned to Rhiannon. "You should stay with them. Keep them safe."

"Screw that. I'm going with you and keeping *you* guys safe. I plan on pouring this shitty djinn right back in the bottle."

Damian turned to the uncertain group of slaves. "Stay here unless there is immediate danger. You're free now, and that's something. We'll come back and get you once we have the djinn."

They nodded, and we departed, the three of us running back down the passage.

"Follow me. I can sense the djinn again." Damian looked to Rhiannon. "Neve and I will ambush him. Can you keep him distracted while I cast the spell to trap him?"

She grinned and nodded. "This sounds dangerous. I'm all in."

"Do you have a weapon?" he asked as we ran.

Rhiannon materialized Hercules in her hand. "I

have my bolas." She looked down at her hand. "Good to see you, Herc."

"I don't think that's going to be effective on a djinn. Take my bow." He pulled the glowing weapon from the ether and handed it to her. "Just point and shoot. It manifests its own arrows. Doesn't matter if it hits, we just need to keep him moving."

"Kick-*ass*." Rhia loved weapons, and I knew she was immediately infatuated with the bow.

Trepidation curled around my spine, but Rhiannon was here, and that made all the difference. With her and Damian at my side, we could do anything.

After a moment, we reached a small door, and Damian motioned for us to stop. "He's nearby. Do you know where we are?"

"Right back where we started," Rhiannon said. "Almost. This door leads to the colonnaded room in front of the baths."

"Then we'll charge out, distract him, and put him in the box. Ready?" Damian said.

My trepidation suddenly turned to a low, throbbing terror, vibrating along with the beat of my heart. My palms were damp. This was it. Go time. Live or die.

Turning to Rhiannon, I gave a concerted nod. At least we were doing it together.

Damian opened the door, and we burst through.

The djinn wasn't there. There were, however, two blue devils lurking in the center of the room, each with cobalt skin and frost-coated wings, but we had the drop on them. Rhiannon threw her bolas, and it wrapped around the legs of the closest devil, which lurched forward and dropped to its knees. I dashed toward it, slicing its throat with my khanjar. The creature's eyes bulged, and its body crumpled.

Damian crossed the distance to the other devil, his blade ringing as it arced through the air. The devil jumped back. It wielded a large glaive—a wicked metal blade mounted on the end of a long pole. The devil struck out, whirling the weapon like the wind.

Damian ducked and rolled, swiping out to cut its ankle, but the devil was too quick and leapt into the air. It swung its glaive again, sparking the floor where Damian had been.

Damian jumped up and slashed through its wing. The devil's flight faltered, and I dove underneath its talons, trying to flank it.

The injured devil turned but had one of us on either side. It spun the glaive back and forth to protect its flanks, but I hit it with a burst of air. That gave Damian an opening, and he ran it through the chest.

That was f-ing teamwork.

Rumbling filled the air, and smoke swirled into the room. It wound around the colonnades, and the air grew hazy and pungent. Like incense burning in reverse, the smoke shot to the floor, and the djinn took form. An ornate orange and red tunic draped over his broad shoulders. Smoke poured off his sky-blue skin, pooling both on the ceiling and floor. His eyes burned with an unidentifiable emotion—perhaps rage, amusement, or desire.

"It is delightful to watch you dance with my soldiers," he roared. "You are talented. Perhaps I should make you fight each other for my entertainment."

"Go ahead and try." My skin itched, and I fought back the strange feeling that formed in my gut, drawing me toward him.

"Fools," he rumbled. "Do you not understand? You are playthings. I am not bound by the rules of your world."

I had prepared a really good taunt for this moment. I was not prepared, however, for the world to turn upside down.

Literally.

I fell upward and crashed face-first into the ceiling. Rhiannon landed beside me. The bow fell from her hand, vanishing in a puff of smoke.

I tried to fly down but collapsed on the ceiling, completely nauseated. I tumbled downhill to the top of the domed room.

Up was down. Down was up. The djinn had inverted gravity.

Damian and Rhiannon staggered to their feet.

"Same plan," I said, through clenched teeth, "just upside down."

I staggered upright and leapt into the air, flying upward toward the djinn, which was simultaneously downward toward the floor.

He casually turned his open palm over, and gravity reversed again.

Now being pulled down, I accelerated and flew headfirst into the floor. Pain exploded in my forehead, and I gasped.

Half a second later, Damian and Rhiannon crashed beside me.

The djinn flipped his hand. We slammed into the ceiling.

Rhiannon cried out as she landed awkwardly. I barely managed to stop myself in midair.

The djinn was toying with us. He laughed in delight and flipped his hand again. We plummeted—and then everything slowed. The smoke rose off the djinn's body like a stream of molasses.

Rhiannon had slowed time.

"It only lasts a second!" she shouted. "Prepare to land right."

We flipped over, and time resumed. Though we landed hard, we managed to maintain our footing. Damian pulled his bow from the ether and prepared to shoot—but gravity flipped.

Time slowed again.

"I can't do this much more!" Rhiannon yelled. "We have to get out of here."

I flew to her and grabbed her around the waist, heading for the open hallway. "Damian, let's go. We can't win here."

He followed.

Time resumed, and we crashed to the floor as we left the djinn's gravity bubble.

Damian pulled Rhiannon and me to our feet, and we ran for our lives.

25

Laughter followed us down the corridor, and then a roar of wind.

I looked back. "Holy shit!"

A massive dust storm raged behind us, rendering columns into flying bits of stone and ripping decorations and torches from the walls.

Rhiannon screamed.

Damian turned back and dropped to one knee, then fired an arrow at the oncoming storm. The arrow exploded in a glowing bubble that filled the corridor, and the storm collided with the force field, dust and smoke roiling against an impenetrable transparent wall.

"Hell, yeah!" Rhia shouted.

Then the djinn was there, all-powerful and motionless in the midst of the raging storm. He reached out to touch the bubble, which sizzled as it started to dissolve.

"Run!" Damian barked, then turned and sped toward us.

We charged down the hall, driven by terror and the mad whistling of the wind as it leaked through the dissolving force field. Overwhelmed with panic, we rounded the corner and burst forth into bright sunlight, racing across a stone-arched walkway that led into another open-air garden.

The djinn blew through the archway in a rush of wind that knocked me off my feet. Rhiannon tumbled alongside me. I rolled and took cover behind the lip of the central pool. Rhiannon and Damian crouched behind a bush across the way. Damian pulled the brass box out of his backpack. His eyes met mine, and I nodded.

The air swirled into a small tornado, and the djinn manifested into his humanoid form.

It was go time.

I would need to distract the djinn while Damian cast the binding spell. Matthias had said it would take at least thirty seconds. Or was it a minute? *Shit,* that was a long time.

Heart pounding, I stood on shaky legs and slammed him with a gust of wind. It barely affected him, like a gentle midsummer breeze.

The djinn's kohl-lined eyes narrowed, and an evil smile stretched across his face. "Nevaeh."

The way he said my name, slowly and emphatically,

made my skin prickle.

I shot a side glance at Damian. He had begun the spell.

"Why are you doing this?" I asked. It was a stupid question, but I needed to stall and keep the djinn focused on me.

"Because I was a captive. And now, I will have vengeance. You will all bow before me, in chains."

"It sounds like you're just an asshole."

He growled and whipped a gust of wind back at me.

I leapt into the air and darted down behind a low wall.

"You brought this fate on yourself, Nevaeh," he continued. "You raided my palace. You stole from me. And yet, I would have ignored you, as I owe Damian a great debt for releasing me. But now you have returned to trap me again."

Shock raced through me, chilling me from my skin to my bones.

Damian freed him.

No. It couldn't be.

I spun toward Damian. His face, racked by guilt, told me everything I needed to know. Of course. This was why he'd risked everything. *He* was the one responsible for letting the monster loose. *He* was the one responsible for the consequences—for the missing supes, for Rhiannon's abduction. All of it.

Rage boiled within me.

This was all *his* fault.

"You didn't know, did you?" The djinn laughed—a terrible sound, like the roar of an avalanche. "Of course you didn't know. He has been using you all along. You need to learn that, to them, our kind will always be a thing to be used, to be exploited—even a weak little half-breed like yourself."

Anger coursed through my body—at the djinn, at Damian, at the world.

The djinn first, I decided. Then the rest.

"You hypocrite," I snarled. "You did to my friend what was done to you." Fury threatened to split me at the seams. I shot my hand forward, releasing my anger in a blast of wind.

The djinn slammed backward into the palace's wall with a crash. He righted himself and sneered. "I was captive for a thousand years, and I demand retribution. With your friend's power, I will travel through time. I will find every mortal who extracted a wish from me and repay their impudence tenfold."

"I understand your desire for vengeance. It was *wrong* how you were treated. But what you're doing right now is insanity!"

I shot another gust of wind into him. It whipped about his body, and he laughed. He waved his hand, and a force slammed into my chest, lifting me off the ground.

Rhiannon screamed as I hurled through the air. I

landed on my back with a crack that forced the wind from my lungs and left my head ringing.

A dozen yards to the left, Damian kept chanting, his face ashen.

I had to buy him more time, and so I sat up, gasping in agony.

Rhiannon threw her bolas at the djinn, but he knocked it from the air with a swipe of his arm.

Scrambling to my feet, I dodged another strike, then fell into my defensive stance.

The djinn strode toward me. Magic swirled around his fists. "You are a pathetic excuse for one of our kind. You have inherited your family's rage and impetuousness, but none of their wisdom or power. Did you really think you could defeat me?"

He slammed me into a column with another gust of air. My ribs cracked, but the whirling words in my mind drowned out the pain.

My family?

I was paralyzed. "What do you know about my family?"

"That they do not know what a worthless shadow you are and will pay dearly to have you back. You cannot imagine my delight to have you barge into my domain. I will not let you go. I will chain you to the ground with a blade over your neck. Your kin will not touch me as long as your throat is mine."

"Not if I chain you first." I broke loose and shot across the garden, pulling my khanjar from its sheath.

The djinn lifted his hands and summoned a blast of sand. I raised my arms and blocked the onslaught with a wall of wind, but his power was overwhelming. The sandstorm inched toward me, and I struggled to stay upright, my feet skidding across the ground. The force made my arms ache.

"Damian," I panted, "how much longer?"

His face was grim, and his lips were moving.

"Almost!" Rhiannon shouted over the tempest.

I steadied my feet and pushed forward, forcing the sandstorm back an inch, and then another. This was not my strength's doing—the djinn was losing focus.

The binding spell must be working, I told myself. *Just hold on...*

The djinn looked around wildly as his legs began to dissipate into blue smoke. He caught Damian's gaze and snarled. In an instant, the djinn was in the air, and the force I was holding back let up. The sandstorm blew backward under my power and blasted into the wall.

The djinn rocketed upward toward the palace's roof, breaking away from Damian's hold. Escaping.

Shit. He was so fast.

But so was I.

Adrenaline pumping, I bolted to Rhiannon and Damian. "Give me the box!"

Damian was on his feet in seconds. He pushed the

box into my arms, regret flickering in his eyes. My chest ached, but I ignored it. There was no time. I pulled the box out of his grasp. "Get everyone together."

Closing my eyes, I cleared my mind. The storm rose within me, and I shot into the air. The wind tore at my hair as I flew above the palace domes. Rhiannon and Damian became specks in the garden below.

I smashed through the translucent dome of magic. I was of this place, and it could not hold me back.

The sky was bright, but the thunderclouds around the palace were dark and foreboding. "Where are you, you son of a bitch?" I screamed, scanning the empty expanse.

Lightning flashed behind towering gray clouds, and the distant crack of thunder rumbled.

There!

The djinn raced toward the lightning storm. I took off after him, flying faster than I'd ever flown before. Adrenaline pushed me to the limit, and the thrill of the fight coursed through my body.

The binding spell appeared to have weakened him. I was gaining on him and could make out the tattoos on his body.

The binding spell!

Clutching the box more tightly, I began reciting the spell, repeating it over and over.

The djinn sensed the magical bonds forming again and blasted me with a flurry of hail. I darted to the side and evaded the assault. Chunks of ice whirled past my head. I dodged, narrowly avoiding them.

Freaking *hell*, that was close.

The djinn sneered and bolted into the thundercloud. I broke through after him and was jolted by turbulence so strong, my legs felt like they'd be ripped off. Still, I clutched the box, desperate not to drop it.

A blinding flash cracked through the air ahead, and a shockwave sent me wheeling downward. The ensuing crash of thunder pounded my eardrums and reverberated through my bones. Pain forced a scream from my lungs, but I only heard ringing.

I stopped my free fall and spotted the djinn in the distance. His body jerked left and right, also caught in the grip of the unsteady air.

Pain pounded through my ears, but I whipped after him.

I began reciting the spell again, this time screaming it, though I could only faintly hear my voice.

The djinn raced ahead, disappearing into a rising puff of vapor—except it wasn't part of the clouds. Two giant serpent heads appeared out of the mist. One lunged forward with an open mouth. I shifted the box under my arm and blasted the cloud beast with a gale. The serpent's head dissipated, but exhaustion pulled at me, dragging me down.

Using the fall to my advantage, I dove downward. The cloud serpent raced after me, and I twisted and turned, breaking through the clouds into clear sky. The cloud creature strained its jaws to reach me, but I darted out of its grasp. Away from the thunderheads, it slowly evaporated.

I slowed to a hover and scanned the empty sky.

"Looking for me?" The ominous voice sounded close, but it was hard to tell since my hearing wasn't right.

I whipped around, but a hand gripped my throat, squeezing tightly. His magic rippled over me in waves. The scent of frankincense filled my nose, and tobacco burned my tongue. The djinn peered down at the box under my arm.

"You thought you could trap me?" He quaked with laughter. My throat ached under his grip.

He reached for the box, but I blocked his hand with my free arm and twisted my body to move it out of his reach. His grip around my neck loosened, but my arm was pinned behind my back. I thrashed, trying to break free.

"I told you last time that I would tear your limbs off," he hissed at my ear. "I wasn't lying."

I heard a crack, and pain pierced through my arm. My vision darkened, agony tearing a scream from my throat.

I struggled to retain consciousness. The djinn roared, and I slipped from his grasp. My arm was broken. Snapped like a twig.

I dropped through the sky like a stone, clutching my broken arm and the magic box, struggling to command the wind. To save myself. But the pain overwhelmed me, nearly blackening my vision.

Through bleary eyes, I spotted something falling toward me. Just a blur, but it was closing in.

Two arms suddenly wrapped around me and slowed my fall.

Damian.

His face was set in tortured lines, but he didn't seem injured.

"Neve!" He cradled me in his arms. "Give me the box. I'll finish it."

Though my broken arm screamed in agony, my senses came rushing back, and rage dulled the pain.

"No! I've got to do this." I shot upright and pushed him away with my elbow, breaking free of his grasp and flying on my own.

The djinn hovered several hundred feet above us. He was enraged, but so was I. He hurled a gust of wind at us, followed by a shower of baseball-sized hail.

We darted sideways, but Damian was hit by a chunk of ice. He plummeted downward.

No!

Another blast of wind whirled toward me, then another. I ducked the onslaught and looked down. Damian was out of sight. Gone.

Heart racing, I dashed toward the djinn. My anger

erupted, and I recited the spell in a roar. His face contorted, and he dove toward me.

I ducked into a ball, and we crashed together, spinning through the air. He latched onto my leg, and I grimaced, but I continued to reel off the spell from memory. Using the grip he had on my leg, he pulled himself up and reached for my neck.

An ear-piercing screech rocked our bodies, and something flashed past my vision. I craned my neck but saw nothing.

The djinn was suddenly ripped from me.

I spun around, scanning the sky, and gasped. A magnificent white beast soared through the air, clutching the djinn in its massive talons.

The cloud dragon.

With no time to lose, I opened the lid of the chest and flew toward them, the spell echoing off my lips.

The djinn bellowed and struggled to free himself from the dragon's grasp. He managed to loosen his arm and shot a burst of hail at the dragon's belly.

The beast screeched and released the djinn, then fell from the sky.

I kept chanting but cursed the djinn in my mind. Cradling the opened chest in my broken arm, I raced toward him. I used my free hand to summon my remaining energy and focused it on the djinn, creating a spinning vortex around him. Every muscle in my body burned, and every part of my mind was stretched to the limit, but the djinn was pinned in the air. I raised my free arm and clenched my fist. The djinn writhed in pain as I squeezed, my nails digging into my palm.

My power was suddenly ripped from my body as the spell took hold. The vortex vanished, but the enchantment bound the djinn. He roared as his legs dissipated into blue smoke, trailing through the air and into the chest. With a wail, his body followed, sucked into the chest with a force so powerful that it shot me back several feet. Pain surged through my broken arm, but I managed to shut the lid. It clicked closed.

I stared at the chest in disbelief.

We did it.

My heart sank as I looked around me. I was alone.

Damian. No.

He'd betrayed me, but I didn't want him dead. A rush of air blew me forward. I clenched the chest and whipped around as another wave hit me, this time from above.

I looked up and saw a pair of silver wings and a reptilian belly.

The dragon screeched and swooped down. Damian rode on its back, his dark hair blowing in the wind and his gaze pinned on me.

I silently thanked the fates, though my heart ached.

The cloud dragon glided downward toward the palace, the trip fast and smooth. The throbbing in my arm had dulled, but my muscles screamed with pain. Had my mind not been so fuzzy from exhaustion, I would have reveled in the chance to soar on the back of a dragon.

Instead, I was in agony, with my betrayer behind me. It took all my strength to sit so we didn't touch, but I couldn't stop hearing Damian's voice. "Let me heal you."

I wanted to refuse, damn it, but that would be cutting off my nose to spite my face. "Fine," I snapped.

His hand moved to my broken arm. The dull aching subsided, and warmth flowed in its place. I hated the shiver that raced up my arm, the awareness of him so close to me. I swallowed hard, *really* hating that I could still feel anything for him after what he had done.

"Thank you." The words felt like gravel in my throat.

He lied to me. *He* had set the djinn free. How could I trust him?

I leaned forward, urging the dragon to go faster.

The storm clouds behind us churned and rumbled, and lightening flashed in the distance. As we drew closer to the palace, the wind surged around us.

"Oh, no," Damian whispered.

I followed his gaze. "Oh, *shit*."

The edges of the island were crumbling away, the waterfalls boiling into steam. The djinn had crafted this place from his magic, and now that he was gone, it was falling apart.

The walls of the palace fractured, and pieces crashed to the ground. The vines of the maze lashed out and twisted. Fear lanced me. Where was Rhiannon? I searched for her as the dragon slowed its pace and hovered over the open garden.

Rhiannon stood below with the four supes the djinn had captured.

"Neve...this looks bad!" Rhiannon screamed.

Damian and I jumped off the dragon's back, and I flew to its face, touching its cheek. "Thank you."

It met my gaze for one brief second, then took off into the clouds. I shot down to Rhiannon. As I neared, the ground quaked, and one of the palace's domes collapsed in a thunderous rumble, sending dust billowing into the air.

"Neve!" Rhiannon ran up to me. "Did you get him? Can we bail?"

"Yeah, let's go." I hurried toward the other supes, who stood with Damian. "Everybody gather around me and hold on tight. It's going to be a rough ride."

With everyone in place, I closed my eyes and focused on Magic Side. The universe melted away with a roar.

26

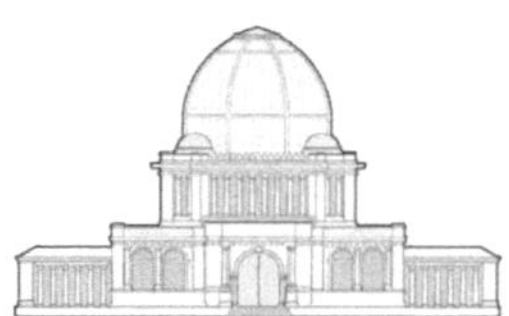

The familiar world wheeled around me, and my feet hit the pavement. My arm ached where I clutched the box. Damian and I had been prepared for the rigors of the journey—the others, not so much. Most staggered about, and two fell to their knees, heads down, trying to stop the spinning. The shifter was still wailing in terror, though she quickly clamped it down once she realized that the universe was no longer attempting to pull her to pieces.

Rhiannon had her head between her legs. "Oh, fates...Neve...that was horrible. No wonder you never use your powers."

"Sorry."

"I much preferred the ride there with the djinn. Much less being turned inside out."

"He's had a thousand years of practice." I looked

around. "Anyway, we're all here and on target. That's what counts."

I had dropped us in the courtyard outside the Order of Magica's Hall of Inquiry, near the entrance to my office. The gray stone building had that neoclassical Chicago look that I loved so much.

Several of the Order's enforcers marched down the front steps toward us.

Rhiannon hugged me, refusing to let go. "I can't believe we lived! I thought the djinn was going to blast us into oblivion. You were amazing. Thanks for coming for me. I didn't want you to risk yourself, but I'm so thankful you did."

I squeezed her back. "I would never, ever leave you."

I traded hugs with the others, whose names I didn't even know. The commotion drew even more attention.

Soon, I was face to face with Lieutenant Bitchface—Gretchen—herself. "Neve! Where have you been?" she demanded. "Fates, is that Rhiannon? Who are these people? What's going on here?"

I grinned. "We caught the djinn."

"We caught the djinn!" Rhiannon echoed.

Gretchen frowned at us. "*What* djinn?"

Of course, I had never told her what was going on. "The djinn that was abducting supes," I explained.

"And me," Rhiannon added. "I was a captive in his palace. Neve tracked me down and saved me. Us." She motioned to the other supes around us.

Gretchen looked dumbfounded. "You? *You* caught a djinn?"

Rhiannon quickly recounted the battle, taking artistic liberties with explosions and whooshing noises. Glowing from within, I looked around for Damian. He stood beneath a shaded tree across the courtyard. The branches covered him in a dark shadow that mirrored his eyes.

Anger and betrayal flared within me as I crossed the distance between us.

"What are we doing here?" he demanded, his jaw tense.

What the hell was his problem? I knew he wasn't a fan of the Order, but someone had to fix this mess. I tossed my hair. "We're returning these people. And I'm handing the djinn over to Order custody."

"*What?*"

"It needs to be locked away where it can't harm anyone."

"That wasn't the deal." Anger echoed in his voice as rage flashed in his eyes. He loomed larger, and the shadows coalesced around him. Trepidation rose in my stomach—I had never seen him like this.

"Well, I'm not trusting *you* with it," I snapped. All the stress of the escape finally boiled over. "Is it true that you released it?"

He glared, saying nothing.

Fury bubbled up inside me, sick and dark. "*Is. It. True*? Did you release it? Did you command it?"

He dragged a hand through his hair. "I released it. I didn't know that..."

"Didn't know what?"

"That it would go this way."

That was no excuse. "You fool! Why did you do that?"

His face turned to stone. "I can't tell you."

"No, you *won't* tell me."

He clamped his mouth shut, and that just pissed me off. Nix had told me not to trust him. I should have listened. "Did you have anything to do with the abductions?"

"Of course not," he growled. "Is that what you think?"

"I don't know what to think. You've lied to me this *entire* time." I slammed my finger into his broad chest. "This is your fault. I almost lost my best friend. I almost lost my *life*. You released this curse on us, and then you duped me into putting it right."

"I'm sorry. I can explain. Just give me the djinn, and let's get out of here."

"You've got to be kidding. It's way too dangerous to be anywhere but under Order custody." He gripped my arm, gently but firmly, and I jerked away. "No!"

From the edge of my vision, I caught sight of heads

turning toward us, the crowd's attention drawn by my shout. Rhiannon started over.

I choked back tears as rage and betrayal and exhaustion formed a toxic mess in my soul. "Are you insane? I'm not giving it to you. Your wicked wish caused this mess. You lied to me. I don't know if you're *still* lying to me. I don't know what you're hiding. You're a deceiver, a thief, and you're standing outside the Hall of Inquiry, so if you don't want to be asked any questions harder than mine, I would get the hell out of here."

I was a hurricane, except there was no calm in the middle of this storm. Wind whipped around me, a shield of rage. Damian backed away. He fixed me with a lingering glare that twisted my stomach, and then he turned and strode off.

I watched him go, my mind a mess. Memories flashed. Damian, fighting at my side. Damian, healing me. I swore I'd sensed goodness in him. Honor.

Fat lot of good my senses did.

"Where's he going?" Rhiannon asked.

"I don't know. He wanted the djinn, but I wouldn't let him have it. He released it in the first place. This was all his fault, Rhia. How could I trust him with it?"

"Should I go after him?"

"Yes. No." I raked a hand through my hair. "I don't think so. I...don't know what to do."

"It's okay," she said, grabbing my hand.

He had saved my life, again and again, but he had

released the djinn, and it had taken my best friend. He had opened the door to new worlds, but he had also deceived me from the start. Could I trust that he had nothing to do with the abductions? I had no idea. He hadn't been honest about his motives or how he was entangled in all this. He'd led me along into peril with no warning. I wouldn't have known if the djinn hadn't told me.

I forced back a sob. This moment should have been so different. A triumph. Instead, I was in turmoil, a cyclone turned inward.

Lieutenant Bitchface came over. "What was that ruckus about?"

"Nothing. Personal stuff. It's been a long day." I turned to her and produced the ornate brass box. "This is the djinn." She reached out to take it, but I pulled it back just slightly. "No one should touch it. The bonds haven't yet fully set. It needs to be locked away in the strongest vault we have and never released."

Bitchface considered me for a moment, then nodded. "Okay, then. Let's go."

Ten minutes later, Gretchen, Rhiannon, and I made our way to the Vault. I clutched the brass box, unwilling to let it out of my sight for even a second.

"Your knuckles have gone white, Neve. Relax," Rhiannon whispered.

"I'm scared that if I let go, the bonds will break. I don't know how this works. He *can't* escape again."

"It's going to be fine."

"You don't know that." My nerves were getting the best of me. Screw this djinn. I wanted him buried.

We walked on in silence.

A heavy brass door marked the gateway to the Vault. Every inch was engraved with arcane sigils, and protection magic thrummed almost violently around it.

A weathered old man with gray muttonchops met us. It looked like he had spent his life tied to the mast of a ship. I couldn't get much sense of his magic.

Gretchen bowed her head in respect, something I'd never seen her do before to anyone. "Archmage DeLoren, we have something for your vaults."

"So I've heard." The grizzled man turned to me. "You must be Neve. This is the djinn?"

He reached to take the little brass box, but I jerked it back.

He raised a hoary eyebrow that looked like it wanted to crawl off his face and make a chrysalis somewhere.

"How do I know it'll be safe in there?" I asked, and nodded to the door. Gretchen gaped at my impertinence, but I just stared at the archmage. This was too important to screw around with.

When DeLoren responded, it was almost in a growl.

"The Vault is the most secure place in Magic Side. It's an arcane labyrinth filled with dangers and permanently sealed chambers. Very few have access, and none of us knows its true extent. It's a place to lock things away and forget about them."

He reached out, but I didn't hand it over. DeLoren radiated danger. I gestured down to the box. "The djinn is unimaginably powerful. Someone could just open it, and we'd be trapped in this nightmare again. Who's going to say no to three wishes? Would you?"

Gretchen nodded slightly, as if I had a point.

I pinned the archmage with a stare. "So how do I know I can trust you?"

His eyes flared, revealing a deep, repressed font of magic. As if to emphasize his point, he let just a fraction of his signature show, and it was like the air around us became stone. I couldn't breathe, I couldn't move. It was like being crushed beneath the depths of the ocean.

"Magic Side's archmages have guarded the Vault safely for more than a century," he said. "There are things worse than a djinn locked in the recesses, and they have never escaped." DeLoren gently placed a hand on my shoulder. "Each one of us has something in that Vault we never want released. Let me assure you, we all believe that there are things that don't belong in this world and shouldn't go free. Like this djinn."

He took the box from my open hand with his disfigured, knobby fingers. I hadn't even realized that I'd been holding it out. "Now, if you will excuse me, I need to lock it up."

DeLoren turned and traced runes upon the gateway. The brass door didn't open, but rather bulged outward, sucking him through with a thunderclap.

It took a moment for the three of us to recover once he left. I felt like someone had backed over me with a steamroller. Rhiannon looked at me wide-eyed, and then at Gretchen. "Whew. Well, I guess that seems legit."

"Yeah." I nodded. "I really don't want to know what else they have locked up in there."

"Me, neither," Gretchen said. "I could use some air."

Together, we climbed the stairs to a tower balcony. The neoclassical stone walls of the Hall of Inquiry loomed over the wide courtyard. Night had fallen. The few lonely lamps in the park across the street formed islands of light in a sea of shadowy trees. Beyond the foliage, Magic Side stretched out, lit by sodium streetlights that gave the low overhanging clouds a dull pinkish-yellow glow.

I leaned on the railing. "I need a drink."

"You deserve it." Gretchen looked me in the eyes. "There might be some hell from the higher-ups, but I'm going to push for a promotion to detective for you. You've earned it."

"Detective?" I was shocked.

"Of course. Hell, I've been trying for over a year. You're a great researcher, Neve, but I need my best people on the street, solving crime. I don't think they'll be able to turn it down this time—you just rescued Order personnel and several civilians, and solved a major kidnapping."

"Gretchen...thanks."

She nodded, satisfied. "The pack is back together again. That's what matters to me." She slapped me on the shoulder and left.

Rhiannon beamed back at me after the door closed. "That went well."

I leaned on the rail, letting my breath out. "I have to say I'm shocked. I was pretty sure she hated me."

"No, she's just prickly. I've been telling you that for years."

"I suppose I have to take back some of the things I've said." *And stop calling her Lieutenant Bitchface.*

"Promoted, Neve. A detective! We can solve crime side by side. Cagney and Lacey!"

"More like Turner and Hooch."

Rhiannon laughed, and it lifted my soul.

"How do you want to celebrate?" she asked. "Want to go out?"

"Honestly, I want to turn into a potato. I'm so burned out, I don't think I can even manage an intelligible conversation at this point."

"Perfect." Rhiannon clapped her hands. "I'm half a potato at this point as it is. How about pizza and a movie? My place? Let's watch a chick flick and pass out on the couch."

"Perfect."

As she'd predicted, Rhiannon passed out about twenty-five minutes into *Bridget Jones's Diary*. I loved the movie but couldn't focus. I was exhausted but restless, miserable on the couch.

What I needed was a walk.

I let myself out of Rhiannon's place and headed down the street, the cold night air revitalizing me. Warm sodium lights lit the shuttered storefronts. My thoughts churned. A promotion? Maybe. I didn't want to get ahead of myself. Half of my heart was giddy. The other half was...well, a mess.

Damian.

He'd lied to me. Betrayed me, effectively. He used me to get to the djinn and put me in harm's way while concealing his true motives and role. And yet, part of me still wanted him.

Idiot.

I had other troubles, though. I looked down at the white tattoos that wove around my arm. What was happening to me? I'd pushed it out of my mind before, but it was going to be staring back at me every time I looked in the mirror. Would it stop growing? Was it linked to my powers or to something else entirely?

The djinn's words about my family drifted to the front of my mind. A deep ache tore at my chest. His words had almost suggested that they were still out there somewhere. Alive. Looking for me.

The street felt closed in, claustrophobic and stifling. A light breeze rustled the trees above, as if a suggestion. The sidewalk behind me was empty.

Good.

I looked up into the cloudy sky and leapt. A slight gust caught me as I soared past the tops of the buildings in Old Mud City. The wind rushed around me and calmed my mind in a way that no movie, no drink, no euphoria could.

I was actually flying now, instead of just pushing myself along with the wind. Thank goodness I'd run into the wind sprites. I wasn't as strong here as in the Realm of Air, but I could still fly, and that made my heart sing.

The old trees lining the streets below melted into formless black masses backlit by the golden lights. As I pulled away from the earth, their shadows merged with the buildings until the city itself was simply a sea of stars.

I was home.

EPILOGUE

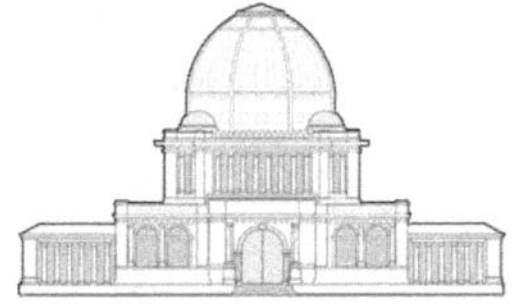

The Thief

I strode through the Hall of Inquiry.

Sometimes, stealing in broad daylight was just easier than breaking in.

Frustration gnawed at the back of my mind. I'd come so close to possessing the djinn, only to have her hand it over to be locked up in the Vault. Weeks of planning, ruined.

"This is it. The entrance to the Vault," the security guard in front of me slurred, mesmerized by the charm I'd hypnotized him with.

No one guarded the bronze door that led to the Vault. It didn't need it. If I entered the wrong access code, the door would instantly devour me and digest my body in some strange, otherworldly dimension.

The giant bronze face on the door grinned, as if reading my mind.

I turned to the guard. "You're done here. Go back to the other end of the building and create a distraction."

He stared at me blankly then left.

Deftly, I wove runes in the air to disentangle the invisible spells that surrounded the door. If I dispelled the wrong one, the rest would trigger. I wasn't certain what all the spells did, but I was sure they would collectively blast me to kingdom come.

A minute later, fire alarms sounded in the distance.

Good.

The silver eyes of the bad-tempered door watched me as I worked, waiting for an excuse to bite.

Quite an intelligent creation, aren't we?

Luckily, intelligent things were easy to manipulate. I pulled a charm from my pocket, and slowly hypnotized the door. Once it was under my spell, it told me the access code with a conspiratorial chuckle. I pressed them, and the door sucked me through the ether, ejecting me into a poorly lit stone corridor.

The air hung lifeless and heavy, sapping my power. An anti-magic room. I was prepared for that, of course.

Flicking on a flashlight, I stepped forward. The stone slab beneath my foot shifted, and with a hiss, a heavy yellow gas began leaking into the room, and an acrid scent rose into the air.

Well, shit.

A poison gas trap.

I sprinted toward the bronze door at the end of the corridor. The large keyhole in the center of the door had to be a ruse. I checked the ornate vine decoration for a concealed button and found a loose bronze leaf. I pushed it aside, revealing a small slit—a hidden keyhole. Satisfaction rippled through me, and I pulled the long, hooked lockpick from my pocket and slowly slid it into the keyhole.

There was a click.

I ducked as a tiny dart whipped past my head.

Fuck. That was close.

A low, grating sound echoed from the door, and it sprang open a millimeter. Pushing it open, I stepped out from the claustrophobic darkness into a brightly lit, snowy wasteland. The bitter cold burned my lungs.

The door stood alone, unconnected to a wall or structure of any kind. It was isolated, surrounded by a field of clean snow.

Bizarre.

Similar solitary doors perched atop nearby mounds, while the silhouettes of others were visible in the far distance. How many were there? Hundreds? And this was only the entryway into the Vault, a labyrinth of hundreds of perilous chambers connected across the ether.

Suddenly, a mound of snow shifted on my left, then fell motionless.

Cursed fates.

I summoned my black blade from the ether just as the giant, blood-red eel erupted from the drift, jaws aiming for my chest. The eel dodged my first blow and dove toward me with another attack. Rolling out of the way, I brought my blade down on its neck, hacking once, twice, three times until it was severed. Splotches of bright red blood hissed in the snow.

What a hellhole.

My whole body was numb by the time I reached the closest door. It was unmarked, and there was no indication where it led. Irritation flared as I scanned the frozen wasteland, catching sight of dozens of similar isolated doors.

So much for this plan.

I hadn't assumed that I could crack the Vault and its myriad of pathways, but I had hoped to make it a little farther than the entrance. But time was short.

Frustrated, I retrieved the twisted green bottle from my satchel. It was amazing that such a fragile thing of beauty could trap the cosmic powers of a genie—*my* genie.

I sighed. I'd been so close to getting the djinn. Now that it was sealed in this hell-forsaken Vault, I'd have to burn a wish to recover it. It was a net gain, but still ironic, and an inconvenient waste of a wish.

I uncorked the glass bottle and rubbed it with my frozen palm. "I summon you, Adrazar, great efreet of the bottle."

Black, noxious smoke poured out of the spout, and flashes of flame burst within the dark clouds. The air exploded, and a billowing pillar of fire erupted, driving me backward and melting a crater in the snow.

The pillar of fire took the form of a man who spoke with a thunderous, crackling voice. "What does my master command?"

"Adrazar, son of fire, I will have you bestow upon me a wish."

"And what is it that you wish of me?" The efreet's eyes raged with desire, no doubt sensing an opportunity to betray me.

Making a wish was dangerous. The efreet obeyed my simple commands, but he was malicious by nature. And like all genies, he would twist my words if he could.

But I was prepared. I'd written my wish down on a clay tablet to ensure there were no mistakes. Paper would have burned. I'd considered every loophole and distortion and written a watertight contract.

It was still extremely risky.

Flames licked up my palm as I handed the tablet to the efreet, the heat from his fingers baking the clay. Rage burned in his eyes as he read. "You have written an iron contract. I am bound to your service. I will grant you this wish."

The efreet grabbed me with fiery hands, and we exploded through the air, leaving a trail of melted snow in our wake.

Searing pain racked my body as we flew on and on, passing from door to door, chamber to chamber, through a rapidly progressing labyrinth. Traversing it would have been impossible without the wish—to imagine otherwise would have been sheer insanity.

At last, he landed in a small cave occupied by a solitary black iron chest. Still burning from the efreet's touch, I stalked forward. *Finally.*

Impatience tore at me as I wove runes in the air, recklessly ripping away the protection wards. *So close.* I summoned my magic and dissolved the lock into dust.

The chest creaked faintly as the lid released. Careful not to touch the chest, I drew my blade and flipped the lid open.

The small ornate brass box lay within.

I lifted it gently from the chest as if, like the efreet bottle, it were made of glass.

At last, it was mine. The djinn—master of the winds. I would rule it as I ruled the efreet, master of fire.

Only two more remained.

We hope you enjoyed *Wicked Wish!* The sequel, *Dark Storm,* is already out! Get it here: mybook.to/Dark-Storm

Would you like to read Damian's point of view on the kiss in the maze? Sign up for our newsletter to get access to an exclusive deleted scene that didn't fit in the book: http://hyperurl.co/wickedwishscene (you can unsubscribe anytime).

Finally, if you'd like to chat more about the books, interact with fellow readers, and get the scoop on what's up next, join the Veronica Douglas Facebook group here:

https://www.facebook.com/groups/veronicadouglas

THANK YOU!

Thanks for joining us on this adventure! It means a lot to us! If you've got an extra minute, we'd appreciate it if you would leave us a review on Amazon (http://mybook. to/Wicked-Wish). Reviews make a *huge* impact. They help us become better writers and keep us going through the difficult pages!

And if you're ready for more, the series is now complete and you can find books 2-4 here:

Dark Storm: mybook.to/Dark-Storm

Cursed Angel: mybook.to/Cursed-Angel

Broken Skies: mybook.to/Broken-Skies

Also, be sure to check out the sequel Wolf Bound series:

Wolf Marked: mybook.to/Wolf-Marked

AUTHOR'S NOTE

Thanks so much for reading *Wicked Wish*. We hope you had as much fun reading it as we had writing it! We dreamed up this series last summer with our bestie Linsey Hall, and took much of our inspiration from our research and adventures in Chicago and the Middle East.

Magic Side is our little slice of Chicago. Sometimes when we're out running along the Lakefront Trail, we feel as if the island and its fantastical world are right offshore. Magic Side gives us a chance to explore the things that make the Windy City unique and bring its rich history back to life. While Chicago phased out its trolley lines in the 40s and 50s, we made sure they were still up and running in Magic Side. The design of the Hall of Inquiry is partially based on the Administration building from the 1893 World's Fair, as well as the

Museum of Science and Industry—the only remaining buildings from the Exposition. We'll be exploring the curiosities and culture of Magic Side more in future books, as well as Linsey's Guild City series!

Now, for some facts. The Oriental Institute Museum, where Neve and her friends battle the gallu demons, is one of Chicago's treasures. In addition to the countless objects from the ancient Near East that are on display (and hidden in the basement), the OI Museum has numerous artifacts associated with demons and has even held several "demon hunts" as part of their public outreach programs. The most iconic demon from their collection is a Mesopotamian figurine depicting the four-winged Pazuzu—king of the evil winds. The gallu in our book are based on another type of Mesopotamian demon known for dragging their hapless victims into the underworld.

As archaeologists and lovers of stories, we added a little history to our book for flavor. The magic portal that Neve uses to travel to the Library of Alexandria is based on the 4,300-year-old Egyptian chapel of Netjer-User that is currently housed in a break room in the Field Museum. The Library of Alexandria is based on the ancient library built by the Ptolemaic rulers of Egypt. And while the structure sadly no longer exists, stories about it are still vividly alive. According to Greek sources, the Ptolemies went to great lengths to purchase and acquire books for the library, even going so far as confiscating books that arrived at the port. After copying the texts, the royal scribes reportedly returned the copies, keeping the original books for the library—how rude!

If you've ever visited or seen pictures of Cappadocia, you'll immediately recognize the region's alien-like landscape comprised of what are known as Fairy Chimneys —bizarre spires of volcanic tuff that rise out of the earth like towers. Gizli Tepe is a fictional site inspired by the ancient cities that were carved into Cappadocia's soft volcanic rock. Over the centuries, these underground cities were used by the inhabitants of the region as safe havens, even into Ottoman times. During the early Medieval Period, Cappadocia was located along the Byzantine-Islamic frontier, and subject to frequent Arab raids. Naturally, the region's underground cities were advantageous places to live and avoid potentially dangerous border skirmishes. This fascinating history provided the inspiration for the clues leading up to Neve and Damian's trip to Gizli Tepe.

And finally, a few words about our world. *Wicked Wish* is set in the Dragon's Gift universe created by Linsey Hall. We're huge fans of her writing and are super excited that we were able to weave Magic Side into her world. This book gave us a chance to return to our favorite bar and coffee shop, Potions & Pastilles, and catch up with some of Linsey's characters. Nix and Connor are each featured in their own series. You should check out Dragon's Gift: The Protector to learn about Nix and her past, and *Secrets & Alchemy* to learn more about the spark between Connor and Sora. We started writing this series while Linsey was working on Shadow Guild: The Rebel, so Neve and Damian first appear in the adventures of Grey and Carrow. They'll be popping up again in Linsey's new series, Shadow Guild: Wolf Queen, and you can definitely expect more exciting crossovers in the future!

Thank you for reading and sign up for our newsletter for sneak peaks, extra scenes, and super exclusive content!

Book 2, now available! mybook.to/Dark-Storm

I've been betrayed.

I spent years hiding my magic from the world, but now I've got new powers I can't control. Everyone around me is at risk, and if my secret is revealed, I'll be hunted.

But I don't have time to worry about the monster I might become.

Someone has stolen a dangerous artifact that could turn my world upside down. It could get me and my friends killed and bring destruction down on my city.

Is Damien Malek to blame?

He's a fallen angel. Handsome and lethal. A thief and a liar. And he's betrayed me before. The heat between us keeps pulling us together, but his lies always tear us apart.

If I want answers, I will have to risk everything. My job. My magic. My life.

There's a riddle to solve. An ancient city to find. A deadly genie to defeat, and a dark storm rising in the burning sands.

An action-packed urban fantasy, Dark Storm features a rebel heroine, a dark angel hero, and slow burn romance. Dive into the mysteries of the Arabian Nights and prepare yourself for edge-of-your-seat adventure amongst the shifting sands.

If you enjoyed the archaeology, history, and daring in Linsey Hall's original Dragon's Gift books, this adventure is for you!

Read *Dark Storm*: mybook.to/Dark-Storm

ACKNOWLEDGMENTS
VERONICA DOUGLAS

Linsey and Ben—when we dreamed this up on your bluff, we never thought this might become real. Thank you for your endless words of encouragement and tireless work. We couldn't have done it without you!

Thank you to Jena O'Connor and Ash Fitzsimmons for your amazing editing. We learned SO much from you, and our writing is better for it!

Thank you to the amazing readers on our advanced review team!

And finally, thank you to Orina Kafe for the gorgeous cover art.

ACKNOWLEDGMENTS
LINSEY HALL

Thank you so much to Veronica and Doug for the amazing, fun journey! I had the best time creating this story with you and I love every page.

And as usual, thank you to Ben. There would be no books without you.

Thank you to Jena O'Connor and Ash Fitzsimmons for your amazing editing. And to Orina Kafe for the beautiful cover.

ABOUT VERONICA DOUGLAS

Veronica Douglas is a duo of professional archaeologists that love writing and digging together. After spending an inordinate amount of time doing painstaking research for academia, they suddenly discovered a passion for letting their imaginations go wild! A cocktail of magic, romance, and ancient mystery (shaken, not stirred), their books are inspired, in part, by their life in Chicago and their archaeological adventures from around the globe.

ABOUT LINSEY HALL

Before becoming a writer, Linsey Hall was a nautical archaeologist who studied shipwrecks from Hawaii and the Yukon to the UK and the Mediterranean. She credits fantasy and historical romances with her love of history and her career as an archaeologist. After a decade of tromping around the globe in search of old bits of stuff that people left lying about, she settled down and started penning her own romance novels. Her series draw upon her love of history and the paranormal elements that she can't help but include.

COPYRIGHT